KILLER IN CONTROL

A KEY WEST MYSTERY

KILLER IN CONTROL

DOROTHY FRANCIS

FIVE STAR
A part of Gale, Cengage Learning

GALE
CENGAGE Learning™

Detroit • New York • San Francisco • New Haven, Conn • Waterville, Maine • London

GALE
CENGAGE Learning™

Copyright © 2011 by Dorothy Francis.
Scripture taken from the New King James Version, Corinthians 1:13. Used by permission. All rights reserved.
Five Star Publishing, a part of Gale, Cengage Learning.

LIBRARY OF CONGRESS CATALOGING-IN-PUBLICATION DATA

Francis, Dorothy Brenner.
    Killer in control : a Key West mystery / Dorothy Francis. — 1st ed.
        p. cm.
    ISBN-13: 978-1-4328-2502-7 (hardcover)
    ISBN-10: 1-4328-2502-X (hardcover)
    1. Policewomen—Fiction. 2. Bed and breakfast accommoda-tions—Florida—Key West—Fiction. 3. Murder—Investigation—Fiction. 4. Key West (Fla.)—Fiction. I. Title.
PS3556.R327K56 2011
813'.54—dc22   2011007698

First Edition. First Printing: June 2011.
Published in 2011 in conjunction with Tekno Books and Ed Gorman.

Printed in the United States of America
1 2 3 4 5 6 7 15 14 13 12 11

KILLER IN CONTROL

1

The eerie night flashes by the frosted squad car window. My hands ache from clutching the car seat as I, Sgt. Katherine Morgan, and my partner., Sgt. Hank Burdock, do a U-ie. We zoom toward Water Street to answer the call spewing from our radio—a call we've expected and dreaded for weeks.

No lights flash.

No sirens wail. Yet.

"Burglary in progress. Four-twenty South Water. Burglary in progress."

Our headlights glare on the black ribbon of ice decorating the street like a package of death, on week-old snow banks nasty with slush from passing traffic, on a flank of steel-soldier parking meters, marching along the sidewalk's edge. Typical small-town Iowa. Typical January weather. Dumb criminals. You'd think they'd be smart enough to hang it up until spring.

Again I clutch the frayed seat covers in our blue and white.

Hank's fingers choke the padded cover on the steering wheel.

Muddied burger cartons crunch underfoot. If second-hand smoke kills, we'll die soon. Or we may die from Hank's crazy driving.

With feet against floorboards, my weight shifts side to side as we careen around a corner, fishtail, regain traction.

Our headlights show the outside of the store at 420 South Water Street, Wayland's Pet Shop. Tan paint peeling. Cracked front window. Storm door sagging on rusty hinges. Nothing but a rundown hole-in-the-wall. I never go near the place if I can avoid it. And most of

Dorothy Francis

the time I can. The PD's had the shop under long-time surveillance as a suspected cover for drug operations.

We are last to arrive.

Two squad cars sit in front of the shop.

Officers on foot surround the place with drawn guns.

We park in the back alley and skin from the car while Chief Gilmore bellows through a bullhorn.

"Come out with your hands up! Now. Come out with your hands up and nobody gets hurt."

"Now!"

"Come out now!"

Nobody leaves the shop. How many are inside?

Gilmore shouts orders again and we wait—coiled springs ready for action.

Seconds pass.

A couple of minutes tick by before Hank and I follow orders to storm the store from the rear.

Others smash through the front entry and broken glass crashes against concrete.

One kick fractures the door lock and we rush inside. My hand feels clammy against my pistol. A heightened sense of the imminent danger lurking inside this shop kicks in as does my eidetic memory of white mice—a childhood memory I fight to keep buried.

But the memory explodes into my thoughts.

I may vomit.

No! Choke it back!

I won't let the squad say that the token female on the force caused a distraction that allowed these scumbags to escape. How could I explain my heaving to Hank, to any of the guys? I swallow the bitter taste rising in the back of my throat as the stench of animals and urine overcomes the faint smell of air freshener and sweeping compound.

8

I see movement from the periphery of my right eye and whirl to face it.

A street light outside illumines a gunman. He lifts his arm, raises a pistol, points it at my head.

An atavistic impulse prompts me to fire first. The gunman drops like a stone. The stench of gunpowder fills my nostrils, overcoming the animal odors.

Pandemonium.

Shouts.

Pounding feet and more gunshots.

The coppery stench of blood.

The snap of a light switch.

Sudden overhead light bathes the scene as Gilmore barks orders, takes command of two intruders who drop their guns and raise their hands. It's over—for the moment.

The perp lies prone on the floor. Living? Dead? I can't tell. But now it's plain that his gun is nothing more than a child's plastic toy.

I've shot another human being.

I've shot an unarmed man.

I close my eyes to the blackness that washes over me—a murderer. In only a few minutes my world has changed. My thoughts are like vultures that flutter overhead but never perch. I can't cope.

I vomit.

I was a few miles from Key West when I heard the siren and saw blue lights flashing in my rearview mirror. I snapped from thoughts of my two failed career dreams, thoughts that had plagued me all the way from Iowa to Florida. I straightened my shoulders. I might be down, but I wasn't out. My tires crunched against gravel when I pulled onto the scant shoulder beside the highway. I didn't need this encounter.

I lowered my window. I smiled.

My stomach clenched like a fist when the patrolman eased

from his tan car and strolled toward me. He was of medium height. My own five feet and eleven inches usually gave me confidence, but right now I felt miniscule. In a crunch, sometimes I could buoy myself with pleasant memories of my long-ago Miss Iowa crown and the recognition of my singing talent. That ploy didn't work now. This patrolman wouldn't be interested in the incompetent ENT surgeons who had quashed my potential blues-singing career. He might be interested in knowing I had squelched my police officer career with my own gun. But I wasn't telling. To him, I was just another minor law breaker.

"Do you realize you're traveling above the speed limit, ma'am?"

"No, sir. I didn't realize. I'm sorry." Sorry I was caught, I thought, hating to be on the receiving end of a traffic ticket, but knowing a heavy pedal foot marked one of my failings. Right now I didn't want to think of failings. Down deep, I knew neither of my two career failings was my fault. Surgeons and criminals were to blame. People of my past. I was headed toward a bright future—although I didn't know yet what it might be.

"Your name, please." He raised his voice so it would carry above the din of trucks, motorcycles, open convertibles with boom boxes blaring rap.

"Kitt Morgan." No point in telling him I'm Police Sgt. Katherine Morgan from Marshalltown, Iowa. No point in telling him I'm a law-abiding citizen who seldom ignored speed limits. I concentrated on keeping my smile in place.

"May I see your driver's license, please?"

I dug into my purse, jerked out my billfold, opened it and flashed the license toward him. He took his time reading. A Winn Dixie truck driver honked as he passed.

"May I see your car registration, please?"

I leaned to open the glove box. The car was so new the box

had nothing in it except the owner's manual and the registration form. He read the registration carefully then smiled as he returned it to me.

"I clocked you at ten miles over the speed limit, ma'am."

"I didn't realize I was speeding."

He smiled. "It can happen—especially when you're driving a new car. Since you're from out of state, I'll let you off with a warning this time. Easy with the foot from now on, okay?"

"Thank you, Officer. I'll set the cruise control."

"Good idea."

I hesitated then I risked some small talk. "I know you pulled me over for speeding, but I'm guessing you also wanted to get a good look at my Prius, right?"

He grinned. "That was secondary in my thinking, of course, but I'll admit it's the first hybrid car I've had a chance to observe up close and personal. You like it?"

"Love it. Smooth ride. Classy looking."

"Like its owner." He grinned. "Mileage?"

For an instant, his compliment flustered me at the same time it buoyed my spirits. I grinned back and answered his question quickly. "Gets around fifty mpg on the highway. You may not believe it, but it does even better in the stop-and-go city traffic."

"In another place, another time, I might ask you for a demo ride. The public needs to give this type of car serious attention."

"Agreed. It's time the public took some meaningful steps toward energy conservation, especially after all the tragedies our servicemen are experiencing in Iraq."

Still smiling and eyeing the car, the officer backed off and waved me on my way. "Easy on the gas pedal, okay?"

"Right."

He followed me a few miles down Highway One, one of the most dangerous highways in Florida, but I didn't relax until he turned off at the Quik Chik on Boca Chica, leaving me alone with my thoughts, worries, and frustrations. I had a bundle of them, and Shelby Cox, my ex-boyfriend, nudged his way to the head of the list.

Although I'm thirty-two and thinking now and then about marriage and family, Shelby and I weren't into a strong relationship. We didn't live together, but we enjoyed each other's company—I thought—until the pet shop shooting. With a casual see-you-around following our first date after my suspension from the force, he disappeared from my life. No good-night kiss. None of his usual compliments about my slim figure, my flame-red hair, my smooth complexion. No morning follow-up call. Nothing. Was he afraid of me?

Did he think *armed and dangerous* whenever I came to mind?

But forget Shelby Cox. I dumped him from my mind. Or at least I tried to. Most of my problems hinged on my shooting the perp.

My gun bucks in my hand.

I smell the stench of burnt gunpowder.

And the blood. The blood. The blood.

I jerked my thoughts back to the present. The perp. I refused to humanize him by remembering his name. How could I deal with gunning down another human being? Yes, he was still alive and recovering. Yes, he'd been trying to pull a drug deal. Yes, he had a rap sheet a mile long. But those mitigating circumstances were secondary to the fact that I'd shot a man. My guilt felt like an evil fungus, an ever-expanding mushroom crowding my lungs until I could hardly breathe. But I was determined to get over those feelings, to move on with my life. I had to find a new direction.

"Retired after thirty-four years on the force and never fired my gun."

In spite of my determination, Dad's proud words replayed in my mind. He'd been dead five years and I missed him, yet I was glad he'd never know I shot a man. He'd never know my position on the force depended on the decision of a grand jury. If I was permanently cut from the force, what would I do then? I'd faced challenges before, and I could do it again. I *would* find a new direction.

A car zoomed by me in a no-passing zone, but I kept my cool, my thoughts back in Iowa. At home, when a cop shoots a perp, that cop's relieved of duty with pay while a grand jury or a Civilian Review Board investigates the case and decides if the shooting was justified. And if the perp is unarmed? It's a bad scene. I'd testified under oath that I believed I shot in self-defense. Now I could only wait and worry—pray that the members of the jury believed me, and endure the suspension. I loved my job. I wanted nothing to change it or my world. Even before I joined the force I'd read and studied books about the criminal mind, about murderers, their personalities, and what made them tick. Murderers. I never dreamed that one day I might be one of them. I prayed the perp would live.

"How about them Hawkeyes!" A car with blue and white Iowa plates zoomed by me—in a no-passing zone—the guy in the passenger's seat tossing me a thumbs-up along with a big grin.

I beeped my horn in response, but I smiled to see the accident-waiting-to-happen driver stuck behind the same Strunk Lumber truck I had been following for miles.

As I drove on toward my sister Janell's home, news stories of past police shootings flashed through my mind. After one Iowa police chase, a policeman shot and killed an armed robber as the perp abandoned his car and fired at the officer. A grand jury declined to recommend charges against the officer. In another instance, a sheriff's deputy shot an unarmed man dead after a car chase crash. The case came before a grand jury that charged the deputy with voluntary manslaughter.

I hit my brakes when the lumber truck suddenly slowed. Two books flew from my passenger seat to the floor. I'd tossed them into my car before I'd headed south. The black one, which I'd placed in a velvet bag, slipped out and the cover flipped open.

Be fair. Be generous. In all situations, seek the right and the good.

Dad had penned those words he lived by on the inside page of the diary in shimmering gold ink. A great guy. A great cop. He'd given me the diary before he died and I read snatches from it whenever I needed hope and inspiration.

The other book concerned a type of criminal unfamiliar to me. The sociopath. I wanted to learn more and I'd been studying the book for several weeks. Its contents left me feeling unsettled and wary.

After I'd replaced the books beside me on the passenger seat, I noticed Dad's retirement medallion had slipped from the velvet bag where I'd placed it for safekeeping. I scooped it up and tucked it into my pocket. In the past, I'd worn the medallion on a chain hidden under my shirt, but since the shooting I felt unworthy of it. I'd tucked it into the bag with the diary. My neck felt bare without it.

I looked forward to spending a few days of my enforced suspension with my sister and brother-in-law. I had asked to visit them because I needed to take some action on my own behalf. I was not hiding from my problems. I needed to examine my life and find direction. I had every intention of returning to Iowa and facing whatever awaited me there. Sometimes Janell played the part of bossy-older-sister, her BOS act I'd called it as a kid, but I'd see to it that we'd get along fine for a few days. She and her husband, Rex, had agreed to my coming for a visit and I intended to help with daily chores while I was a guest at their bed-and-breakfast, The Poinsettia.

On the right side of the highway, the sun sparkled on waters in the Gulf of Mexico. On the left side, it shone on Hawk

Channel and the Atlantic Ocean. Bay side. Ocean side. That's how the locals designated their addresses. Who, I wondered, decided where the ocean ended and the bay began?

I'd always seen Key West as a fun-and-games, anything-goes island. But today when I watched pelicans perching statue-like on gray coral rocks protruding from bay waters, I tried to avoid seeing it as a haven for the woebegone. But anyone wanting to hide out from the world could find no better place. I hung another right at Garrison Bight and marveled at the hundreds of yachts, sailboats, and runabouts bobbing in their slips.

I felt small.

A traffic snarl involving a Conch Train and an RV with Michigan plates caused near chaos on Duval Street. It made me glad to turn onto the quiet of Caroline Street—an ominous, waiting quiet, I thought. Inching forward slowly, I ignored the kids in the rusty Conch cruiser threatening to drive up my tailpipe as I scanned house numbers. The street had changed in the years since I'd last seen Key West.

I parked in the only space available, a clearly marked tow-away zone.

"Yo, Mama!" a kid in the cruiser shouted, burning rubber when he zoomed past me. "You askin' for a ticket!"

"Your Iowa tags won't save you," his passenger shouted. "The cops suck up tourist tow-away fees like margaritas."

I didn't dignify their comments with a reply.

Janell and Rex's old Conch house sat back from the street. Thorny date palms and a seagrape strangling with bougainvillea vines showered blood red blossoms onto the pea-graveled yard. The home with its white paint, its steep tin roof, and its wrap-around verandas was reminiscent of old Key West. A few feet in front of the house, a sidewalk rimmed a flourishing bed of poinsettia plants, their leaves looking like scarlet spears in the late afternoon sunshine.

Where was everyone? I gave a brief toot on my horn, then slid from the Prius and started walking toward the house. I felt eager to call it home for a few days even though I knew my visit was only a stopgap between my past and my future—whatever it might be.

"Janell? Rex?" Where were they? I knew they were expecting me. Hadn't they seen me arrive? Heard my horn?

In moments Janell appeared in her doorway, tall, willowy, hurrying to greet me, and elegant as always, today in an ankle-length caftan that skimmed her slim body. A broad smile chased a worried frown from her face.

"Kitt! At last! Thought you'd never get here." Our eyes met on a level before we exchanged kisses, but I felt tenseness in her arms and shoulders when I snuggled into her warm embrace. At forty-five, Janell was thirteen years older than I, but her fiery red hair was still as bright as mine. We both chose casual blow-and-go cuts that suited our lifestyles. Nobody would have any trouble believing we were sisters.

Janell had gone off to college after our mother died. Dad had raised me, and now I saw Janell more as a fairy godmother than a sister. We broke apart only when Rex followed her from the house ready to give me an additional hug. He looked pale and tired and I tried not to stare at his shiny head, although Janell had assured me he was bald by choice.

"Welcome! Welcome!" Rex exclaimed. "Glad you made it . . . safely."

"Come on inside," Janell invited. "But first let's get that new car off the street before the cops tow it—at the owner's expense, of course." Rex hurried to unlock and open a white pine gate at the side of the yard. I slipped beneath my steering wheel and followed him to a carport in the tropical garden behind the home they called The Poinsettia.

16

2

Dark vines snaked up skeleton-thin poles that supported the carport roof, and Rex directed me to a parking place on the concrete slab next to their Ford sedan. Their two bicycles propped on kickstands stood nearby. Space was at a premium on Key West, and Janell and Rex had made the most of their garden. Garden—that's what the locals called their backyards.

"You've made lots of changes since I was here." I eyed the vine-covered guest house with picture windows that overlooked a postage stamp–size pool and patio. "Neat. Very neat."

"Rex finished building the B&B a few years ago, and we reclaimed the privacy of our house, bedding our guests out here, setting up their breakfast buffet beside the pool."

"And I'm sure they love it—and their landlords. Going to show me the rooms—or is that inconvenient right now?" I shivered a bit in a sudden breeze and watched the dark shadows a cypress tree cast onto the pool.

Janell took a step toward the B&B, but Rex reached for her hand and urged her toward the main house. "Showtime later, okay? One room's vacant, and Hella Flusher, our permanent guest, watches a favorite TV program at this time every day. *Wheel of Fortune.*"

Janell and I followed Rex's lead toward the back door. I wondered if something was amiss in the B&B. Trouble keeping both rooms rented? Hella Flusher? Strange name. But Hella

17

and I would have something in common. I was a big *Wheel* fan, too.

Rex paused, turning toward my car. "Shall we take your suitcase inside now, Kitt?"

I smiled, stepped back to unlock the trunk, and then picked up my books from the passenger seat while Rex retrieved my bag. "Nice wheels, Kitt. Very nice. We'll expect a spin in your chariot later."

"Sure thing." I grinned at his compliment. I worried about Janell fussing because I was living in hock up to my eyebrows because of that car. And if I lost my job? It was easy to read Janell's mind. It was even easier to envy their comfortable life.

Rex and Janell had known each other since elementary school days, discovered in high school they were soul mates, and had loved each other ever since. They'd earned college degrees at Iowa State, Janell's in psychology, Rex's in business administration. But when Rex inherited this picturesque home from his grandparents, who had inherited it from their parents, he and Janell moved to the Keys.

In those years the house was a rundown fixer-upper. To generate some much-needed income while they worked on improving it, they opened a bed and breakfast inn in their upstairs, turning two unused bedrooms into rental units, and serving Janell's sweet rolls along with coffee and fresh fruit in their dining room.

I thought it strange that Rex hadn't asked me more about the Prius, but he seemed distracted. Maybe he didn't realize it was a gas/electric hybrid. Or maybe he viewed it as just another car to clog Key West's narrow streets. I peered over my shoulder at a black cat slinking into a weathered shed. Sometimes Old Town locals painted only the fronts of their houses, leaving the sides, backs, and utility sheds unpainted and allowing them to weather to a gray-silver sheen.

"What's in the shed?"

"Tools and fishing gear," Rex said, "and I let Phud, our yard man, use part of it for his gardening equipment and plant containers. We used to keep our boat in it, but since we built the B&B I need more space here. I have to keep our boat at the marina. We'll show it to you tomorrow."

Phud? I almost laughed as I tried to imagine the sort of person who would answer to such a name.

"Let's go on inside." In her BOS way, Janell urged me ahead of her, blocking the entry to their open-air patio café that Rex had attached to the side of the house. A swinging door separated the café from their kitchen. Through a diamond-shaped window in the swinging door I glimpsed a small snack bar, a dance floor and a slightly raised platform holding a trap drum set. I wanted to see more of this new addition, but Janell didn't offer a tour.

"Rex usually makes supper, but tonight I have a pot of conch chowder simmering on the stove." Janell followed me inside. "I knew you'd probably be hungry when you arrived. This way, it'll only be moments before 'soup's on.' "

The spicy fragrance of the chowder filled the kitchen—bay leaf, tomato, onion. I inhaled the heady smell and my mouth watered. I could imagine the taste. Janell had set three trays on the countertop.

"Thought we'd carry our chowder outside to the café and dine under the stars," she said. "We're closed for business tonight, so the place is all ours."

"Great idea," I agreed, wondering why they were closed for business. I hoped my arrival hadn't caused a change in their plans.

Janell and Rex had decorated the inside of the house until it looked like a page from *Southern Living*. In the combination living room and dining room, I admired the pine wainscoting. It reached from floor to waist high, forming the bottom half of the walls. A plate rail, holding antique plates and mugs that Rex's great-grandfather had salvaged from reef wrecks, separated the wainscoting from the painted ecru-toned walls above.

I felt the sagging centers of the old stair treads when we climbed to the second floor where Janell led me into one of three bedrooms—the hibiscus room. The lavender, red-and-pink-flowered wallpaper made me feel as if I were in the center of a tropical bouquet.

"Take your time unpacking, Kitt. No hurry. When you're finished, come on downstairs and join us for chowder."

Her voice said "take your time," but her BOS inflection said "hurry." I hoped my visit wasn't inconveniencing them in some way. I had invited myself here and they'd agreed to my visit, but maybe their generosity came from pity and sympathy for my precarious position in Iowa.

Plastic hangers clicked together when I hung shorts, slacks, and shirts in the pine-scented closet. I dumped underwear into a dresser drawer fragrant with the scent of lavender before I set my cosmetic bag beside the sink in the bathroom. I took only a moment to wash up before I shoved my suitcase into the closet and hurried downstairs.

The minute I stepped into the kitchen, Janell began dipping the chowder into bisque-colored bowls that contrasted with the tropical print placemats already on the trays. Rex dropped ice cubes into glasses and filled them with iced tea, adding a slice of lemon to each glass.

"Follow me outside," Rex invited.

Rex speaks quietly, but when he talks, people pay attention. I followed his directions, and we sat at one of the guest tables in the empty café. Lighted torches flickered from sand-filled ollas placed around the perimeter of the dance floor, lending a party-like atmosphere to our meal.

Rex'd been like an anchor in the family since Dad died, the firm steadying weight that held us in place. Although Janell had made the chowder, Rex wore a red chef's apron. It didn't hide his twill cargo slacks with their zip-off lower legs and zippered back pockets, but it protected his hand-print shirt. He sliced a loaf of the crusty Cuban bread he'd already brought outside, buttered it and passed it to each of us before he took a piece for himself.

I couldn't help wondering if his bald head, now gleaming in torchlight, was his idea of a current men's hairstyle, or if he was on some powerful chemo and they were withholding the bad news from me until later. So far nobody had mentioned Rex's head or my PD suspension, and I didn't bring the subjects up now. Instead, I looked into the calmness of the star-studded sky and enjoyed Janell's chowder.

I remembered the quick way night fell in the Keys once the sun set. A soft twilight had settled around us and I felt as if we might be the last three people on earth. We took our time savoring the chowder—a Key West specialty—and we all enjoyed an extra piece of bread slathered with garlic butter.

"You dive for the conch?" I asked.

"You know better than that." Rex laughed. "They're still an endangered species—at least in Key West waters. I bought it at the Waterfront Market. I think they ship it in from the Bahamas."

"The chowder's delicious, Janell," I said as she brought out a tureen and we lingered over second helpings. "You'll have to share your recipe and teach me how to make it, so I can help out with a few meals while I'm visiting. I'm not here on vacation, you know. I'm here to consider a new direction for my life if my suspension is permanent."

"Don't worry about helping us. We have plenty of plans for you."

"And what might they be?" I leaned forward. "Tell all."

Janell and Rex exchanged enigmatic glances before Janell stepped back inside and then returned with a tin of cookies.

Her shoulders slumped after she opened the tin, set the cookies on the table, and joined us again. I braced myself for bad news and tried not to look at Rex's head.

"I hate to end our meal with bad news, but . . ."

"What is it?" I laid my cookie down, awaiting her next words. Nobody moved during the long pause before Janell spoke.

"Someone murdered one of our guests."

For a moment nobody spoke.

"Who?" I broke the silence, although I admit I felt a flood of relief when I realized Janell's bad news didn't involve Rex or an illness. "Who? When did it happen? Where? Right here at The Poinsettia? That the reason for the empty rental? The closed café? Details, please. Details."

"One question at a time, Kitt." Janell gave a mirthless laugh "Abra Barrie. That's the woman's name." Janell pursed her lips, looked down at her hands and let Rex continue.

"Last Thursday she arrived in Key West on business and had booked one of our rooms. She'd seen our B&B ad on the Internet.

"A big Midwest corporation making wind turbines sent her here. They're promoting their business and feeling out the Key West attitude concerning the use of off-shore wind machines to create a renewable source of energy."

"Wind turbines? As in windmills like Iowa farmers sometimes use to pump water for livestock?"

"Yes," Rex said, "only on a much more sophisticated level. Some of the commercial turbines are huge machines with blades longer than a football field—maybe longer than two or three football fields. But that's beside the point right now. Abra Barrie flew here to speak at a City Commissioner's meeting early Friday morning, and also to say a few words at a women's club brunch later in the day. On Saturday, her schedule included a brief morning speech at the monthly meeting of the Power Boat

Association and after that, she planned to take the afternoon off for a ride on the Conch Train and maybe enjoy more sightseeing during the weekend."

"She had more meetings scheduled for Monday that included an important presentation at the naval station," Janell said.

"And after that she planned to fly back to Nebraska." Rex paused for a sip of tea.

"We liked what we saw of her on Thursday night," Janell said. "She ate at our snack bar, visited with us and the combo musicians and retired early."

"As far as we know, she kept her Friday morning appointment," Rex said. "I helped her get a taxi."

"But she never kept her Saturday appointments," Janell said. "She failed to return here after her Friday brunch meeting. We don't keep tabs on our guests. They're free to come and go as they please, but Abra told me she'd like to hear the combo again on Friday night—said she played the piano. I had told her that Mama Gomez might let her sit in for a set, and she seemed pleased and excited about that."

Rex broke in. "So when she didn't show up here on Friday as planned, I reported her absence to the police. They fluffed me off, said they'd keep an eye out for her, but that she'd probably just gone off somewhere on her own to do a little sightseeing. Chief Ramsey helps run the Power Boat meetings, and it wasn't until Abra failed to appear for her Saturday morning speech for that group that he began to take my missing-person report seriously."

"But the police never found her," I said, knowing I had stated the obvious.

"They found her body—late Saturday evening washed ashore, lying dead and mutilated on Smathers Beach." Janell's hand shook as she lifted her iced tea glass. "I knew when she failed to show up to hear the combo on Friday evening that something had happened to her. The medical examiner estimated the time of death as mid-afternoon on Friday. Here we were getting ready to open our patio café for the evening. I'd even mentioned to Mama G that Abra might want to sit in on piano for a few numbers. And all the time we were making plans for her, she was dead. Dead. It's still like a bad dream. I can hardly believe it."

"I suppose the police have searched your place thoroughly, looking for clues and leads."

"Right." Rex scowled. "On Saturday night, they surrounded the place with crime scene tape even though her body wasn't found here. Didn't remove the tape until early this morning. Her parents flew in from Nebraska as soon as they heard the news. Even by flying, they couldn't get here until yesterday afternoon. When the medical examiner and the police released her body, her parents made funeral arrangements."

"I felt so sorry for them," Janell said. "Their only daughter. Their only child. Life's unfair. A young woman simply here doing her job, enjoying Key West—and now she's gone."

"Her room?" I asked.

"Her parents cleared and packed up her things. She traveled light. Not much there. I offered to help, but they didn't want my help. Don't blame them."

Janell's eyes began to tear and I broke in quickly. "So now the police are investigating her murder?"

"Right." Rex pounded the table, making the tea glasses jump. "Investigating, now that it's too late. If they'd listened to me in the first place . . ."

"Can't blame you for feeling that way," Janell said. "But Key West has so many attractions that might have caught her eye, pulled her off her planned course. I can understand police reluctance to begin an extensive search."

"And now we're all under suspicion," Rex said. "All of us.

Not you, of course, since you just arrived, but the rest of us."

"You and Janell," I said. "Who else?"

"Hella in the other rental, the three combo musicians, Phud the yard man. All of us. Good thing you didn't arrive early, Kitt, or they'd be fingerprinting you, too. Once they get started, they're very thorough."

"They have any leads?"

"None that they're revealing," Janell said. "But I heard the chief muttering about a serial killer. South Florida's had several unexplained murders in the last few years. The police think there may be a serial killer on the loose."

"Hadn't heard about that," I said, "but lots of times big news in Florida doesn't reach Iowa."

"And you'll probably never read anything about those murders in the *Citizen,* either." Janell sighed. "They keep the bad stuff in small type on the back pages if they bother to publish it at all. Don't want to scare off the tourists."

"But news is news," I said. "People need to know what's going on in their community—or at least what the police think might be going on. They need any knowledge that will help them protect themselves. Where has this supposed serial killer struck?"

"Fort Meyers Beach." Rex began ticking the cities off on his fingers. "Miami, of course. Ft. Lauderdale. Stewart. Orlando. At this point, they're not sure the same guy committed all the murders. But some of the mutilations were similar enough to make them think serial killer."

Janell put a hand on his shoulder and shook her head to try to stop his words, but he continued.

"Breasts sliced off. Pubic hair shaved. Ears and eyes mutilated. Oh, he was a real sport."

I shuddered. "You're sure it was a he? Murder's an equal opportunity employer. Could have been a woman."

"Not likely." Rex stood and began pacing the wide expanse of café floor. "Not at all likely. I don't think a woman would have had the strength."

"So if everyone connected with The Poinsettia is suspect, I want to meet those people. I want a good look at them. You plan to open the place to the public tomorrow, right?"

"Right," Janell said. "Had to close tonight. Didn't know when the police would give permission or when they'd remove the crime scene tape. Hella's here tonight, of course, but you can meet her tomorrow."

"I'm surprised she hasn't moved out," Rex said. "We may have trouble keeping the inn rented for a while."

"It's not as if the woman was murdered in her room," I said.

"No," Janell agreed, "but there's one more thing we haven't told you yet." Janell hesitated until Rex shrugged and nodded.

"Go ahead. She has to hear it sometime."

Janell's voice dropped so low I could hardly hear it.

"A small item appeared on a back page of today's paper. The police announced they've found blood stains on Rex's boat."

3

Blood stains. Rex's boat. The words hit my eardrums then ricocheted, hanging suspended in air for a few moments before I allowed them to invade my brain. Even then, I tried to deny their import. Were the police trying to lay Abra Barrie's murder on Rex's doorstep?

"Rex?" I hesitated. "The police were wrong, weren't they? Or if they found blood on your boat, it must have been fish blood, or maybe blood from an injured gull or pelican. I remember how those birds hang around boats waiting for a handout."

"Police have confirmed it's human blood," Rex stood. "They called me last night with that news."

"Rex!" Janell exclaimed. "You didn't tell me."

"Didn't want to upset you any more than you already were upset. There has to be a logical explanation for that blood. I know nothing about it or how it might have been smeared on our boat. Haven't been around *Poinsettia Two* for a couple of weeks. Haven't had time to use it."

"*Poinsettia Two?*"

"Yeah. We named the boat after our B&B. Thought the name painted in red on the boat side would be good advertising."

Janell stepped closer to Rex and he curled his arm around her waist, drawing her closer. "We drove to the marina early this morning," Janell said. "Saw the bloodstains, saw where the police had scraped samples from the console and the deck. I'm with you, Kitt. I thought it must be animal blood—fish or fowl.

27

Maybe the police made a big mistake in their lab."

"I doubt that," Rex said. "And it'll only be a matter of time until they do DNA testing."

"We'll all have to undergo tests?" Janell asked.

"I'm guessing we might," Rex said. "Or maybe just me. I want to get back to the marina and clean up the mess, but when I asked the police for permission, they refused. They want to snap more pictures. Said I couldn't do the cleaning until tomorrow morning. You can bet I'll be at the marina early with a scrub brush and bucket."

Janell scowled. "And in the meantime, all the curious sensation seekers on the island can go ogle the boat and take their own pictures to send up north to their relatives and friends."

"So everyone connected with your B&B is under scrutiny," I said. "Not just you and Janell, Rex. Everybody who works here. And then there may be an unknown serial killer to consider. I've been reading *The Sociopath Next Door*. I think it's a book everyone should read. It concerns a type of person who's been born without a conscience."

"Be real, Kitt," Janell said. "In college, I studied a lot of psychology books and articles—even wrote a thesis on serial killers. I never read anything about people being born without a conscience."

"It's been quite a few years since you were in school," I said. "This theory—no. The book I read said it was more than a theory, that it's a fact. Some people are born without a conscience. The serial killer, if there is one at large in Florida, may be a sociopath."

"Hmmm," Rex muttered. "I'm not doubting your word, Kitt, or the book you read, but I can't imagine a person without a conscience."

"That's because you have a conscience, as do Janell and I and most of the people we associate with. It's hard to imagine something you've never been aware of—especially such a basic thing. Some scientists now believe that one person out of twenty-five is born conscience free—that they can do anything they please—lie, cheat, steal—and they feel no guilt or remorse."

"At that rate there'd be a serial killer on every corner," Janell said. "I don't buy into the 'no conscience' theory."

"Sociopaths are frequently spotted early on as children who get their kicks from abusing animals. They do horrendous things to defenseless creatures."

"But there are laws against that kind of thing," Janell said.

"Many times adults overlook such crimes with a kids-will-be-kids attitude."

"And later those kids turn to abusing people?" Rex asked.

"Not always. When the abusers grow up, they may use their lack of conscience in many other ways. They may manage to set themselves up as authority figures to be respected and admired. According to the book I read, they're the world's liars, the flatterers who can mesmerize you with a guileless gaze until you tend to believe their words."

"We all know people who might fit those categories," Janell said. "But we don't call them serial killers."

"They don't always turn to serial killing to express themselves. You probably know friends who've experienced rotten situations in their everyday lives. A sociopath could be a dirty-dealing co-worker who steals others' ideas. Or he or she could be the CEO of a humongous corporation who embezzles the profits and bilks his workers out of their life savings, believing he's done nothing wrong."

"And smiles all the way to the bank, as the saying goes." Rex laughed. "There's lots of that going on."

"Poke fun if you want to," I said, "but sometimes my instincts warn me of people to beware of and I give them a wide berth. It's called self-preservation." I grinned at them. "Don't lie to me. Don't seek my pity. Don't flatter me. Or I'm likely to put you on my 'watch-out-for-that-person' list."

Neither Janell nor Rex laughed, but I sensed them humoring me and I changed the subject. "We need to narrow our thoughts to the here and now," I said. "Can you think of anyone working at the B&B who would have had both the motive and the opportunity to murder Abra Barrie?"

"No," Janell said. "Our workers are our friends. Friends we've known for years. Hella, for instance. She retired years ago from teaching music in the public schools in Nebraska. Said she's lived frugally all her life and has come to the Keys for a change of scene. She's lived in our B&B for five years."

"You called her a permanent renter," I said. "Why's she permanent?"

"Because she asked to be," Rex said. "We've given her a reduced rate because she pays her rent on time, and she even insists on taking care of her own laundry and room cleaning."

"We'd hate to lose Hella," Janell added, "even though some people find her a bit strange."

Rex stepped inside, then returned to freshen our iced-tea glasses and grinned, commenting on Janell's last statement. "More than a bit strange, I'd say."

"Strange in what way?" I bit into another cookie.

Rex thought for a few moments before he tried to explain. "Hella claims to be a clairvoyant—you know, one of those gifted people who can read tarot cards and see future happenings before they take place. But hey! Hella's a kind and honest person and she wouldn't hurt a soul. If she believes she can see into the future, I say more power to her."

"Agreed," Janell said. "She's even president of a nationally known clairvoyants' organization. She gets lots of mail. Guess she's highly respected in that field."

"She sounds very interesting, Janell. An authority figure in her field. I'm eager to meet her."

"She has fun with her talent, too," Janell said. "On some evenings, she goes to Mallory Dock for the sunset celebrations. I'm guessing she reads a few palms to help pay her rent."

"She ever read yours?" I asked.

"No." Janell laughed. "Nor Rex's. We've never been deeply involved in fortune telling."

"Some people really are psychic," I said. "A psychic from Chicago once helped Chief Gilmore solve a case in Iowa. But you mentioned a person working for you named Phud. The name fascinates me. What sort of a person is he?"

"Phud's just a nickname for Ph.D." Rex grinned. "He has a doctorate degree and he's a professor emeritus from Yale."

"He's a highly respected botanist," Janell said. "A walking green thumb. We're lucky to have him as our gardener. He's a busy person, but he fits us in when he has time. He writes a weekly column on plants and gardening for the *Citizen* and he lectures once a month for garden club members both here at West Martello and in Marathon's new center. You've been to West Martello years ago. Remember?"

"Of course. A very neat place."

"Right. And Phud's a very neat person. I volunteer at West Martello at least once a week, passing out brochures and show-ing guests the grounds. I'll give you a special tour before you leave. The club's made some changes, added lots of new plant-ings since you last saw the place."

"I'll look forward to that. But let's keep our talk on murder suspects. So there's Hella and Phud, both respected authority figures in their fields. What about the combo musicians? Old friends, too? And how many of them are there?"

"There are three of them, and they're all old friends." Rex poured himself yet another glass of tea and offered me another cookie. "There's Ace, our drummer. That's his trap set on the bandstand. He leaves it here to save having to move it back and forth and also for the advertising it might bring him. You may have noticed his logo on the drum head—*THE ACE— Freshest Shrimp in the Keys.*"

"So shrimping's his real business," I said.

"Right." Janell nodded. "He calls himself a drum bum, but he's a serious and respected businessman. He's a happy-go-lucky sort, and he often shares some shrimp with us. It's fun having him around."

"When he *is* around," Rex added. "Sometimes I think he misses as many gigs as he plays. When his boat, the *Ace,* is on a run, he's aboard, charting the course, winching in the nets."

"So what do you do without a drummer?"

"Hella fills in for him."

"Psychic and drummer. Some combination. That I want to see!"

Janell pushed her chair under the table, making it clear she was ready to go back inside. "Hella used to teach music and she does okay on the drums. Keeps a steady beat. Says she played in an all-girl dance band for a while after she left college— answered an ad in *Downbeat,* hired on with an all-girl swing band. *Says* she went on the road with them, playing one-night stands."

Rex broke in before Janell could say anymore about Hella and her drumming. "Then there's Mama Gomez. Mama G we call her, another old friend and another talented lady."

"I remember you mentioned you told Abra Barrie that Mama G might let Abra sit in for a few numbers on Friday night."

"Yes," Janell said. "Of course, Mama Gomez might have had other ideas about that when the time came. She has a mindset of her own. If she wants something to happen, it'll usually happen. If she wants something not to happen, it usually doesn't happen."

"That's a kind way of saying she's opinionated and bossy." Rex laughed. "Janell gets along with her better than I do."

"I like her, but I also need her. In addition to playing the piano, she has secret recipes for the sandwich fillings I serve almost every night at our snack bar. She claims to have smuggled the recipes into Florida from Cuba. I've never dared ask for the recipes, but sometimes I can taste capers and black olives and ground conch. In addition to making sandwich fillings and playing piano, she also cleans on some days at the Lighthouse Museum."

"A busy bee," I said.

"Most service people in Key West hold several jobs," Rex said. "They have to if they've formed the bad habit of eating."

Janell nodded. "Mama G has her fingers in lots of pies, but murder isn't one of them."

"So there's one more musician you've not mentioned. Who?"

"Teach Quinn, the bass player," Janell said. "Everyone calls him Teach because he talks nonstop, spieling facts about Fort Jefferson near the Tortugas. You remember going there, right?"

"Right. Why's this guy so interested in Fort Jefferson?"

"He's deeply in debt for his seaplane. He makes his living flying tourists to the fort for day trips, and he gives them information on the old fort at every opportunity, hoping they'll pass some of it on to friends and thus give him some word-of-mouth advertising."

"Probably tells them more info than they're interested in." Rex began stacking our dishes and trays. "Teach's short and he's sensitive about it. Really ticks him off if I call him a banty rooster."

"That nickname might tick me off, too, Rex, but thank you both for all the mini-intros. I'll try to remember them when I meet these key people tomorrow—I will be meeting them tomorrow, won't I?

"Sure," Janelle said. "They'll be hard to avoid."

"Then I'll feel that I almost know them. But I won't let on that we've discussed them. What I want to know now is if you think any of these people had a motive for killing Abra Barrie."

"No strong motive that I can see, that's for sure." Rex picked up our trays. "The woman came here to talk up the use of off-shore wind turbines. She pointed out the nation's need for renewable energy and she told of other on-the-seaside communities that were using the turbines effectively. That set Ace and Teach on edge immediately."

"They're both very possessive of the sea," Janell said. "You'd think they owned it, or at least a big share of it."

"They thought wind turbines would pollute the sea?" I asked as Janell and I began gathering the rest of our supper things.

"Ace thought the turbines' sound, or the vibrations from them, might affect water in his shrimping area. Guess you can't fault a guy for worrying about anything that might interfere with his livelihood."

"And Teach?"

"Teach felt the sight of huge turbines might ruin the tourist business for him as well as for everyone else." Rex nodded. "Key West depends on tourists. I think Teach also visualized accidentally flying his plane into one of those whirling blades. I saw him arguing with Abra Barrie last Thursday night. I think he was trying to talk her into booking a flight to Fort Jefferson, and I'm guessing her schedule didn't allow time for that. Either that or she wasn't interested."

"That's two viewpoints for you," Janell said. "I know you must be exhausted after your long trip, Kitt. Why don't we call it a night?" She led the way to the back door while Rex walked to the torches and extinguished them. For a few minutes the odor of lighter fluid hung in the air before I followed Janell into the kitchen.

"I'm ready to crash. That's for sure. But are you saying Ace and Teach are the only two working here who objected to the turbine idea?"

"Far as I know." Once inside, Janell gathered the place mats and gave them a shake out the back door. "But I certainly don't consider their objections as motives for murder. That'd be a far stretch."

I agreed. I was ready to retire for the night, and I told them goodnight and headed upstairs. Listening to Janell and Rex talk had shifted my mind from my problem to theirs. Until now. Before I showered, I pulled my dad's medallion from my pocket and tucked it into the velvet bag with his diary. After I showered and slipped between the sheets, I lay awake for a long time wondering if The Perp had lived or died. I didn't know his name. Didn't want to know his name. Didn't want to know anymore about him—only if he'd lived or died.

Whenever my thoughts threatened to go to Shelby Cox, I reined them in, refusing to let him remain a part of my life. I tried to tell myself I wouldn't miss him. Who needed Shelby Cox?

4

I realized I was having a nightmare. I always know. I tried to fight my way to wakefulness but dark fragments of the dream clung to my mind. I turned face down onto my pillow to muffle my crying as a death-like miasma floated like black fog in the periphery of my conscious mind.

The snake hangs dangling around his neck. Its skin touches his skin. I shiver in the August heat, imagining what a snake skin would feel like against my neck.

The snake's head sways from side to side.

Donald keeps walking toward me.

Donald. That's the boy's name. Don't know his last name. It's long and too hard to remember. Mama doesn't like for me to play with Donald, but she never says exactly why.

"Why not, Mama?"

"He's too old to be your playmate, Kitt."

"Why does being older make a difference?"

"He should find boys his own age to play with."

Mama makes me curious about Donald.

Right now I've never been so scared, but I stand straight and put on a brave act for Donald—and for me. My dad's a cop, and he says acting brave will help make me brave. I try to believe him. Cops know about stuff like that. But in my heart I doubt. Being tall for my age also helps me act brave. I'm three years old and Donald's five, but I'm taller than he is.

I want to run home, but I force myself to stay. He steps carefully from stone to stone, crossing the shallow stream that flows through this meadow on its way to Ott's pond. Sometimes in the hot weather of summer the stream disappears until the cooler weather of fall. Although the meadow and the pond are only a block from my house, they are off limits for me.

"Katherine, you're not to go near Ott's pond. You hear me?"

Mama's voice is loud and clear when it replays inside my head. Mama ties lots of nots into my life. How can I miss hearing her?

"Yes, Mama, I hear you."

"Promise me you won't go near Ott's pond. It's deep this time of year. Over your head. You could fall in and drown. Promise me. I want to hear you say the words." She stands with her hands on her hips, waiting.

"I won't go near the pond, Mama." I promise, but I cross my fingers behind my back. Promises don't count when you have crossed fingers. That's what the big girls tell me and I believe them.

Now Donald reaches my side of the creek, but I don't back away. And I don't run. If I run, I can reach Mama and the safety of my backyard quickly. I can probably outrun Donald, especially since my legs are longer than his and he has the snake hanging around his neck. But I stand there waiting. Yesterday he promised to let me watch him feed his snake. He said I didn't have to touch it. He promised he'd do the touching and I could stand there and watch.

So that's what I plan to do today. Stand there and watch. I wonder what snakes eat. Grass? Special snake food that comes in boxes like cereal?

"Hi, Kitt."

"Hi, Donald."

"You afraid of snakes?"

"No," I lie.

"Want to touch it?"

"No." And that's no lie.

"If you won't touch it, I know you're afraid of it. Come on. Prove

37

you're not a scaredy cat. Give it a pat on the head."

"No. It might bite me."

"Well, I suppose it might," Donald says. "But you can see it's not biting me."

"It knows you. It doesn't know me."

"Then touch it on its side away from its head. Bet you think snakes are cold and slimy."

"That's what I think."

"You're wrong. Their skin's warm and dry." He steps closer. "Give it a pat. I call it Homer."

I grit my teeth, reach out and give Homer a very brief pat. Donald is right. His snake feels warm and dry. I wonder why it looks cold and slimy.

"Hey, you're pretty brave for a girl. I'll let you help me feed Homer, if you want to—unless you're afraid of mice."

"Mice? You're kidding, right?"

Donald reaches into his jeans pocket and pulls out a tiny white mouse. It wiggles and tries to escape from his hand. "This's Homer's lunch"

"But it's alive." I back off. The back of my neck feels cold, but my face feels sunburn hot. I'm sorry I disobeyed my mother. Sorry I disobeyed and came here like I promised my mother I wouldn't.

"Homer likes live mice, Kitt. Won't eat 'em dead. He'd starve first. Homer wants them alive."

I start to back farther from him, but Donald grabs my wrist. I try to jerk away, but I can't break his grip. I might be taller, but his hands are stronger than mine. Donald holds the mouse by its tail, dangling it above Homer's head with his hand that isn't holding my hand. Homer lifts his head and opens his mouth. I never knew snakes had such big mouths. It looks big enough to hold a tennis ball—well at least a ping-pong ball. I can't bear to watch. I squint my eyes shut.

The mouse screams. It doesn't shriek. It doesn't squeal. It screams. I know it's screaming for help and I want to help it, but I can't.

When I force my eyes open, I'm crying. The mouse is inside the snake's mouth, making the snake's head bulge. Donald holds onto the mouse's tail, grinning until the snake moves its head and pulls the mouse all the way inside. I imagine that mouse still screaming inside the snake, but Donald doesn't act sorry for killing the mouse.

My stomach churns and I throw up my breakfast on Donald's shoes. Orange juice, oatmeal with raisins, toast with grape jam. The mess puddles on Donald's red and white tennies. My throat aches. I don't care if I've ruined his tennies, except that I don't want him to tell his mother and have her call my mother so my mother will know I disobeyed her.

Donald scowls and drops my wrist while he tries to wipe my vomit from his shoes onto the grass.

I run.

I rub the bitter taste in my mouth onto my shirt tail.

I wipe my eyes with my undershirt.

I run all the way home with the sound of mouse screams echoing in my head. When I reach my yard, Mama comes to the door, smiles and asks if I've been running a race. I nod a yes.

I can't tell Mama what happened without admitting I disobeyed her. I bury the snake and the screaming mouse scene in a corner of my mind and never speak of it to anyone. It lives there to haunt my dreams.

When I forced myself fully awake, I lay drenched with sweat. I rose and grabbed a big drink of water as if I could wash the nightmare into oblivion forever. While I took another shower, I wondered about Donald. Where did he live now? I shuddered. He had showed no remorse for torturing that mouse. None. He had laughed. How could he have laughed? Was he a sociopath—a kid born without a conscience? I shuddered, trying not to think of a little kid without a conscience. Today Donald could be a serial killer at large. Or he might be the CEO of a Fortune 500 corporation. According to the *Sociopath Next Door,* all sociopaths weren't killers, but serial killers were usually sociopaths.

Once I had calmed down, I dressed and prepared to face the day. Shorts. Sandals. Green tank top. When I'm out of uniform, I wear lots of green. Shelby says it brings out my eyes. But I no longer care what Shelby says. I wear green because I like green and because it calms down the red of my hair. After I made my bed, I laid my two books on the bedside table, pulled Dad's medallion from the velvet bag where I'd hidden it with his diary, and thrust it into my pocket. Maybe sometime later in my life I could bring myself to wear it around my neck as I used to, but not yet, not while I remained on suspension.

"Have a good night?" Janell asked when I entered the kitchen where she stood at the stove already making coffee and warming cinnamon rolls in the microwave. I knew if there had been any word from home about The Perp, she would have told me, so I didn't ask.

"Had a great night," I lied before I spoke the truth. "I like waking up in Florida with family. I'd forgotten how close The Poinsettia is to the sea. I can smell the ocean on the trade wind and hear the gulls laughing."

Janell smiled and poked a tendril of fiery hair behind her ear. "Every morning I pause at our bedroom window. I can see the ocean from there and I don't ever want to take that view for granted. It has a different look every day. Unique colors. Unique shapes in the waves. If I ever get homesick for Iowa, I look at the sea, and it reminds me of how lucky I am to be here."

"How can I help you this morning, Janell?" I eyed the electric orange juicer lying on the countertop, the orange rinds in the sink. "You carry breakfast out to the pool every morning?"

"Right. If you'll tote the coffee pot and the rolls, I'll bring a pitcher of juice and the fresh fruit. Some things are already out there."

"Will do." I picked up the coffee and rolls and followed Janell

40

to the poolside patio where we set our breakfast treats on a white iron table surrounded by white all-weather chairs. Janell seemed not to notice when the morning dew dampened the hem of her blue caftan, but she grabbed a napkin and wiped the dampness from the table top and the chair seats.

Sun filtering between palm fronds warmed my head and shoulders, but the dark shadows it cast into the pool matched my thoughts. The greenness of the plants in the Cummings's tropical garden bespoke the careful attention of both Janell and the groundskeeper. Elephant ears. Aloes. Cactus? I could do without thorns, but how could I have overlooked the banana plant and the fruit tree laden with oranges!

I glanced from this Eden to the B&B at the side of the patio, hating to think about Abra Barrie, who had slept there only a few nights ago. I liked the woman without ever having met her or known her—liked anyone interested in finding renewable energy sources. My blood boiled if I thought too much about all the millions we taxpayers paid the Arabs for their oil. We give them our help in establishing a democracy—they give us three-dollar oil. I liked the days when oil was cheap and people were valuable. I'd wondered if that time would ever come again.

"Will Hella Flusher be having breakfast with us?" I snapped my attention back to the iron table and the breakfast goodies.

"Not this morning. She begged off after enjoying a glass of orange juice, saying she needed an early morning walk on the dock. I think she's allowing us to have a little more family-only time before the morning engulfs us."

"Think the police will come around here again today?"

"They may. But I hope not. Rex will join us in a few minutes. He's doing some repairs on the café. High winds hit us fairly hard last summer and fall, but we've been able to open for business every night. We plan to open as usual tonight and hope some customers show up in spite of—everything."

"Janell?"

She paused at my tone and the question in my voice.

"What were you and Rex doing last Friday afternoon when the ME says Abra Barrie died?"

"You don't think we're into murdering our guests, do you?"

"Of course not, but I was wondering if you both had air-tight alibis."

"No. We don't. We have alibis of sorts, but I'm afraid they're both a long way from being air-tight."

Before I could learn more about their alibis, air-tight or otherwise, Rex approached from the café, the sun gleaming on his baldness.

"Morning, women. Got a handout for a hungry working man?"

Janell poured Rex a glass of juice and offered him a roll while he reached for a cup and the coffee pot. I spooned chunks of fresh strawberries, banana, and papaya onto my plate and sat back to enjoy the treat. We'd only been sipping and munching for a few minutes when Rex spoke. As usual, his tone was quiet, but it riveted me to my chair as did his words.

"Kitt, Janell and I are going to ask a big favor of you. We hope it won't turn your stay here into a busman's holiday, but we'd like you to help us find the person who murdered Abra Barrie. No, maybe that's not exactly what we want. Maybe we just want you to help us prove that we and our workers are innocent, and that the guilty one has nothing to do with The Poinsettia. You've been in police work and law enforcement for several years now. We need you, especially since the police keep dwelling on the human blood they found on my boat."

"How about it, Kitt?" Janell said. "If you'll help us, we'll do a private investigation of the people connected with The Poinsettia."

"Right," Rex agreed. "With your police background, you've

got the skills, the know-how. I hope guilt doesn't point a finger at any of our people, and if we can prove their innocence, the police will feel free to leave us alone and start searching elsewhere. What do you think?"

"I think I'd like to help—very much like to help and, under the present circumstances, I'm flattered you've asked me."

"The present circumstances you refer to will soon be past circumstances. We'll have to work quickly while you're still in Florida. The minute your suspension ends, they'll want you back in Iowa."

"You're surer of that than I."

"Be a positive thinker," Janell ordered.

"Janell made notes on the alibis our workers gave the police on Saturday. They called us all in and talked to us together. No *Miranda* warning. Strictly off the cuff—they said. The info Janell has came right from their mouths. Will you take a careful look at those alibis and then do some in-depth checking on each person?"

"Yes," I agreed. "Janell's notes will be a good starting place. Glad you took careful notes."

"I'll help, too, in any way I can," Rex said, "but I'm still repairing wind damage on our dance floor and snack bar. We were hit hard last summer and it could happen again."

"I remember watching the Weather Channel for well over a month and worrying about you."

"We're lucky the damage wasn't worse," Rex said. "I'll help all I can with an investigation. We want to see this murder solved. One of our largest fears is that it might turn into a cold case that will have the locals gossiping and speculating for years to come."

"We want to see justice done," Janell said, "but at the same time we need to see our business continue to succeed."

"Of course. Good thing your business thrives on tourist trade.

The murder, if it's like most murders, will soon fall out of the news. Cops may remember it, but most tourists will never hear of it."

"The locals have long memories," Janell said. "I'll help you all I can, but I'm no detective and time's of an essence."

"Not only must we consider your being called home soon," Rex said, "but we must also consider the way our police department sometimes works. S-l-o-w-l-y. I think they'd prefer to push the murder under a palm branch, weight it down with coconuts and forget about it."

"I'm guessing they do their best," I said. "Most police departments do, if they're anything like the one I work for—worked for."

"They can't stall in trying to solve this case," Rex said. "Police from other areas are searching for a serial killer. Right now the search is pointing to Key West."

5

"Of course I'll help you in any way I can," I said. "You're family. Where will we start? When do we get started?"

"Great, Kitt." Janell gave my arm a squeeze. "We'll get started as soon as possible. We need all the help we can get."

"And all the locals are family where this murder's concerned," Rex said.

Suddenly the tropical garden I'd seen as warm and comforting morphed into a jungle-like prison. All its green vines and thorns were closing in on me, holding me in place. I wanted to help solve Abra Barrie's murder. Yes. I wanted to help get a serial killer off the streets. Yes. But I didn't want to offer help that might place Janell or Rex under closer scrutiny. Janell had started to tell me where they were last Friday afternoon, but she'd been interrupted and I didn't want to ask again. The fact that the police had found human blood on Rex's boat loomed large in my mind, although I couldn't imagine him harming anyone. They hadn't proved that the blood was Rex's.

"You realize I have a selfish reason for wanting to help, don't you?" I looked at the ground, unable to meet their eyes. "Maybe working on this murder will help me atone for my mistake back home." I got off the subject of that shooting quickly before either of them could comment.

"And another reason. I can identify with Abra Barrie. I'd like to help find her killer. She was working to improve our environment. Helping make people aware of sources of renewable energy is a good and logical place to start. It's one reason I'm driving the Prius. I want people to notice it, to ask about it. I wish I could have known Abra. I think we had a lot in common."

Janell stood and laid a hand on my shoulder. "Whatever your reasons for helping find this killer, they all boil down to the fact that you're a good person, Kitt. Never forget that."

Rex's cell phone rang and he spoke to a caller briefly before he pocketed the phone and turned to us again. "Police. They want me at headquarters—again. Now. Didn't say why, but I don't think they're serving tea and toast."

"I thought they'd asked all their questions last Saturday," Janell said. "I hope their questioning isn't going to be an ongoing thing."

"Maybe they're going to give you the go-ahead for cleaning up your boat." I wished I could forget about that blood, his boat.

"They could have mentioned that over the phone. But they didn't." Rex gulped the last of his coffee then strode toward the carport and wheeled his bicycle onto the path to the front gate.

"Why don't you take the car?" Janell called. "I won't need it to get supplies until later in the morning."

"And we could take the Prius for that errand," I added.

"Arriving in the car would tell the chief I place extra importance on this meeting. Going to play it cool. Going to ride the bike as usual."

Rex left and I pushed my plate and juice glass aside, no longer interested in breakfast. Janell refilled her coffee cup and settled back in her chair.

"During tourist season, we only use the car for essential driving—usually to the grocery store or the lumberyard for supplies. If we're lucky, we can find side streets with little traffic and a parking slot at Fausto's or Strunk's. But for ordinary errands, we ride our bicycles."

"I noticed heavy traffic when I arrived yesterday."

"Right. The traffic's hard to deal with—SUVs and live-in campers clog streets originally designed for horses and buggies. But we smile and tell tourists our crowded streets are a part of Key West's charm. And while parking places are hard to find, I'm sure there'll be one waiting for Rex at the police station. Wish I could have gone with him."

"Maybe he'll be back soon. In the meantime, how about giving me the scoop on your workers and their alibis?" I hoped that would take our minds off Rex's command performance at the police station.

"Sure. We'll get to that, but first let's stop pussyfooting around your problems back home. You must have had good reason for shooting that guy. Want to tell me about it?"

"I hate thinking about it, hate talking about it. But maybe it'll be a relief to tell you the whole story. You and Rex are the only family I have left."

"So give. What happened?"

I gave her all the details leading to the shooting. "And there we were with guns drawn in this dark, smelly pet shop." The thought of the animal odor reminded me of last night's nightmare, and I had to gulp more juice before I could continue. "I saw The Perp raise his arm, point his gun at my head—and I fired first. Several minutes later we discovered he wasn't armed. Had a phony pistol, a child's toy. Can't understand why he risked pointing a fake gun at a police officer. Dumb butt. Didn't he know he was putting his life on the line?"

Janell took my hand, clasping it in both of hers. "I'm so sorry this happened, Kitt. I know the kind of person you are. Straight arrow all the way. What kind of a person was this man?"

"The scum of the earth, as far as I'm concerned. A crook. A druggie. A scofflaw with a long rap sheet. And maybe a sociopath. He'd appeared in court many times before. Chief Gilmore told me he'd never seen the guy show any remorse for his crimes."

"And in spite of his record, he was still on the street."

"Yes. Janell, there's a whole underbelly of society that law-abiding citizens like you and Rex know little about. The police arrest the same people for the same types of offenses time after time. We risk our lives to get criminals off the street only to have the courts release them all too soon back into society where they're free to commit their crimes again. And again. They get by with no more than a slap on the wrist. It's discouraging, but it's no reason for me to have shot a man."

I frowned, irritated at myself. "Guess I need to rent a hall and give lectures to the public. Sorry I ran off at the mouth like that."

"Surely the review committee will rule that you shot in self defense. Surely you'll be reinstated on the force."

"Maybe. Maybe not. But either way, I'll know I'm capable of shooting another person. That's hard knowledge to live with. I've disgraced the family as well as myself. 'Thirty-four years on the force and I never fired my gun.' That's what Dad said after he retired. If I heard him say it once, I heard it a hundred times. How can I go on being a cop? Even if the review committee allows me the chance?"

"You can do it because it's the right thing to do and because you're a strong person, Kitt. You're not going to let your spur-of-the-minute reaction to a threat to your life ruin the rest of your years on this earth. You have lots to offer today's society. Think about your future."

"Sometimes I think I've lost my future. With one shot I lost everything—everything of value."

"Not so. You'll always have Rex and me."

"I'll also have an all-knowing God."

"And an all-loving God," Janell said. "Never forget that."

"Sometimes that's very hard to remember. And I'm not sure I'm deserving."

Janell refilled her coffee cup before she spoke again. "What do you really want from life, Kitt? What are your long-term goals and dreams?"

I didn't spout a glib reply, and I wished she'd stop prodding me for answers to questions I didn't want to face—or to share. I waited moments before I spoke again, wondering how I could change the subject, but I saw Janell lean forward. I felt her pushing me for a reply.

"I wanted to have a career like Dad's—unblemished. I want my life to count for something. I want a husband and children and a family life, but I'm thirty-two and the clock's ticking. I hate the thought of Shelby Cox. Where's he disappeared to all of a sudden? Some friend! I feel like my life ended with that gunshot. I have little hope of ever getting it back on track again."

Janell didn't speak, and I followed her gaze when she looked over her shoulder. A big burly woman opened the garden gate. I squelched my inner vision of a female wrestler, but I welcomed the end of our discussion.

"Hella," Janell called. "Good morning." Then turning to me again, she whispered, "Have hope, Kitt. We'll talk again later. Right now, I want to introduce you to our B&B guest."

Hella looked like a mountain of muscle—a big-boned person who captured me with her direct gaze. She wore her hair in a thick brown braid that hung down the back of her cream-colored shift. *TUESDAY.* The name of the day was embroidered on the sleeve. Did she have a different shift for each day of the week? The tan fanny-pack belted loosely around her waist matched clunky leather shoes that gave her avoirdupois firm footing as she headed toward the poolside patio.

"Hella," Janell called again. "Do come meet my sister. Kitt, this's Hella Flusher. Do sit down and join us for a few minutes."

Hella and I exchanged greetings while Janell filled a coffee cup and pushed the plate of rolls toward her. Hella chose the chair next to me, and I jumped, startled when I saw movement in the straw tote bag she set on the patio beside her.

"Relax, child. It's just Voodoo." A black cat with startling green eyes peeked over the edge of Hella's tote then ran, disappearing into the tropical greenery at the side of the pool.

"Voodoo?"

Janell laughed. "A neighborhood cat."

"Belongs to the family next door who recently moved here from Louisiana," Hella said. "I sometimes take Voodoo with me on my morning stroll. Cats are good company for old ladies."

All the time the three of us sat visiting, I wanted to ask Hella where she'd been last Friday afternoon. She had the muscle and probably the opportunity to overcome Abra Barrie, but I could think of no motive.

"Janell tells me you're from Iowa," Hella said.

"Right. Very cold up there right now. Snow. Ice. Slush. I'm lucky to be here in the sunshine."

Hella nodded and smiled. "I know all about Iowa winters." She gave a mock shudder. "As a child I lived in Des Moines. And castles are hard to heat in Iowa even on a fairly warm day."

"Castles? You lived in a castle? In Des Moines?"

"Right. Years ago, of course. Balmoral Castle. Some folks claimed it was haunted." Hella looked directly at me, waiting for my response.

Janell raised her eyebrows. "Hella likes to tease."

I'd never heard of a castle in Des Moines. Hella had dark eyes that seemed to look right into my soul. I fought a desire to squirm under her gaze. Was this woman a liar? If I hadn't left my computer in an Iowa shop for repair, I'd have looked up Balmoral Castle at my first chance.

"Tell me about your castle."

"Over a hundred years ago, a self-promoting doctor built it in the style of Scotland's Balmoral Castle. Later, a senator bought it. His son died there, and people say it's the son's ghost that still haunts the castle. I lived there when new owners converted it into apartments."

"And did you ever see the ghost?"

Hella looked directly into my eyes for several moments before she spoke. "Perhaps I did. Perhaps I didn't. Doesn't matter a lot one way or the other. People always doubt what a clairvoyant says."

Questions sizzled inside me, but Hella stood and changed the subject before I could ask more about the castles, ghosts, or clairvoyants.

"Janell, I see that you've brought your croton bush back from death." Hella stepped off the patio onto one of the flagstones that decorated the garden. "It's looking much better than it did last week."

I looked at the plant Hella had stooped to touch. Its vibrant multicolored leaves looked healthy enough to me—reds, yellows, greens, pinks. I wished I knew more about tropical plants.

"I've really been babying that croton," Janell said. "It's hard to get rid of mites and mealy bugs, but I've developed a new pesticide. And just in time. Those pests were destroying the plant."

"You telling all?" Hella asked. "Or are you planning to patent your new formula?"

Janell grinned. "I'll tell all. It's really a simple remedy—my own variation on an old standby. I take three cigarettes and soak them in water overnight, instead of just for an hour or two, in a pint of tepid tap water. The next day I strain that water through a sieve, add it to a pint of warm soapy water, and spray or wipe it onto the underside of the croton leaves. So far, it's been working."

"You and Phud both have green thumbs," Hella said, "but don't tell Phud I gave him a compliment."

Janell laughed. "You and Phud need to bury the machete. Don't know what we'd do around here without him—or you, Hella. But Kitt, now would be a good time to see inside the B&B—now while there's an empty apartment. I've placed an ad in the *Citizen,* and I hope to have it rented soon."

The B&B had flower boxes attached to the front windows that overlooked the pool, each box boasting an array of brightly blooming petunias. The entry to the apartments opened on the back of the unit, and I followed Janell inside the room Abra Barrie had rented. I'd expected only one room, but there were two—a tiny living room big enough for a couch and a TV, and a bedroom with a bath attached. Janell had applied her usual *Southern Living* touch to the rooms with pastel-colored walls and big windows that could be left open to catch the ocean breeze and the sunlight, or closed for privacy with vertical panels on a pull cord.

"It's lovely, Janell. Wouldn't mind renting it myself—maybe for the rest of my life. Are the units alike?"

"No. Each has its own decorating scheme."

I hoped Hella might offer to show me her unit, but no. When we left Abra's rooms, Hella stood firm in front of her doorway. She didn't budge. It was almost as if she were daring us to ask to enter.

We didn't ask.

"It's been nice meeting you, Hella. Maybe we'll be seeing more of each other before my stay comes to an end."

"That's quite probable." Hella let her dark, probing eyes meet mine in a long gaze. "People never meet by accident, Kitt. There's a purpose. Maybe we'll have time to discover what it is."

6

Rex rode his bike into the garden and on toward the carport moments before I saw a tall man wearing a camouflage jumpsuit and a navy blue tam approach the tool shed at the back of the Cummings's lot, entering on foot by way of an alley and a small opening in the fence.

"Who's the stranger?" I touched Janell's arm to get her attention as she headed toward Rex.

"Oh, Phud's here!" she exclaimed. "Let me introduce you. You two can get acquainted while I go hear what Rex learned from the police."

I felt uncomfortable—wary of being left alone with the yard man, but I knew Janell wanted a few minutes of privacy with Rex, so I smiled and followed her toward the tool shed. The caretaker towered a few inches above both of us, and with his height and the fringe of salt-and-pepper hair peeking from beneath his tam, he looked distinguished even in his casual work attire. I'd always pictured artists in tams, but maybe this guy was an artist with plants and flowers. His piercing blue eyes and aquiline nose gave character to his face, and his cleft chin reminded me of my dad. Janell had chosen a handsome yard man.

"Kitt, I want you to meet Dr. Whitney Ashby. He knows his way around plants and trees, and lots of my friends are on a waiting list for his landscaping services. Phud, meet my sister, Kitt."

I extended my hand and he responded with a firm handshake. "Pleased to meet you, Dr. Ashby."

"The pleasure is mutual, Kitt. Janell's told me a lot about you—all good, of course. Do feel free to call me Phud. Dr. Ashby sounds far too formal for a guy who spends his prime time digging in the dirt."

"Thank you, Phud." The name didn't become him, and I could hardly say it without laughing.

"If you two will excuse me, I need to talk with Rex. Help yourself to a roll and a cup of coffee, Phud. Or maybe you prefer orange juice. Think there's still a little in the pitcher."

"Thanks, but no thanks." He smiled at Janell as she left us, then turned to me. "Before I start whacking down coconuts—my goal for this morning—I'd like to check on my starter plot of double impatiens. It's back beside the tool shed. I'm hoping they'll soon be ready to transplant."

"Where will you plant them? Your home garden?"

"No. I live in a condo in the Truman Annex. No room for more flower beds there. I've promised to design a flower bed on the grounds of the Lighthouse Museum in front of the entryway, a sort of colorful welcome to visitors. That's the place I've planned for the impatiens. They were thriving yesterday and sometimes they seem they grow overnight."

"You must have a magic touch."

"These plants are my current pride and joy. You a flower person, Kitt?"

"I enjoy looking at them, but my thumb is more brown than green. I admire people who can get plants to grow and bloom."

"Your eyes make up for any small deficiency people might find in your thumb." He smiled when he looked into my eyes, and it was easy to smile back. I noticed his slight limp when I followed him to the plot of loamy soil he had staked off as his impatiens bed.

"Look as if they'll be blooming soon. There are lots of buds."

I'd expected to hear Phud agree with me, but he'd stooped to grab a clod of earth and hurl it toward the backyard fence. In the next moment I saw Voodoo take a flying leap and land hidden in the greenery of the garden across the alley.

"That darned cat!" Phud took a threatening step toward the fence before he stopped and turned to face me again. "Insists on using my impatiens bed as a litter box. Someday . . ." He sighed. "I never manage to hit it, probably don't come close or it wouldn't keep prowling here. But at least I scare it off temporarily."

"Does it really damage your plants?"

"Smashes them flat. Takes them a day or so to recover. And sometimes it even claws them from the ground." Phud scowled, peering toward the spot where Voodoo had disappeared. "Think Hella coaxes him here, but of course she denies that and I've never actually caught her at it. Neighbors ought to keep the nuisance on a leash."

"So tell me about your gardening goal for today. The coconuts?" I tried to change the subject from Hella and Voodoo, but I wondered if what he said about her coaxing the cat was true.

"Going to cut the coconuts from the palms that border the sides of the property. Those out front are date palms. Nothing to do out there." Phud stepped inside the tool shed and returned wearing a pair of cotton work gloves and carrying a long-handled machete and a cardboard box. "I'll drop the coconuts into the box and set them in front of the house. On Tuesdays, Cubans cruise the neighborhoods in pickup trucks and haul them away for us."

"They take them and pay you, or do you pay them for the cleanup?"

"No pay." Phud laughed. "We're glad to get rid of them

before they fall and hurt someone or damage other plantings. The Cubans are glad to get them."

"And what do they do with them?"

"Sometimes they sell them to local craftsmen who paint or carve them into souvenirs they sell at art fairs. You've probably seen plenty of those."

"Right. In fact, Janell sent me one that I use as a doorstop back home."

"Other times they haul them to a processing plant near Miami, market them there to workers who turn them into something edible. Coconut meat. Coconut milk. Palm oil. Whatever."

"Maybe I can help you." I thought about his limp and wondered if gathering coconuts made his leg hurt. "I could pick the nuts up and toss them into the box for you if that would help."

"If you care to do that, I'd welcome the help—not that I can't do it myself. Do it every few weeks."

"Be glad to assist."

"Okay, but stand back several feet while I whack," Phud warned. "The nuts usually fall straight down, but I wouldn't want one to fly astray and hit you."

I watched until he had slashed three coconuts from the tree nearest his shed. He worked deftly with the machete, taking careful aim and bringing the nuts down on the first whack. If a dead frond blocked his aim, he whacked it down, too. It was no big deal for me to toss the coconuts into the box.

What were you doing last Friday afternoon, Phud? Any other use you've found for that machete?

My questions died in my mind, unasked when I saw Janell on the back steps near the café, motioning me toward her.

"Got to go now, Phud." I nodded toward the house. "Nice meeting you. I'll tell Janell I think her garden's in good hands."

56

Phud winked at me. "Janell knows." He turned back to the palms and continued harvesting coconuts.

His wink left me feeling off center. He *had* winked at me, hadn't he? Or maybe I'd imagined it. I followed Janell into the café where Rex stood with his cell phone to his ear, shouting, "Can you hear me now?"

"He's talking to the guy from Strunk Lumber about supplies," Janell said. "But he wants to tell us both about his visit with the police. Doesn't want to have to tell it twice."

"Good news or bad?" I asked.

Janell shrugged. "Don't know yet."

"What are all the rolls of plastic for?"

"Side curtains," Janell said. "Customers like the open-air ambience of the café, so the plastic hooks to the side framework so we can raise and lower the curtains against chilly winds. Most of the time we don't need them, but when a cold front moves in, they help protect our customers."

"You lost the curtains last fall in the hurricane?"

"Right. For a long time Rex had trouble getting supplies. Everyone on the island needed building materials. Now that Rex has the plastic, he has trouble finding time to tack it in place."

When Rex pocketed his phone, Janell and I both stepped closer to him. "What happened at the PD?" Janell asked. "What did they want? Blood sample?"

"No blood. They wanted to hear my alibi one more time."

"Wonder why they didn't want to hear mine again."

"Guess they figured there was nothing you could say that would give yours more credibility. You were at West Martello talking to tourists. No way could the police expect you to locate transients for corroboration."

"So what did they say to you?" Janell asked.

Rex met her gaze. "I've got a confession. I lied to them that first time they talked to everyone, Janell."

I swallowed a gasp and forced myself to keep looking at him without changing my expression. Rex a liar?

"You *lied?*" Janell asked. "What were you thinking? On Friday, you were at Strunk's looking at catalogs, going over a list of supplies you'd ordered and not received, weren't you?"

"No. I wasn't. Lying's never been my style, but I thought I might get by with that little white one. I've been in and out of that lumberyard so often since September, I thought some clerk might vouch for my presence by mistake, believing he had seen me there on Friday. When an officer went to Strunk's to check on my alibi, they could find no clerk there who'd vouch for me. No fault of Strunk's. I'll be first to admit I did a dumb thing."

"Okay, Rex." Janell took a step away from him. "I want the truth. Where were you on Friday afternoon?"

Janell stood tapping her toe on the concrete floor, and I hoped I wasn't about to witness a family quarrel. I looked toward the door and took a step in that direction, but Rex called me back.

"Stay here, Kitt. I want you to hear this. I lied for a good cause—at least it seemed like a good cause at the time. The officers had said the questioning was informal. Janell, you remember that painting you saw at the art fair on Whitehead Street last week?"

"Of course I remember it. A lone pelican perched on a dock piling. Beautiful work. Such a typical Key West scene. We both liked it, right? But I thought it was too expensive for our pocketbooks right now while we're buying so many repair supplies. I passed it by."

"But I knew you liked it and I wanted you to have it. It'll look great in our living room. I measured the wall space beside the bookcase. I knew it would fit. You have a birthday coming up in March, and I wanted to surprise you with that painting as a birthday gift."

Rex began talking faster and faster, and Janell stopped toe tapping.

"The artist's from up in the islands—Big Pine Key. I went back to talk to her later on the day of the art show. She said she displays her work at the co-op gallery in the Winn Dixie plaza."

"So you drove there on Friday afternoon while I was busy volunteering at West Martello."

"Right, Janell. I did. But the painting was gone. The artist gave me the name of the buyer—a woman in Marathon. I drove there, thinking maybe I could talk her out of the painting—buy it from her."

"So did you?" I asked.

"No such luck. The woman wasn't home. Nobody answered my knock. I was going to try again later, phone first the next time, but . . . there's been no time."

"So you drove home without the painting," Janell said.

"Right. And without an alibi I was willing to give the police while you sat there listening. It would have spoiled my surprise. I still had hope of talking to the woman in Marathon and buying the painting from her. I thought I could tell the police my true alibi later when you weren't around and that nothing more would be said about it—at least not to you."

She gave Rex a hug. "But it didn't work out that way. I appreciate your effort to surprise me on my birthday, and I'm sorry it backfired."

"Right. It's caused me grief and it may cause more. Although the police had said that the initial questioning was informal, I began feeling the seriousness of my statement when a detective announced they'd found blood on my boat. I knew then I was in for another questioning—a *Miranda* warning–type questioning."

"Rex! I think we need a lawyer."

"You may be right, but it's too late for that now. Without being asked, I went to the station privately and without a lawyer and gave the police chief my true alibi, expecting them to believe it."

"They didn't believe you?" Janell asked. "The people at the Big Pine gallery would corroborate your story, wouldn't they?"

"Yes. The police checked with them and they vouched for me. The volunteer on duty even said I spent an hour in the museum looking at other paintings I thought you might like."

"So why did the police call you in this morning?"

"They wanted to hear me tell my story again—wanted to see if I'd change it in any way or if I'd stick to it."

"And you stuck to it, I hope," Janell said.

"Right. The police were satisfied, and they gave me permission to clean up my boat. They also told me, warned me, that they had ordered DNA testing on the blood on the boat to see if it matched Abra Barrie's DNA."

7

"Hola, amigos! Hola!" The swinging door between the house and the patio café opened with a whoosh. A plump woman with a braided crown of bottle-black hair anchored to the top of her head by tortoise-shell pins distracted us from Rex's DNA announcement.

"Mama Gomez is here!" The woman stepped into the café and plunked a willow basket onto the snack bar near the refrigerator as if it might contain the gold of Pizarro. *"Tasting time. Gustoso! Bueno!"*

Janell smiled and stepped toward the woman who'd been spouting orders. "Good morning, Mama G."

"Morning? The woman snorted and tapped her wristwatch with a fat forefinger. *"Es mediodia!"*

"Mama G," Janell smiled. "Please let me introduce you to my sister, Kitt Morgan." I looked down at Mama G, whose crowning glory reached barely to my chin, ready to exchange greetings.

"Hola, Kitt!" Mama G looked up at me, but gave me no time to respond. *"Bienvenida!* You're in for a treat today. And Janell, your customers are in for a treat tonight. I've made two of my specials. The C and C and the E and F. Now you will taste both kinds. Bring me some *galletas."*

I guessed the word "please" wasn't in this woman's vocabulary. It didn't surprise me that Janell hurried to the kitchen and returned with a plate of crackers. I supposed from Mama G's tone and her body language that in dealing with her, Janell needed to save her refusals for more important occasions.

"Here, here, *amigos*. Come." Mama G opened her basket with a flourish to reveal two plastic-covered bowls. "You'll be tasting the C and C first. And I expect compliments." By now her Cuban lingo had diminished. She opened the first bowl of a coarse pinkish paste.

"C and C?" I hung back, refusing to let *Senora* Boss Lady order my life as she seemed so intent on doing.

"Conch and capers." Mama G lifted a knife from her basket and spread a generous amount of sandwich filling onto three crackers. She paused, then fixed a third cracker and then a fourth as Hella and Phud stepped onto the patio. "Welcome one, welcome all."

Mama G turned to me. "As you can see, people come from all directions to taste my creations of the day. *Attencion* now! Line up, please."

I couldn't believe everyone was obeying this loudmouth as if she were a theater master and they were puppets on a string. I stood in line with the others, and we sampled the conch and caper spread.

"Wonderful!" everyone exclaimed, more or less in unison. I wanted to say "turdy and terrible." Those words slipped into my thinking vocabulary now and then, but never into my verbal vocabulary. I said nothing.

"And you, Kitt Morgan?" Mama G glared at me. "What do you think of my sandwich filling?"

Not wanting to embarrass Janell, I rose to the occasion with a very dingy white lie. "It's wonderful, Mama G. Delicious."

"Mama Gomez to you is my name." The woman lifted her chin and scowled. "One must earn the right to call me Mama G."

"Mama Gomez." I stood corrected, wondering how one

"earned the right."

"And now the E and F." Mama G opened the second bowl and spread a dark mixture onto the crackers.

"What's in it, Mama G?" Rex asked. "Tell all if you expect me to taste. Never seen this one before."

"Correct. I've never honored you with this specialty before. Is a secret recipe from *Tia* Louisa, my great-great-aunt who resides in Havana." She thrust the plate of crackers toward Rex."

"I asked you what's *in* it." By cocking his head and refusing to lift a hand toward the plate, Rex called her bluff.

"It's a special mixture of escargot and feta cheese."

"Count me out." Rex shook his head and backed away from the rest of us. "Not my thing."

"I'll try it." Phud reached for a sample then passed the plate to Hella, who shook her head and eased closer to Rex. I waited for an explosion from Mama G, but Voodoo saved us all, jumping from Hella's tote, where he'd been hiding, knocking the crackers to the floor and snarfing them down as if they were the last supper.

"I'm sorry, Mama G," Janell said. "I'm sure tonight's guests will enjoy your treat. I'll refrigerate the bowls, and Kitt will help me make the sandwiches for this evening."

Mama G drew herself to her full height and, in turn, glared at each one of us. "Another scene like this, and it's *adios*. I won't be upstaged by a cat." She flounced from the patio and stomped through the garden toward a rusty Chevy parked out front in the tow-away zone. I doubted she'd ever been towed. What cop would have had the nerve!

"Janell, how do you and Rex tolerate that woman?" I asked. "Where does she get the intestinal fortitude to come on so strong?"

Janell laughed. "When you know her better, you'll find she's an interesting person, Kitt. Proud of her sandwich mixes. You'll get used to her. She thrives on attention. She claims her mama stitched secret family recipes into the hem of her dress in order to smuggle them out of Cuba when Castro took over. Her parents sent her as a child from their home in Havana to a Miami orphanage."

"They abandoned her?" I asked.

"No, she wasn't an abandoned child," Rex said. "She'll be more than willing to tell you all about the 1959 Pedro Pan airlift for kids. Parents didn't like what Castro was doing to the Cuban school system. If I were you, I wouldn't ask. She'll talk your ear off. And I wouldn't eat any of her escargot and feta cheese, either."

"She'll calm down by tonight," Janell said. "She's good on the piano, and she sings along on some numbers."

"And she sings, too?" I corked my envy.

"Yes, she sings," Rex said. "But forget about her calming down. Tonight she'll vent her orders on Teach and Ace. They pretend to obey her. Or, at least, they figure out ways to ignore her orders."

"I'm checking out for today, Janell," Phud said. "Put a large box of coconuts out front ready for pickup."

"Thanks, Phud. I appreciate it."

"I'll drop around tonight," Hella promised as she headed back toward the B&B. "Want to see if bad publicity attracts or repels."

"A true psychic and clairvoyant would know the answer to that beforehand." Phud tossed Hella a superior glance.

"My work speaks for itself." Hella straightened her shoulders, letting her baleful glance speak for itself.

"When does your snack bar open?" I asked, wondering if the relationship between Hella and Phud was a stormy one. "I'm ready to make sandwiches any time you are."

"We open at six," Janell said. "That's about the time lots of people begin passing to and from the sunset celebration on Mallory. We advertise as a family café. Parents want and need a soda bar for minors where their kids can have fun without risking an encounter with alcohol—or drugs."

"We're zoned for business," Rex said, "and we close at ten. Neighbors don't complain about late-night noise. We usually do a good business."

"In spite of Mama Gomez and her conch and capers sandwiches—escargot and feta?" I asked.

Janell grinned. "Right. Many parents enjoy taste adventures. I keep plenty of pimento cheese and peanut butter and jelly on hand for the kids if they want it."

"Key West's an island of history and mystery," Rex said. "Mama G's sandwich fillings fit right in."

"So, shall we make sandwiches now?" I asked.

"Later, Kitt. Right now I need to go to Fausto's for fresh bread. Want to come along?"

"Sure. I've been waiting for a chance to drive around the island. How about taking my car?"

"Fine with me," Janell said. "Rex, you need anything from the store?"

"No, but thanks. I've got plenty right here to keep me busy for an hour or so. Then I'll go to the marina and start cleaning up my boat." Rex turned to the roll of plastic he'd been working with, then looked up again. "On second thought, you might pick up a jar of dill relish at Fausto's. I'll grill some grouper for supper. Give Kitt a taste of the best fish in the Keys."

"Will do." Janell turned to me. "Grouper. It's a favorite around here, and Rex does a great job of grilling it, but first let's freshen up inside and have a bite of lunch."

"Rex, could I help you work on your boat?" I hoped he'd say yes. I wanted to see the boat exactly as the police had seen it. "Two people working together could get the job done faster than one person working alone."

"Thanks, Kitt, but it's a job I need to do alone. No task for any woman. I'm not looking forward to it, but I'll get it behind me today."

"Come on, Kitt. I'll bring out a salad for Rex."

So much had happened this morning that I'd forgotten about lunch. When we left the café and started into the kitchen, Phud was standing near the carport looking at my car. I joined him, and Janell went on inside.

"Ever seen a Prius before?" I asked.

"Yes," Phud said. "I've even been thinking of buying one—expensive though they may be. I like the idea of an electric motor combined with a gasoline engine. You enjoying this model?"

"Very much. Less pollution and better mileage." I enjoyed telling people about the car, pointing out some of its special hybrid features. But when I ran out of facts and turned to face Phud again, he was studying me, not the car. I shifted from one foot to the other, then looked away.

"A beautiful car for a beautiful woman, Kitt. Any chance of you taking me for a ride some day?"

My face flushed at his compliment, and I stooped to pick a twig from the front tire, giving myself a few moments of thinking time before answering him. "Sure, Phud. Janell and Rex haven't had time to ride it in yet, so maybe we all can go out for a spin around the island soon."

"Wonderful," Phud said. "I'll look forward to it." He tweaked a broken poinsettia leaf from a nearby plant.

"What a garden full of brilliant blossoms!" I watched as he tossed the broken leaf into a trash basket.

Phud laughed. "I'm guessing you think the showy red leaves are the plant's blossoms."

"Sure," I said. "They are, aren't they?"

"Take a closer look." Phud touched a tiny while flower on a

nearby plant. "These are the poinsettia flowers. The red leaves are just that—leaves."

"Oh." My face flushed again.

"Lots of people don't know that. Guess it doesn't make a lot of difference, though. All parts of the plant are beautiful."

"Right." I started toward the back door.

"See you tomorrow." Phud winked and walked toward the street, and I gazed after him. This time I was sure he had winked. It had been a long time since anyone had winked at me—and called me beautiful. Certainly not Shelby Cox. But I was through with Shelby Cox, and I was certainly in no mood to be thinking about a new boyfriend. Any minute the phone might ring, telling me I'd killed a man.

"Let's have a salad, Kitt," Janell said when I stepped into the house. "Not a good plan to skip meals, but with so much going on around here lately, it's been easy to do."

We enjoyed a simple lettuce, tomato, and avocado salad and a piece of toast before we got into my car and headed out. Easing into the traffic on Whitehead Street, we soon passed the wrought iron presidential gates near Truman's Little White House. "We have time to scoop a loop or two?"

"Sure, Kitt. Enjoy while you can. The rest of this day will be crammed with have-to-dos, and tomorrow I want the two of us to start some careful thinking about Abra Barrie's death and about who might have killed her. I hope we can provide the police with airtight alibis for our friends working at The Poinsettia."

"Right. I'm sure that's uppermost in your mind." It would have been uppermost in my mind too, if it hadn't been for The Perp hovering between life and death in Iowa. I turned to drive by Mallory Square, where an island boy with corn-row braids sang a calypso melody to his beat on a set of steel drums.

"Day-o-day-o." His soft singing and beguiling smile had many girls stopping to listen. Even older women and men gave him their rapt attention. Others milled about, patronizing vendors and kiosks. I wondered if any of the coconut shell masks on display had come from Janell's trees.

"In spite of our lunch, my mouth's watering at the fragrance of those hotdogs grilling at a lunch stand."

"Want to stop for one?" Janell asked.

"No, we better get on with our errands." I hung a left and felt the Prius thump onto a narrow bricked street next to the square. Stopping behind a white Bone Island Shuttle loading passengers, I peered into the shell warehouse on our right. The pungent odor of dried sea shells wafted from the building and the wide-planked flooring begged us to enter.

"Remember when you took me in there to buy shells to string on fishing line to create a necklace? And look, Janell. I think that's still the same exhibit of conch shells and sponges out front."

"You may be right. Some things stay the same. It's people who change, people who suddenly become murder suspects."

A woman stood laughing and posing beside the life-size sculpture of a fisherman. The bus driver waited until her companion snapped a picture and they boarded the shuttle. Traffic inched forward.

On Duval, we slowed in front of Sloppy Joe's bar. The blare from the rock band inside floated in the air along with the scent of shrimp steamed in beer. The amplified guitars drowned out the bells pealing from St. Paul's Episcopal, a few blocks away. A Conch Train rumbled along ahead of us and I followed.

"Can you get around it?" Janell leaned forward.

"No room to pass. Too many mopeds. And how about that horse-drawn cart!"

I could tell Janell wasn't enjoying the loop scooping, so at the first chance I headed toward Fleming Street and Fausto's. Luckily, we found a parking slot close to the door. Once inside, I shivered, remembering Fausto's had the coldest air-conditioning on the island.

Janell made fast work of the grocery shopping and I welcomed the warmth of the January sunshine as we returned to the car and headed home. Rex was nowhere in sight, and I guessed he'd gone to the marina. We toted groceries from car to house and once they were put away, Janell began making sandwiches.

"Kitt, you go on upstairs and rest or you'll be too tired to enjoy the activities later. I'll only make and wrap a few sandwiches right now. I can make more as we need them tonight—if we need them."

I felt guilty leaving Janell to make the sandwiches, but all my travel along with the change of climate took its toll. I felt ready to rest. Once I stretched out on my bed I fell asleep, awaking only when I heard an eerie moaning outside my window.

8

Slipping quickly into the clothes I'd removed before my nap, I rushed to look out the window. Although it was only a little after five o'clock, the sun hung low in the sky. Seeing nothing unusual below, I ran downstairs to the kitchen, feeling sure someone lay injured. Janell stood calmly loading the dishwasher while Rex handed her plates from the table.

"What's going on?" I asked. "That moaning! What's making it?"

Janell laughed. "Guess we should have warned you. It's Mama G playing a conch shell."

"Didn't know people played conch shells."

"Most people don't," Rex said. "My dad said folks used to call their kids in from play by blowing on a conch shell. Each kid knew the sound of his family's shell and reported home immediately."

"Mama G's carried conch blowing a step farther." Janell added detergent to the machine and started the washer. "Listen carefully and you'll hear her playing a diatonic scale. She claims it's in the key of C-major."

"How does she do that?"

"By blowing hard into a cut end of the shell and then adjusting her hands inside the shell opening," Rex said.

I listened, but I could hear only weird moaning. "I'd think the sound would scare people away."

"No," Janell began filling a supper plate for me. "It attracts kids. They come running to see what's going on. Mama G's good publicity for us. But, Kitt, do sit down and eat. We have to eat supper early in order to open the café on time. We didn't call you when we ate because you were sleeping so soundly we hated to awaken you. Kept the food warm."

"Thanks a bunch." I inhaled the enticing fragrance of the grouper, sat down, and began eating. "Wonderful, Rex. Didn't realize how hungry I was." I finished the fish and chips quickly, spooned up a helping of fresh strawberries, then placed my dishes on top of the dishwasher.

"Come outside to the patio and brag a little about Mama G's conch shell music. As you may have guessed from her comments earlier, she thrives on compliments."

"And compliments are usually forthcoming—at least for her sandwich fillings, if not for her conch shell music." Rex hung his apron on a hook on the back of the door.

"Ace and Teach have arrived, so I'll introduce you." Janell opened the door between the house and the café, and I followed her onto the patio and to the edge of the snack bar. Rex had already lit the patio torches, and their light flickered against Mama G's face, which still glowed a dull red from blowing on the conch. She looked ready for a break—or a massive stroke.

"*Hola*, Mama Gomez!" I greeted her in her specified way, careful to use her full name. "You get an interesting sound from your shell."

"Not a sound, Kitt Morgan. I play a well-known musical scale. You no hear the scale?"

"Yes, of course I heard it. Of course." No point in antagonizing the woman.

"Want to try?" After wiping the point of the shell on her caftan as if that would make the shell sterile, she thrust it toward me.

"No thanks, Mama Gomez. I'm sure I couldn't make a sound."

"Try," she insisted. "Now. I want you to know for yourself how hard to do is this music I make."

I took the shell and put it to my lips and blew. No sound. I blew again. And again. At last a faint moan wavered from the shell, and when I paused for more breath, Mama G grabbed the shell from me.

"You see, Kitt Morgan, it takes both talent and perseverance to play a melody on a conch shell."

"Indeed it does. You have many talents."

"And so does Ace, Kitt," Janell said, urging me toward the bandstand. "Come meet our drummer."

A tall shaggy-haired blond wearing black jeans and a black tank top was pulling a trap set closer to the side of a piano. At our approach, he stopped tugging at the drums and turned toward me. Turned reluctantly, I thought. I guessed him to be in his early thirties. Big. Broad shouldered. Muscular. Our eyes met on a level. I wondered what he'd been doing last Friday afternoon.

Janell performed the introductions.

Ace shook my hand with a bone-grinding grip. When he looked at me, his eyes twinkled, reminding me of someone I couldn't quite place. Crazy thinking. I'd never met anyone like this guy before.

"Glad to have you aboard." Ace grinned at me then opened a black cordura case and pulled out two black drumsticks, which he twirled into the air for a moment, caught and laid carefully on the piano. Then his face sobered. He pulled a black bandana from his hip pocket and used it to protect his fingers when he began to twist the screws set on the rim of his snare. "Hard to keep the drums in tune in all this humidity."

"I didn't know musicians had to tune drums. Thought they

came from the factory ready to go."

"I'm a drum bum." Ace grinned. "I take my time setting up for a job, and I work toward a certain sound, a certain tone."

Twist. Rat-a-tat. Twist. Rat-a-tat. I watched while he twisted and tested the drum head for sound. He said nothing more to keep the conversation going. Janell had left us to answer a telephone, so I read words stenciled on the bass drum head in bold blue beside the likeness of a shrimp boat. *"THE ACE— Freshest Shrimp in the Keys."*

"Pays to advertise, ma'am. Always see people waiting on shore when the *Ace* comes in from a run." Ace pulled up a chair behind the trap set and, using a foot pedal, tested the bass drum."

"Kitt. Just call me Kitt." Janell had disappeared into the house, and I felt uncomfortable talking to this guy. I'd felt uncomfortable around Phud. Maybe I'd feel uncomfortable talking to any guy who'd been around the B&B when Abra had been in residence. "Rather unusual for a shrimp captain to play drums, isn't it?"

"Drumming's my hobby, Kitt. It's my thing, you might say. If I hadn't already scrimped and saved to buy my boat, I might have bought a trap set and some lessons and taken up professional drumming. A red hot drummer can make it into the big time on either coast. Gene Krupa. Buddy Rich. Louie Belson."

"Guess it's never too late to change occupations."

"Too late for me. I love shrimping too much to make a change. Love shrimping when I'm at sea—love the drum-bum scene when I'm ashore."

"So how'd you get started on drums?"

"Won the traps in a poker game at Captain Tony's several years ago—snare, bass, and lignum vitae sticks. Ironwood. Hardest sticks ever made. Wouldn't take a ton of money for 'em. The Buddy Rich band was playing at Pier House, one of the island's top beach hotels, and one night while the sidemen took a break, I talked Buddy into giving me a few lessons in exchange for a short run on the *Ace.*"

I laughed. "And, as they say, the rest is history?"

"Right. History."

Ace had a charisma that made me like him—an engaging smile, a direct gaze, a sexy sort of voice. I could tell he enjoyed talking about himself, and I was about to ask more questions about his trap set and his association with Buddy Rich when Mama Gomez interrupted us.

"Drums too close to my piano. Move 'em to the right."

"In your dreams," Ace said. "Those traps are sitting right where they usually sit. Don't you dare touch 'em, woman." He stood, as if his height might give him more authority.

Mama Gomez's face hardened and she scowled, but she turned and flounced toward the snack bar.

"You gotta stand your ground with that broad." Ace grinned. "Hey, here comes Teach." He nodded at a short man wearing a blue jumpsuit, a baseball cap turned backward and mirrored sunglasses. He was struggling to carry a bass viol bigger than he was. When he drew near, I saw that his head barely reached my shoulder.

"Hey, Teach! Meet Kitt Morgan, Janell's sis from Iowa. Told her you'd like a new set of ears to listen to your tales about the fort."

"Yo, Kitt. Pleased to meet you." Teach grinned and rested his bass on the edge of the bandstand. "Janell tells us you're in law enforcement up north. Gonna give the police down here a hand?"

"Hadn't planned to. And so far they haven't asked for any assistance. Can I help you with that jumbo fiddle?"

"I can manage, thanks."

His tone told me to back off, and his mirrored sunglasses put me on edge. I couldn't tell where he was looking or whom he was watching.

"Little man needs no help," Ace said. "Won't let anyone else touch that leviathan of his. But don't let his size fool you. He's a black belt—karate, you know. He could deck a guy twice his size."

"Janell tells me you're a pilot." I tried to direct the conversation away from Teach's size, but I could see that Ace liked to tease.

"Right," he said. "In real life, flying's my job. I make daily flights to Fort Jefferson. In unreal life, I do a little writing and pluck the bass fiddle here at The Poinsettia."

"What sort of plane do you fly?"

"The bank and I own a five-passenger rebuilt Cessna. Amphibious, of course. The *Osprey*. It's tethered at the airport. I'm booked full most days during the season. You been out to the fort?"

"Yes. Years ago our family took a day trip by ferry. As I remember it, most of our time was spent on the water and only a little of it on the fort grounds."

Teach steadied his bass against the piano, pulled a booklet from the back pocket of his jumpsuit and handed it to me. I smiled at the title: *Meet Fort Jefferson*. I flipped through a few pages of the book, noting that it had fifteen chapters and lots of illustrations, both black and white and in color.

Ace sighed. "Don't get the little man started, Kitt. He'll talk you to death. You'd think he'd built the fort himself—single-handed."

Teach ignored him. "I've written this small handbook on the Tortugas and the fort. Got word today that it'll soon be available at the airport. You know—in those racks where the locals advertise their businesses."

"That's great, Teach. I'll look for it."

"No need to. You can keep that copy. Take it along with you."

"Thanks, Teach. I'm sure I'll enjoy reading it."

"I've autographed it. Maybe you'd like to fly to the fort some day. I'll let you know when I have an extra seat. Sometimes tourists book a time and then find reason to chicken out at the last minute. If you'd like to fly along with me, I'd be glad to give you a guided tour of the fort and the grounds."

I hesitated, feeling reluctant to spend time alone with any of these people, although Janell and Rex seemed at ease with them. So what if Teach was short. He'd earned a black belt. It was reasonable to think that he was powerful enough to have overcome Abra Barrie. But I could think of no motivation. Although the word *caution* played in my mind, I refused to live in fear.

"You're very generous, Teach. As for the Fort Jefferson trip, I'll let you know later. Not sure what Janell has planned for us this week. But right now I'm eager to hear this combo." I squelched the temptation to mention that I had once planned a musical career. Still made me sad to think about it. "Have you always played bass, Teach?"

"Not always." He laughed. "But I've played since junior high school days. Started when I was twelve. Most important thing I learned back then was not from books, but from a tough music teacher who was strong on discipline, the use of correct grammar, and daily practice on one's instrument."

"Guess it paid off big time, since you're still playing."

"Off the bandstand, Kitt Morgan," Mama G ordered.

I stepped down, giving her plenty of room.

"Gotta test the amps and get the charts lined up in correct order. Get your fronts in place, men. Almost time to start playing."

"Don't see anyone crowdin' the floor yet," Ace drawled.

"They'll start coming when they hear the music," Mama G

said. "As usual, we'll begin with our theme song—*Hella's Tune* with Hella on drums."

"Hella wrote the song?" I asked.

"Right," Ace said. "A good melody, too."

I backed away from the bandstand and Mama G tugged an amplifier onto the spot where I'd been standing, plugged it in, and started twisting dials, pressing buttons. Neither man helped her set up the heavy equipment nor the silver fronts decorated with music symbols stenciled in black. Nor did she ask for help. Clearly, Mama G thought she was the glue that held the combo together. Teach and Ace grinned at each other and allowed her to do and think whatever she pleased.

"Didn't know Hella played every night, Janell," I said, joining her at the snack bar. "Thought she was a sub."

"She is, but she wrote the theme music, and she likes to sit in on it at the opening and closing of our evenings. Ace never objects. Guess he doesn't dare object since Hella fills in for him when he wants time off to make a shrimp run. She has to use her own drumsticks, though. He never lends his sticks to anyone."

"Big deal." I laughed. "What's so special about his sticks?"

"You'll probably see before the evening's over." Janell went on about her chores and I sat at the snack bar while Hella entered the patio and took her place behind Ace's bass drum. I was sorry *Hella's Tune* was such a dreamy ballad. But that's the way Mama G played it—dreamy. Not much of a tune for showing off a drummer's expertise. Ace joined me at the snack bar while the combo played.

"That Hella! She's quite a gal." Ace grinned.

I smiled my agreement. "Hope I get to hear her hit some hot licks before I go home."

"She can play hot or sweet," Ace said. "Used to teach music. Used to play in a swing band after the war. World War II, that is.

A long time ago." Ace sat with me in an uncomfortable silence until Mama G motioned him back to his traps.

Yes, the crowd had started arriving during the combo's first number, and for the second time that evening I noticed a cop patrolling the block on a motorbike. Maybe the police were giving The Poinsettia special attention tonight. Janell and Rex didn't need to worry about a lack of business. Parents soon filled the tables near the edge of the patio, and kids began dancing to Ace's steady rock beat. When I turned to face the snack bar, it startled me to see Phud sitting on a high stool at the far end and sipping a soda that frothed down the side of the glass.

"Kitt," he called. "Looks like it's going to be a big night at The Poinsettia."

"Hope so." I passed his stool and spoke to Janell who stood some distance away. "Need some help making sandwiches?"

"Thanks, but I'm keeping up with the demand."

"Good." Phud eased his way to my side. "Since Janell doesn't need your help right now, may I have this dance? They're playing a slow one." Easing an arm around my waist, Phud pulled me onto the dance floor before I could think of a polite protest. And maybe I wouldn't have protested. Shelby Cox didn't care for dancing. It was a long time since a man had held me in his arms and hummed into my ear.

Phud was a smooth dancer and I had no trouble following his lead. I liked the fragrance of his lime-scented after shave. Tonight he was wearing silk—cream-colored slacks with a navy blue shirt that matched his jaunty tam. Torchlight glinted sparks onto his fringe of salt and pepper hair. The combo was playing a medley of ballads, and Phud hummed along, pulling me closer to him to avoid a teenage couple heading our way.

"What are you thinking?" he asked, suddenly pushing back from me and looking into my eyes.

"Thinking about what a lovely night this is." I'd been thinking of The Perp and of Shelby Cox, but I wasn't about to mention either man out loud. Phud seized that moment to wink, pull me close again and whirl me toward the garden.

"Kitt!" I felt the wooden dance floor give a bit under Hella's weight when she joined us. Phud had been about to ease us onto stepping stones lying among huge elephant ear plants. "Been searching for you. Janell says you might like to go with me to the sunset celebration tonight." Her heavy shoes scraped on the floor as she took another step toward us.

When I looked into her face, her dark eyes were like magnets holding my gaze. "But it's already past sunset. You'll be giving readings?"

"Perhaps." She turned her back to Phud as if trying to keep him from hearing. "Or perhaps not. People hang around on the dock long after sunset, but if you'd rather stay here and dance, that's fine, too. Janell doesn't want you to be bored."

"If Phud will excuse me, I'd like to tag along with you to the dock this evening. Like to watch . . ."

Phud gave an unbecoming snort and interrupted me. "Watch a phony fortune-teller bilk the tourists." Sarcasm dripped from his voice. "Someone should warn them about her kind."

Hella quelled Phud with a look. "Ignore him, Kitt. As always, my work speaks for itself."

"Excuse me, Phud. I really would like to watch Hella mesmerize the tourists."

"As you choose." Phud bowed and then with a flourish, he kissed my hand.

"And who's calling who a phony?" Hella glared at Phud, then turned toward me. "Shall we go?"

"I'll see you later, Phud," I said, hoping he wouldn't be insulted at being left behind.

"Come with me one minute," Hella said. "Need to talk to Rex for a sec."

When we reached the snack bar where Rex was manning the cash register, he was wearing a tank top instead of the handprint shirt he'd worn earlier. Hella reached into her bulging tote, pulled out the carefully folded handprint shirt and handed it to Rex.

"The spot came out easily, Rex. A little stain remover, a few minutes in the dryer. That's all it took."

Rex stepped behind the swinging door for a moment and then returned wearing the handprint shirt. "Thanks, Hella. You're a doll!"

"Glad to help." Hella hoisted her tote and adjusted the backpack I noticed for the first time.

"Let me carry your tote, Hella. You've got enough of a load." I laughed. "You don't have Voodoo hiding in there somewhere, do you?"

"Not this time, but you can carry the tote if you want to."

I took her tote and we started walking through the twilight toward Mallory Dock. We'd taken only a few steps before a bicycle cop passed us.

"That makes three I've seen this evening," I said.

Hella adjusted her backpack and kept moving forward. "The PD has The Poinsettia under close scrutiny tonight."

9

The sun had set, but a rosy glow hung in the western sky and people were still taking pictures of it and the sailboat silhouetted against it. Clearly, for some people, the sunset had played second fiddle to the juggler. The man wore grease-stained jeans and shirt with hair that hung in stiff tendrils around his face. Tourists still circled him, watching him toss seven oranges into the air, catching them before they hit the concrete. A few watchers dropped dollar bills into the hat he passed around after each round of juggling.

"Makes my head spin to watch him, Hella. How do you suppose he ever learned to do that?"

"My question would be *why* he ever learned."

"Do you think he has to survive on the few dollars he gleans each night from that hat?"

"Maybe. Or maybe not. He might be a homeless guy sleeping under a bridge, or he might be some doting grandfather's trust fund grandbaby. But let's move on. I have a special spot near the footbridge where I like to set up my table and stools."

"A reserved space?"

"No. On most nights, I arrive much earlier than this, but today has been an unusual one. Hope someone else hasn't claimed my place."

"Hella, can you really see into the future and tell people what's going to happen in their lives?"

"Sometimes. Yes, sometimes I can do that."

"But not all the time?"

"That's right. Clairvoyance is a sometimey thing. Sometimes it's there for me. Sometimes it isn't there no matter how hard I call upon it. I study the writings of Edgar Cayce, a famous clairvoyant who lived many years ago. He, too, found his clairvoyance an off-and-on thing. If I depend on its being there at a certain time and place, that'll be the time it disappears."

"So it's a gift. A gift that can't be forced?"

"Right. That's how I view it."

"I've got to know this, Hella. Have you tried to see the person who killed Abra Barrie?"

"Nobody's asked me to do that."

"Wouldn't you *want* to try to see her killer—for your own satisfaction of knowing?"

"Maybe. Maybe not."

It irritated me that Hella was being so evasive. "Why wouldn't you want to see this person? You might be able to help the police solve the case. Maybe they don't know of your ability."

"My so-called ability. That's what many people call clairvoyance. If the police come to me asking for my input on the Abra Barrie case, I'll give it, but with reservations. It's sometimes easy for me to misinterpret the things I see. Sometimes things are not what they appear to be."

I dropped the subject of Abra Barrie's murder. "So if you have a customer sitting before you and your clairvoyance decides to take a vacation for the evening, what do you tell that customer?"

Hella shrugged. "Then I do the only reasonable thing. I turn myself into a common-sense counselor. The patron asks me a question and I give her a common-sense answer."

"Her? Men never ask for your help?"

"Seldom. Around here, it's mostly women I deal with. People could solve most of their problems by using some down-to-earth common sense."

I giggled. "My dad told Janell and me that nothing's more uncommon than common sense."

"Could be that he was right. I don't cheat anyone, Kitt. I admit to customers that sometimes I don't have X-ray vision into the future."

While we headed toward Hella's special spot, we passed giddy little kids up long past their bedtimes, deeply tanned weirdoes sipping from bottles wrapped in brown paper bags, little old ladies in dressy pumps and mid-length gowns. A mime with silver-painted skin stood performing a don't-move-a-muscle statue impersonation near a bass vocalist who droned on and on with no apparent need to take a breath.

"What happened to Tank Island?" I peered across the harbor. "I remember lots of trees—maybe Australian pines and scrub palms.

"Those times are gone. Developers have renamed it Sunset Island, and they hawk the upscale houses and condos they've built there. And of course there's a restaurant with an upscale menu."

"Meaning no burgers or foot-long cheese dogs?"

Hella laughed. "Might find a burger or a dog on the kid's menu. Tourists can take a free water shuttle over for lunch even if they can't afford to buy a million-dollar condo—or even rent one for the weekend. Lots of folks look like big money, haven't got a pot or a window. But here's my place."

Hella stopped beside a seagrape tree near the edge of the dock and sighed in relief when she slipped off her backpack and began digging into it. A mountain of muscles. My first impression of her returned. Right now in this shadowy place, I could be in as much danger from Hella as from any of the men at The Poinsettia. But Janell wouldn't have suggested my accompanying Hella tonight had she thought I'd be in danger. Right? Right.

Once more I decided against being afraid, telling myself there was a big difference between wariness and fear. I took careful note of my surroundings.

"Can I help you unpack?" I asked.

"Better watch this time." From her backpack, Hella pulled a small round table with folding legs and two matching stools. She removed a lacy gold and silver cloth and flicked it onto the table, anchoring it with a crystal ball, a purple scepter, and a deck of tarot cards. With her fat braid of hair, her dark caftan, her heavy shoes, she looked the part of a seer. Too bad she'd left Voodoo at home. A black cat would have completed the picture most people associate with a true fortune-teller.

"You look very professional, Hella. If I wanted my future read, I'd choose you to do the reading."

"The things I've brought with me tonight are common props to attract customers. Visual props do nothing to help my clairvoyance. I either see or I don't see. But few people understand that. If you want to help my business tonight, you can pretend you've come to me as a paying customer."

"How? A few instructions, please."

"Sit on the stool and pull it close to my table as if you want no one to overhear our conversation. I'll lay out the tarot cards. Your acting as a customer will attract the curious to us."

I sat on the stool while Hella spread out the tarot cards and began arranging them in some esoteric fashion known only to her—and perhaps other seers in the tarot-reading business.

When she flipped through the cards, I saw one that said the *Devil*, others that said *Temperance*, the *Empress*, the *Hermit*, the *Chariot*. I couldn't help wondering what the pictures and words meant. When she turned up a card depicting a white horse and a black-clad horseman along with the word *Death*, I looked up at her.

"What do you see, Hella?"

"What I see is in my mind, not in the cards." Hella had a glazed look in her eyes and she stared at a space on my forehead, avoiding my gaze. If this was an act, she was a good actress.

"Kitt Morgan, I see a cold winter night. Much snow and ice and slush. I see you in a car with another man, a policeman. Then I see a store—a very small store in a rundown part of a town. My head aches from the tension of the scene. I smell animals. I hear shouts. I smell gunpowder. I see more police-men . . ."

"Ho!"

I jumped at the sound of Phud's voice coming from behind us. Why had he followed us here? How long had he been trail-ing us? Why had he interrupted us? I wanted to hear what else Hella might have to say. But I didn't want Phud to hear, too. No way. In a few short sentences, Hella had convinced me of her clairvoyant ability. I shivered in spite of the warm evening.

"Ho, yourself," Hella said, glaring at Phud. "The bad penny returns."

By now a small group had gathered around Hella's table. One woman flashed a twenty-dollar bill, insisting in a nasal voice that she was next in line.

"Come on, Kitt," Phud said. "Let's leave Hella to her patsies while I show you around. Lots to see here tonight."

"We've already seen what's here." Hella took the twenty the woman thrust toward her, motioning her to take the stool I had vacated when Phud arrived.

"Bet you haven't seen the trained pigs or the crystal gazer." Phud twined his arm through mine and urged me toward the dock. "I'll have her back safe and sound in an hour or so, Hella. Janell won't mind."

"Go ahead." Hella gave me a nod. "But I'm watching the time, and I expect you to do likewise."

I resented both Hella and Phud treating me like a child. I

could take care of myself without either of them enforcing a curfew. My mind twirled in a spin. Hella had *seen* some things from my past that were correct. At first I had been mesmerized and I'd wanted to hear more. But now I wasn't so sure. Sometimes she was wrong. She'd admitted that. What if she told looked more deeply into my life and told me The Perp was recovering? What if she told me the review committee had ruled that I shot in self-defense? And what if she was wrong? For the moment, I welcomed Phud's intrusion and I gave him my full attention.

"We've missed the sunset," Phud said. "But no matter. It's partly illusion, you know."

"Illusion? No I didn't know."

"The sun always looks larger as it sinks behind the horizon, but it's really the same size it always is. The sudden largeness people think they see is an illusion. Makes one wonder what's real and what isn't."

Phud's comment about the real and the unreal made me wary, but I let him ease us into the crowd. We walked through the soft night to the Hilton Hotel's bricked patio where some acrobats were performing. They looked like teenagers dressed for a gymnastics party. Their leader, dressed in a red leotard, held a lighted baton that she twirled then tossed to the sky, catching it seconds before it splashed into the harbor waters. Her followers performed hand walks, splits, knee crawls. Where were these kids' parents? Or maybe they were older than they looked. One girl performed with a white parrot on her shoulder. Had PETA checked her out? There was lots of applause, and the girl gave the parrot an ample treat.

"This whole scene is amazing," I said. "I remember seeing performers here years ago."

"You probably did," Phud said. "Maybe some of the same ones."

We strolled a while longer, then Phud bought us popcorn and we sat on hard chairs around a wrought iron table to rest.

"Your leg, Phud. Thoughtless of me to let you wear yourself out showing me around."

"No problem. I'm a willing volunteer and I'm doing fine. Would you like a limeade?" He nodded toward a vendor nearby.

"Yes, but let me go get it. You rest for a few minutes."

Phud smiled and thrust a bill into my hand. "Okay. I'll be fine in a minute or two. Get large drinks, right?"

I brought the limeades to our table and dropped the change into Phud's hand. We'd been enjoying the sweet tartness of our treats for a few minutes before a guy walked behind our chairs and tossed a cigarette into the harbor.

"The jerk," Phud said when the man was out of earshot. "Guess he doesn't know what trash receptacles are for."

"Some people don't," I agreed.

"Maybe I should follow him around," Phud said. "I don't smoke and I need a few cigarette butts."

"Whatever for?" I asked.

"Really, I need three whole cigarettes. I've developed this garden pesticide. Need to take a bottle of it to the Lighthouse Museum when I do my plantings there. Told you I was doing an exhibit for them, didn't I?"

"Yes, you mentioned the lighthouse, but nothing about a pesticide. Is it something special?"

Phud grinned. "Oh, it's nothing all that special—except to me. Haven't been able to find anything like it in the garden shops."

"Maybe you can play entrepreneur, bottle it and market it to the public. Is it a complicated formula?"

"No. It's simple. I shake the tobacco from three cigarettes and soak it in water overnight, instead of just for an hour or two. The next day I strain that water through a sieve, add it to a pint of warm soapy water. And that's it. It's easy to use—either as a spray-on or a wipe-on."

Who was pulling my leg, Phud or Janell? I'd heard this idea twice in the same day. My wariness kicked in again and I stood, trying to recall exactly what Janell had said about the pesticide. Had she said she'd developed it? Or had she said it was an idea of Phud's she was using? I made a mental note to ask her more about it.

"Ready to go?" Phud glanced at his watch and carried our drink glasses to a trash container. "Guess our hour has more than passed."

I relaxed as Phud led the way back to the spot where Hella stood folding her small table and sliding it into her backpack.

"I've been waiting for you," Hella said. "About time you showed up."

I wondered if she had worked as long as she wanted to, or if she was making it clear that she wanted to be ready to walk me back to The Poinsettia without Phud's company. A tension twanged between Hella and Phud that I didn't understand. I sensed that it involved more than Voodoo.

I helped Hella slip on her backpack before I picked up her tote bag.

"I want to be back in plenty of time to play the last number with the combo," Hella said, "so I called a cab." She patted her cell phone, then dropped it into the pocket of her caftan. "It should be waiting for us on the corner at Front Street."

"Thanks for the tour, Phud. I enjoyed seeing the dock activity at night again. It's been a long time."

"Pleased to be your guide."

Phud walked alongside us, and I expected Hella to invite him to share our cab. But when she didn't, he left us, wandering into the crowd. The cabbie sat waiting in a pink taxi, and when he saw Hella, he came to take her backpack and tote. We slid onto the back seat.

"Maybe we should have invited Phud to share our cab, Hella. I think his leg was bothering him tonight."

"Too bad. So sad."

I said nothing more about Phud. On the ride home, I thought about the performers I'd seen. Who were they? The gymnasts? The magic man? The mime? Had any of those people planned a career of performing on an open dock? Or had they failed at some other career and accidentally found their way to Key West?

I might lose my job on the police force in Iowa. Or I might succeed in keeping it, but even so, I doubted I could continue in a career that required me to carry a gun. And, although I loved and respected Janell and Rex, I couldn't sponge on them much longer.

When we reached The Poinsettia, Hella called to Mama G.

"Be there for the last number, guys. Don't play it without me."

Mama G scowled, but Ace gave Hella thumbs-up and I carried her tote to the B&B. While she was finding her keys and unlocking her door, I sensed a movement in the flower box at the side of her door. Setting the tote down, I brushed aside the petunia plants and saw Voodoo lying there and chewing on leaves. My approach hadn't startled him. In fact, he barely noticed me.

"Hella! Look at this. I think Voodoo's sick."

Hella dropped her backpack on the doorstep and joined me. She patted Voodoo's head for a moment, then smiled. "Voodoo's not sick. He's just very relaxed and happy."

"But he was eating petunia leaves. Don't cats eat grass or green plants when they're sick?

Hella patted Voodoo again and smiled. "Sometimes Voodoo pigs out on catnip. That's what he's been eating while I've been away. Won't hurt him any, but I'll send him on his way home before the owners miss him."

I began to understand several things. Who but Hella would have hidden catnip in the petunia box? Maybe Phud had a legitimate complaint about her. And maybe she had a legitimate complaint about him—throwing clods at a neighborhood pet she loved.

10

We had arrived back at The Poinsettia in plenty of time to enjoy a sandwich and a soda before the combo played their final set. A few teenage couples performed enthusiastic gyrations to a rock tune while parents sat at the tables enjoying the soft evening. Clearly, any bad publicity about Abra Barrie and the B&B had failed to affect business.

Suddenly, Mama Gomez thumb-nailed a loud piano glissando that silenced the crowd.

"Attention please! One and all! Attention! Before our final number, we now present Ace the Drum Bum and his laser beams."

Rex doused the patio lights and only the glow from the torches flickered across the dance floor. The crowd gathered closer to the bandstand when the combo began playing.

A few bars into their tune, brilliant lights flashed inside Ace's black drumsticks, lights that made him look like a phantom drummer. Gasps went up from the audience and people stepped closer to the bandstand. Ace's entranced admirers clapped when he began an intricate solo, featuring rim shots, flams, paradiddles, and many strokes I couldn't name. His hands moved from cymbals to snare heads, and he tossed his sticks in the air without missing a foot beat on the bass. Laser beams continued to flash as he twirled one stick above his head like a baton while keeping a steady beat on the snare head with the other stick. A triple cymbal crash ended both his solo and the lasers. Rex took his cue and snapped on the patio lights again.

"More! More! Encore!" Although the crowd whistled, stamped and clapped, Ace offered no encore. He stood and bowed before he relinquished the drum seat to Hella. After he packed his sticks into their case, he joined me at the snack bar.

"Some show, Ace." I smiled up at him. "Brilliant. How'd you do that? Or is it a trade secret?"

"No secret. It's my special sticks. Got laser lights set into them. Battery operated. Lights fit in a compartment with an off/on toggle switch."

"No wonder you take such good care of those sticks."

"You bet I take good care of them. Made from lignum vitae. Paid almost two hundred bucks for 'em—and the laser lights were extra. The lignum vitae's unbreakable, so I'll probably never have to replace them."

I was still thinking about Ace's performance when I reached for another snack. To my surprise, customers had depleted Janell's supply of escargot and feta cheese sandwiches.

"So forget the sandwiches. How about the last dance?" With an amused twinkle in his eye, Ace reached for my hand as if he were sure I wouldn't refuse.

And I didn't. He was a good dancer, and for a few minutes he held me tight and tapped the slow rhythm with his fingers on my shoulder. I wished I could relax into his arms, but a wariness I couldn't shake kept me alert and on guard. How had he spent last Friday afternoon?

"You enjoy Mallory?" he asked.

I smiled up at him. "Yes. Very much."

"Our tourist board wants visitors to think the sun doesn't set anywhere but at Mallory Dock in Key West, Florida."

"Maybe it doesn't." I grinned up at him. "Ever thought of that? Yet I feel almost sure I've seen it slip down behind the cornfields and windmills in Iowa."

"Ever been to Dyersville? I remember a cornfield there."

"You've been to Dyersville, Iowa?"

"When I was a kid. Went with a church group on a bus tour to Dyersville when *Field of Dreams* hit in the movie theaters. No sunset that day, though. Our bus arrived at twilight in a misty fog. Eerie. You seen that movie?"

"A couple of times at a movie theater. And several times on TV. It's one of my favorite movies."

"As luck would have it, a group of writing students from the university had arrived in Dyersville by bus that evening along with a mobile TV unit. The writers perched on bleachers near the old farmhouse—same scene as in the movie. A bus driver was joking with one of the professors when a team of local guys dressed as old-time baseball players strolled from the misty cornfield."

"That must have been spectacular."

"Right. Totally awesome. I watched with my nose pressed against the bus window while the guys took their places on the baseball field in silence. It was mind boggling. Even the TV men stared openmouthed for a few moments before they remembered to rev up their cameras."

"And what happened then?"

"The pitcher threw to the catcher. Our tour guide chose that moment to let us kids off the bus and we dashed onto the field. Our leader allowed each of us a turn at bat—with the actors pitching and fielding for us. It's one of my favorite memories. I'll never forget it."

I've never been to Dyersville, but Ace's *Field of Dreams* tale made me feel closer to home—and to him. I left his arms reluctantly when the combo stopped playing and Mama Gomez ordered Ace and Teach to fold up the music stands and unplug the amp. This time they helped.

It was the next afternoon, Wednesday, before Janell and I

finished daily chores and left The Poinsettia.

"The beach will give us privacy while we talk," Janell said. "I have the notes I took at the police questioning right here." She patted her beach bag. "We'll peruse each person's alibi, and I want you to help me decide if any of The Poinsettia people . . ." She hesitated. ". . . if we need to check more deeply into their stories. I hope you'll agree with me that we do."

"Don't you think the police have already done that?"

"Yes, I'm sure they have. But I'm guessing they're probably concentrating most of their thinking and efforts on a suspected serial killer somewhere else in Florida. They'd hate finding anyone from Key West guilty of murder. We're closer to our workers than the police could hope to be. I think we're in a position to get important inside information."

We passed Smathers Beach, but Janell drove on.

"Hey, sis! You missed it."

"Got to deliver some brochures to West Martello. The volunteer guide on duty today ran out of the ones that contained a self-guided map, and I promised to bring her some of my extras. It'll just take a second."

She turned onto the museum grounds, found a visitors' parking slot and cut the engine. "Want to come in with me? The Garden Club's leased the old fort from Monroe County, and it's in much better shape than it was the last time you saw it."

"I've only been in the fort once, Janell. As a teenager, I had little interest in plants and gardening and I found the dark winding walkways clammy and scary, although I wouldn't admit that to anyone at the time." I wanted to add that I had no special interest in West Martello today, that I'd much rather be working on clues that might involve Abra Barrie's killer.

"Our club members cleaned and cleared the place and started a tropical garden by donating plants from our own home gardens."

Janell rattled on about the Garden Club's upbeat projects, and although I wasn't captivated, my senses went on red alert once we stepped through the bricked entryway. This place might thrill Janell, but it still creeped me out big time. Goosebumps prickled my arms. We were the only people in sight and an uncanny quiet made me want to leave immediately.

I found the fort as off-putting as it had been years ago. The smell of penetrating damp and mildew clogged my nose. Sun shining through overhead openings onto greenery thick with vines cast snake-like shadows all around us. Bricked walkways still held a cloying dampness from the night. I shuddered. In spite of Janell's enthusiasm, the fort made me want to run in the other direction.

"Hello." Janell's voice echoed in the silence. "Sue? I'm here with the brochures. Where are you?"

No response.

"Maybe she's in the orchid arbor. Follow me, Kitt. And notice the antique Cuban tiles on the ground. They're priceless as well as exotic. The pond with its waterfall splashing over coral stone is one of my favorite spots."

I let my gaze follow hers, then I concentrated on the orchids. Such an array! I could understand Janell's enthusiasm for this orchid arbor—almost.

"We'll return another day and I'll tell you about the orchids. This's a wonderful place to sit and enjoy the garden, but let's go outside and see if Sue's somewhere on the hill path."

I followed Janell, glad to escape from the shadowy fort to the sunshine again. The path led up a short but steep hill to a roofed gazebo with lots of latticework around its base. A garden of succulents grew on one side of it, and a gnarled tree surrounded by thatch palms shaded the other side. The knoll overlooked the ocean and begged the viewer to sit down, relax, enjoy. But no Sue greeted us, and we had no time to relax.

"I don't see her up here anywhere, sis. Do you?"

"Sometimes she brings visitors up for an ocean view if they're agile enough to make the climb, but I don't see anyone there today. Let's go back down. I'll just leave the brochures inside the entryway where she'll find them. She must have stepped out on an errand."

I'd had enough of West Martello. I slipped and slid down the incline and walked on toward the car while Janell placed the brochures. We drove back to the beach. Today there were plenty of parking places—metered places. Years ago beach parking had been free. We climbed up a few steps from the sidewalk to the sand, glad to be out of the path of walkers, bikers, and skate-boarders.

Janell had brought two beach towels and we spread them in the sparse shade of a scraggly palm. We took care to avoid other sunbathers as well as a volleyball court where teenagers screamed and shouted and kicked up clouds of sand as they vied to whack a ball over the net.

"Now what's the skinny?" I asked once we were settled. "On Friday afternoon, who was doing what and where were they do-ing it? We know now that Rex had driven to Big Pine Key's artist's co-op. What about you, Janell? Where were you?"

"My alibi's as good as no alibi at all. I was at West Martello passing out brochures and answering questions. Lots of people saw me there, but no locals. All tourists. There's no way I could get in touch with any of them now."

"Too bad. Police like to talk to eyewitnesses to verify alibis. Even then, they realize people sometimes didn't see what they thought they saw. Surely they'll realize you didn't murder Abra Barrie."

"Let's hope so."

"What about Hella? Where was she?"

"Out walking. Said she didn't see anyone she knew."

"Not much help there. What about Mama Gomez?"

"She does have an alibi of sorts. She cleans the office at the Lighthouse Museum on Friday afternoons. She says she checked in there as usual—and I feel sure she did, but only the girl selling tickets was there to verify Mama G's presence."

"Maybe one person's enough."

"But the girl was in and out of the office. I checked with her. She said she closed the ticket window between three and four o'clock and left on personal business. Put up one of those be-back-soon signs and asked Mama G to make excuses for her."

I sighed. "I don't think the police are going to find a woman guilty of this murder, Janell. It was too brutal. It required lots of strength. Mama Gomez and Hella are both strong women, but do you think they could overcome a younger woman who was fighting back?"

"No. I think we need to look at the men."

"What about Ace?"

"His story gets sticky very quickly. Rex told the police he lent our boat to Ace for the afternoon."

"A boat owner borrowing someone else's boat?"

"Sure. I can understand that and I didn't mind. Ace owns a working shrimp boat. The old-time shrimp fleet has moved to other territory, but Ace has permission from the city to keep his boat where it's always been as long as he'll open it to tourists one afternoon a week. The harbor committee considers his boat and the long-ago shrimp fleet a colorful part of Key West history."

"They feel tourists and school kids need to see a working shrimp boat and meet its captain, right?"

Janell nodded. "You've got the picture, but a working boat might be smelly and dirty."

"And Ace wanted a boat suitable for taking a girlfriend on a date."

"Right. That night after the afternoon date, he intended to go on a one-night shrimp run, leaving Friday night and returning early Saturday morning. So he asked to borrow *Poinsettia Two* for Friday afternoon."

"And Rex doesn't mind lending your boat?" I wondered who Ace dated and how frequently. Then I wondered why I was so interested in Ace's love life.

"Rex doesn't like lending our boat to casual acquaintances, but he trusts Ace. Ace knows his way around boats and the sea and he's a dependable person. Rex had no qualms about giving Ace the use of the boat for Friday afternoon."

"So what happened?"

"That's what we'll have to find out. Ace told the police that he went to get the boat from the marina and it wasn't in Rex's slip."

"Yet the police say they found it there later—and with blood on it. Human blood."

"Right. The police have talked to Ace, but Rex and I only know what we heard him tell the police late Saturday night— that Rex's boat wasn't in its slip and he rented a boat from the marina for his date. I'm hoping you'll talk to him and see what else you can find out."

"Talk as a policewoman or as your guest in Key West?"

"Whatever works for you." Janell cocked her head and grinned. "You seemed to be getting along well with both Ace and Phud last night on the dance floor."

I felt myself flush. "Come on, Janell. I could hardly turn them down when they asked me to dance. And they both seem like good guys."

"I hope you're right—and I think you are. So let's think about Teach. He has an alibi as holey as a shrimp net. Says he was flying a tourist to Fort Jefferson where they spent the day, returning around five in the afternoon. He gave the police his flight schedule as well as the name and address of the tourist who flew with him—a man from Rhode Island. Easy enough for the police to check on that. But . . ."

"But?"

"But about two-thirty he received a call from a local book distributor concerning his handbook on Fort Jefferson. The distributor wanted Teach to read and maybe sign some papers that might get his book accepted into every independent book store in the Keys and maybe in all of Florida."

"Sounds like a good deal."

"Right. But he had to fly back to Key West to peruse and sign the papers. So he left his passenger-of-the-day, with the passenger's permission, flew to Key West to meet with this business associate. The only problem was that Teach couldn't find the guy. They were to meet in the airport bar. Teach said he waited almost two hours, but the guy didn't show. So he had to return to the fort in time to pick up his passenger and fly back to Key West on schedule."

"He has nobody to corroborate all this?"

"Right. Nobody. I believe him. Rex believes him. But the police point out that he has a large window of time unaccounted for."

I wished I could forget about Teach's black belt, his mirrored sunglasses. I couldn't count him out as a suspect in Barrie's death. Like Ace, Hella and Phud, Teach left an uncomfortable feeling in my mind.

"So that leaves Phud. What did Phud have to say?"

"He said he was at the Marathon Garden Club giving a lecture."

"That sounds easy enough to check out."

"Not really. The lecture took place at a luncheon meeting. He was scheduled to speak from twelve-thirty to one o'clock. There was no question-and-answer period because most of the ladies had to return to work by one."

"Right. And it would take him an hour or maybe less to drive from Marathon back to Key West, depending on traffic flow. Hmm. That could leave an hour or more unaccounted for."

"He told the police he left the garden club and went grocery shopping at Publix and then drove to Sombrero Beach where he sat enjoying the beach scene for awhile. So—no air-tight alibi. You could talk to him, too, Kitt—maybe as a policewoman trying to help her sister. What do you think?"

I checked my watch. "It's getting late. Once we drive home, it'll be time to make sandwiches and prepare for opening the café."

"Right." Janell stood and began shaking the sand from her beach towel. "Maybe tomorrow . . . I don't know where to start."

"Is it okay with you if I talk to Hella? If she's really clairvoyant, she should be able to 'see' what happened to Abra Barrie."

"Did you talk to her about her supposed talent last night? Tell her about your problems in Iowa?"

"No. But she asked me to sit at her table and to pretend to be interested in a reading—said it would attract customers to her. Her eyes took on a glazed look and she began talking in a faraway voice. Said she saw me on a snowy night in a store with policemen. She smelled the odor of animals and gunpowder. She heard shouts. In a non-believing way, I wanted to hear more, and yet I didn't want to hear another word. By then other customers crowded around us—including Phud. I stood, breaking her trance-like gaze."

"You think she's really—a clairvoyant?"

"You hadn't told her about my problems back home, had you?"

"Of course not."

"So how could she have known about the store and the

policemen and the smells unless she saw the scene in her mind? I want to talk to her about Abra Barrie."

11

That night while the combo was playing, I drew Hella aside. "Would you have a moment to talk with me privately, Hella?"

"Of course. Where shall we go? You're welcome to come to my room if you care to."

"Let's sit by the pool."

"Your choice."

I carried two glasses of iced tea as we took the flagstone path to the pool. Moonlight filtered through the palms, casting wavering shadows onto the table and chairs. Somewhere near a dove gave a moaning cry, letting us know we were trespassing. Some small creature kerplunked into the pool and I jumped, startled.

"What was that?"

"Probably a frog," Hella said. "Or a toad that's escaped Voodoo's nocturnal prowling."

I set our tea glasses down, sliding one toward Hella. "You're not giving readings at the dock tonight?"

"No. I skip a few nights now and then. Did you want me to continue your reading?"

I hesitated, not wanting to hurt her feelings. "No, but thanks for the offer. Guess I'm not all that eager to meet my future, but you told me enough last night to convince me of your clairvoyant abilities."

"Go on. You said you wanted to talk to me. How can I help you?"

"Janell, Rex and I want to learn more about Abra Barrie's

murder. As the police investigation stands, everyone working at The Poinsettia is under a cloud of suspicion. I think you can help us."

"The police haven't asked for my help."

"But I'm asking. Now. Surely you've thought about Abra Barrie, wondered who killed her. What do you see with your third eye? Your attitude toward Phud makes me wonder if you suspect him."

"That one! No, I don't suspect him of Abra Barrie's murder. I think he's a big phony. But I don't suspect him of murder."

"A phony?"

"Sure. Watch him at work sometime. His leg doesn't seem to bother him unless there's someone around to offer attention. He gets none from me. I don't like him and Voodoo doesn't like him either."

"The feeling's mutual." I grinned. "And you tease Phud by planting catnip in your flower box so Voodoo will come visiting."

"And I feed him some tidbits every morning before I take my walk, too. Don't like people who don't like cats. It's that simple. You don't need to tell him I coax Voodoo to our garden. I'd rather he thought the cat likes my company."

"Hella, are you willing to help us find Abra Barrie's killer?"

"I'll help in any way I can. But I don't intend to make statements that will cause the police to laugh at me, to laugh at the idea of clairvoyance."

"Great. I appreciate that, but I'm asking you to put your clairvoyance to work. Try to see with your mind's eye, see who might have murdered that woman."

"I've tried to do that. I don't advertise the fact, but I have tried and I see nothing unusual. In turn, I've considered each person who works here. *Nada.* That's what I see. *Nada.*"

My shoulders slumped. "Okay. So you don't see a murderer

among us. But if you had something that had belonged to Abra Barrie, some piece of clothing, perhaps. Could you touch that item and nudge your clairvoyance into action?"

"Perhaps that might be possible. But there's nothing of Abra Barrie's for me to touch. The police came. Then her parents arrived and took everything of Abra's with them. There was nothing belonging to her left in that room. *Nada.* I checked it out. *Nada.*"

Hella seemed to enjoy using the word *nada.* "Okay, Hella, here's my plan B. Could you hold something belonging to each person working at The Poinsettia and perhaps *see* something about that person that might link him to the murder?"

Hella sat in silence. The dove moaned again. A coconut plunked to the ground—a coconut Phud had missed. Good thing nobody was standing under it. Hella cleared her throat.

"Holding a possession of another person might tell me something about that person. True. It might."

"So will you do it? If I bring you a glove, a bandana, a shirt—will you hold the object and see what you can see?"

"Yes. I'll do that. But you must promise not to be too disappointed if I see nothing."

"It's a deal, Hella. I'll see what I can find to bring. Something the person won't miss. I don't want to be accused of petty theft."

"Start with the men first, please. I cannot believe a woman did this murder. I think a man did it, a strong man, but perhaps a man we don't know, a stranger—nobody connected with The Poinsettia."

"I hope you're right."

Hella and I returned to the patio, watched the dancers, listened to the combo, but all the time I was studying the men, trying to figure out what I could borrow that they wouldn't miss. What could I take to Hella tomorrow, or even yet tonight, that might give sight to her third eye?

The next morning Janell and I had already carried breakfast trays to poolside, where Rex and Hella now enjoyed coffee and rolls, when Ace parked his pickup in the tow-away zone and let himself in through the garden gate.

"Care to join us?" Janell called to him.

"Thanks," Ace said, "but I had breakfast at the raw bar."

"Raw oysters for breakfast?" I blurted, then felt myself blushing.

Ace laughed and joined us at the table. "Decided on toast and coffee this morning—no oysters." Then he looked at Rex. "I've come to ask a favor. One of my motors is conking out as if it's not getting enough gas. I usually make my own repairs, but nothing I do helps and Jeb's gone to Miami—best troubleshooter on the rock. I was hoping you might have time to come take a look at it. Didn't you have a similar problem with your boat a few weeks ago?"

"Right, I did. Could be the fuel pump or an alternator, but I'm sure you've already checked those things."

"First thing I did. Didn't help."

"I'll go to the dock with you and take a look-see. There are some wires that may have worn through their casings. I'll be glad to see what I can do."

"Hoped you'd say that. Come on over any time you're free." Ace picked up one of the rolls Janell offered, tasted it, rolled his eyes in pleasure.

"How about right now?" Rex asked.

"Fine with me." Ace finished his roll and looked at me. "Kitt, ever been aboard a working shrimp boat?"

I shook my head. "One of life's pleasures I've somehow managed to miss."

"Come along with us and I'll give you a tour of the *Ace* while Rex takes a look at the motor."

"Wonderful, Ace." Hiding my elation, I tried to act only moderately pleased. Here was my chance to pick up something of Ace's that he wouldn't miss and take it to Hella for close scrutiny.

"I'll go on ahead," Ace said, "before the cops tow my car. You and Rex come whenever it's convenient."

"It's convenient now, right, Kitt?"

I nodded and we finished the last of our rolls and coffee. Rex took a refill on the juice before he stood.

"Rex, may I drive you in the Prius?"

"Sure thing. I've been dying for a ride in that car ever since I saw it. Want to come along with us, Janell?"

"No thanks. Kitt gave me a ride in it yesterday when we went to the beach. I have plenty to do around here this morning."

Rex and I helped carry our breakfast trays to the kitchen before we got into the car. I explained briefly to Rex about the gas to electric capabilities of the Prius as we eased into traffic and headed for Ace's boat.

We turned at the sign that marked Land's End Village, passing a row of tourist shops that lined the narrow road to the docks. Plenty of slots in the parking lot this early in the morning, and I chose one close to the water. Dozens of pleasure crafts bobbed on the greenish brine near a planked walkway, and I followed Rex as we walked toward them. A trade wind fanned my cheeks, and I tasted salt on my tongue and lips and also felt the humidity curl wisps of my hair.

The live-fish smell of the sea filled my nose, even the back of my mouth. For a moment I held my breath then let it out slowly, trying to accustom myself to the strong odor. A flock of gulls rose from the water and flew screaming overhead.

Rex laughed. "Don't look up."

Many of the slips were empty and I guessed the boat owners were already out fishing, but Rex pointed to Ace's shrimp boat and grinned. "There it is."

Pelicans and gulls greeted us, leaving deposits aft of the wheelhouse as they soared lower and lower, hoping for a handout. And they got it. Ace stepped forward and threw a bucket full of shrimp overboard. The birds wheeled and screamed, fighting over the tidbits.

"You threw good shrimp overboard?" I asked.

"Probably trash," Rex said.

"No. I saw fish swimming away from the boat."

"Trash," Ace called. "To a shrimper anything he nets that isn't a shrimp, he calls trash. You may have seen grunts or blue runners that escaped my net."

"Oh." I was glad the trash had caught the attention of the gulls, giving us time to board the *Ace* without getting their line of fire. We paced the length of the short catwalk to the boat, and Rex grabbed a dock piling for support. I waited until he stepped over the gunwale and then turned to offer me a helping hand.

"Welcome aboard!" Ace ducked his head to avoid the doorjamb as he strode from the pilothouse and across the deck to greet us.

Above our heads, heavy iron outriggers were pulled up to form a black V against the blazing blue of the morning sky. I reached up to touch a rough pink substance dangling from the bottom of a net.

"That's chafing gear." Ace answered my unasked question. "Saves wear and tear on the nets as they drag across the ocean bottom. Some of those nets are over sixty feet long. It takes a lot of bread to replace them. Pays to keep them in good repair. When I bought the boat, I had to replace all the nets."

"Former owner hadn't taken care of them?" I asked.

Ace smiled and nodded. "This's an old boat. The former owner abandoned shrimping to take part in the Mariel Boat Lift. Old-timers tell me lots of shrimpers left their nets and went to Cuba to bring back refugees."

"For money, I suppose."

"At two thousand dollars a head, that job paid a lot better than shrimping. All kinds of boats, not just shrimpers, left Garrison Bight by the hundreds and returned to Key West with thousands of people."

"Where did the authorities put them?" Rex asked. "That happened years before Janell and I moved here."

"The Truman Annex docks filled beyond capacity with homeless Cubans. Later officials sent them to Homestead and Miami—until President Carter realized he'd made a mistake and called a halt to his Open Arms, Open Hearts policy. We didn't need any more mentally ill thieves and murderers. That's who Castro allowed to sail to America. He's probably still laughing his head off."

I tried to avoid thinking about the desperate people who had been aboard this boat years ago. As if ready to forget about old times, Ace pointed toward the sky.

"Look up, and you'll see my radio antenna."

The antenna towered above the rest of the rigging like a stark white finger pointing at the sun, but due to the brightness of the sky, we gave the antenna only a casual glance. Rex followed as Ace showed me inside a tiny cabin where the crew slept. Four bunks, a built-in chest of drawers, and four lockers to stow gear. Ace also gave us a quick tour of the galley and the captain's quarters before he offered me a map and a seat in the wheelhouse.

"You might enjoy locating the nearby keys on the chart while Rex and I tinker with the motor."

"Thanks, Ace." I studied the chart until the two of them disappeared into the hold to check on the problem there.

And here was my chance. I laid the chart aside. Ace had left a pair of cotton work gloves near the wheel. I took one of them.

Or maybe Rex had left the gloves. But no, Rex had come to work on the motor. He'd have pulled on his gloves. If Ace missed one, maybe he'd think he'd lost it somewhere. I could take it to Hella, get a reading, then drop the glove at The Poinsettia—maybe beside the pool. When his glove turned up again, Ace would think he'd been careless and dropped it.

I stuffed the glove into my shoulder purse, hoping Ace wouldn't miss it before we returned to The Poinsettia.

12

"Enjoy the shrimp boat?" Janell asked with a laugh. "I practice holding my breath whenever I go there."

"Smells like money to Ace, I guess. Ace was really relieved that Rex could fix the motor. Janell?"

She turned to look at me. "What is it?"

"Any word at all from Iowa? Any news about The Perp?"

Janell stepped close and gave me a hug. "Nothing, Kitt. No calls. But remember the old cliché. No news is good news."

"I hope you're right. I suppose I could call the chief and ask. Or maybe call my partner. Shucks, Hank may already have been assigned a new partner. Can't expect them to wait for me to return."

"Try to forget Iowa for now, Kitt. We've plenty to do right here in Florida." Janell thrust a yellow post-it bearing a name scrawled in green ink toward me.

"Gloria Bishop." I read the name. "Ace's girlfriend, right?"

"Right. She lives on Stock Island. But she waits tables on an early-morning shift at Pier House."

"You've already talked to her?"

"Yes. Caught her at home before she left for Old Town. She'll be reporting for her morning shift today, and she's agreed to talk to us during her break at ten. Says she'll meet us at the outdoor dining deck that overlooks the ocean and the beach. Can you be ready in a few minutes?"

"Sure. I need to freshen up. I feel like my clothes have a

shrimp boat aroma."

"Take your time. I'll be on the patio. Need to rearrange things in the refrig before I add new sandwiches."

I helped carry sandwiches to the patio and when Janell started working in the cooler, I slipped away to the B&B. For some reason, I didn't want her to know I'd asked for Hella's help. Would Janell laugh at that? It didn't matter. I wasn't going to give her a chance to laugh, at least not right now. Plenty of time to tell her about Hella's willingness to help once Hella had discovered something pertinent to our investigation. I waved casually to Phud, who was busily mulching some plants near the tool shed, but I didn't stop to chat, and he didn't try to detain me.

"Hella?" I called as I knocked on her door. "I need to talk to you. Can you spare a minute?"

Hella opened the door so quickly I knew she must have been watching my approach. Or maybe she was watching Phud.

"Come in, child." She opened the door wide, and I stepped inside.

I wondered if I'd passed some sort of a test that had won Hella's trust. A day or so ago she'd been secretive about her apartment, yet now she was opening the door wide and calling me "child."

Stepping inside, I was surprised to see zodiac signs decorating the stark white walls—silver and gold cutouts of the ram, the goat, the bull. I guessed that all twelve symbols were there somewhere. No curtains graced the windows, and white mini-blinds were open to let in the light. A buff-colored rattan mat covered the floor, and a white wicker couch and two matching chairs holding jewel-toned cushions all but filled the small room.

The décor surprised me. I had expected pale walls, low-key tones suitable for a brooding psychic—tones that matched her somber caftans, her Birkenstocks, her dark silences. Hella was a surprise package. Every time I met her, I discovered something new and different. She hadn't invited me to sit down, so I remained standing while I reached deep into my shoulder bag and pulled out the purloined glove for her inspection. It was a working man's glove, cream-colored body, blue knit cuff, slightly stained with grease and dirt. The thumb was almost threadbare and held some mustard-colored stains, but the fingers showed little wear.

"Whose is it?"

"Ace's. Or maybe Rex's. I picked it up from the wheelhouse of Ace's shrimp boat this morning while he and Rex were working on the boat motor." I thrust the glove toward her. "What do you think, Hella? Do you think you might be able to tell something about the owner from holding his glove?"

"It's possible, child. But don't be disappointed if I get nothing from the glove. I make no promises."

"But you'll try? That's all the promise I want, that you'll try."

"You have that promise."

To my disappointment, Hella tried the glove on, studied it for a moment, and then laid it aside. I'd hoped she would clasp the glove in both hands right this minute. I wanted to see her in some sort of psychic action. I'd thought she might press the glove to her forehead as she peered into the distance with glazed eyes. Or maybe she might hold it to her heart while she paced the room.

She did neither of those things. Our police chief back home had at one time called on a psychic for assistance, and although she helped turn his investigation in a different direction, he kept very quiet about it. It never made the newspaper. And he never called on her help again. If Hella had success in spotting a murderer with this glove, maybe I could vouch for the benefits of extrasensory perception. He might use a psychic again. I'd think about that, once I returned to Iowa—if I still had a job.

Janell stood waiting for me once I returned to the house, but she asked no questions. I did a quick change of clothes and we took off in the Prius to meet Gloria Bishop. I doubted that Gloria would have any earth-shaking information about Abra Barrie's murder that she hadn't already shared with the police, but I was eager to meet her. I wondered what sort of girl Ace would choose to date, what sort of girl would he consider so important he'd borrow a boat to take her out?

Pier House was only a few blocks away and when we drew closer to it, Janell despaired of finding a parking place anywhere near.

"We should have walked from home, Kitt. It's not all that far."

I slowed the Prius to a near stop when we came in sight of the Pier House grounds. The white building rose pristine above the palm trees. I came to a complete stop at the gateway into the parking lot where a wine-colored velvet rope held would-be parking seekers at bay.

"No place for us here," Janell said. "See the sign? This lot's reserved for hotel guests only."

"I'll pull into the edge of it anyway, turn around, then head back to the street." I glanced at my watch. "By the time we go back home and walk here, Gloria's break time will have ended."

"May I help you, ma'am?" The parking attendant approached, circumvented the velvet rope and leaned toward my open window.

"Any chance of us parking here for a few minutes while we talk to one of the hotel employees?" I asked

"Just drive on away," Janell advised, sotto voce. "He's not about to let us park here."

"Take that spot right over there." The attendant lowered the rope and pointed to an empty slot. "Belongs to a friend of mine. You can use it for . . . say twenty minutes. Would that help?"

"You're a doll," Janell said, opening her door and leaving the car before the guy could change his mind. I parked the car and joined her.

"Mr. Nice Guy will expect a big tip," Janell said. "Be warned."

I grinned. "Or maybe *he'll tip us* for letting him examine the Prius up close and personal for a few minutes."

Janell turned and we watched the attendant gently kicking the front tire and running his hand over the fender as he looked through the window at the dashboard. "You may be right," she agreed.

We walked on a narrow cement path through tropical greenery, past an aviary of exotic parrots and finches that chattered to us as we passed. We didn't stop, walking on along a section of walkway lined with hibiscus bushes, elephant ears, aloe plants, and ferns I couldn't identify. At last we smelled the aroma of coffee and reached the steps to a rough-planked deck surrounded by a white safety railing where signs warned us not to feed the birds.

Water lapped under the deck, and the aroma of coffee and frying bacon made my mouth water. Round umbrella tables shaded midmorning guests. The tanned waitresses, apparently unaware of melanoma and too much sun, wore white shorts, tennies and silk shirts in a fabric that matched the umbrellas.

"We have an appointment with Gloria Bishop," Janell said to the hostess.

The girl looked around then smiled. "She isn't here at the moment, but if you care to wait, I'll show you to a table."

"Thanks," Janell said. "We'll wait."

We followed the hostess to the only unoccupied table, which was in the sun and only partially shaded by the umbrella. When a waitress approached, we ordered iced coffee. Redheads don't do well in the sun, and when I felt my face flushing, I wished I'd worn my sun hat. We'd waited only a few minutes before a woman stepped onto the deck, paused, then headed toward us.

"Sorry to keep you waiting. I'm Gloria, and you must be Janell and Kitt. Right?"

Tall and willowy, Gloria towered above us until we offered her a chair. I approved of Ace's taste in women. Even dressed in her work uniform, Gloria could have passed for a fashion model. Her chin-length ash-blond hair set off her blue eyes and her flawless complexion.

"How can I help you ladies?" she asked.

"We're deeply concerned about Abra Barrie's murder," Janell said. "Ace made his statement to the police and the police have probably talked to you, too, but we'd like to hear what you have to say about last Friday afternoon."

"We believe that everyone working at The Poinsettia lives under a veil of suspicion," I explained. "If you're willing, maybe you can help us lift that veil."

Gloria sighed then she smiled. "If you've talked to Ace, then you know my story. But I'll review it again for you if you think it'll do any good. I certainly hate the idea of a murderer being on the loose in Key West."

"We all do," Janell said. "May we order you a drink?"

"No, thank you. I've only a few minutes before I go back on duty." She closed her eyes for a moment as if collecting her thoughts before she began talking again. "Ace and I had a picnic date for last Friday afternoon. He told me he'd arranged to use Rex's boat, and we planned to go to a little-known islet he said he'd recently discovered. The sea around here is pockmarked with many uninhabited keys.

"I met Ace at Rex's boat slip and he'd brought a box lunch from Blue Heaven in Bahama Village, but Rex's boat was missing. Rex didn't answer his phone when Ace tried to call him, so Ace decided Rex must have needed his boat at the last minute. Ace rented a marina boat and we went on our picnic a little late, but not late enough to spoil our afternoon plans."

"How long did your picnic last?" I asked.

"By the time we rented a boat, it was one o'clock before we left Key West. We returned at dusk."

"Was Rex's boat in its slip when you returned?" I asked.

"We didn't look. Rex's slip is quite a distance from the rental concession, and we were in a hurry. I needed to report for a late-evening shift here at Pier House, and Ace had last-minute things to do before he took the *Ace* on a Friday night shrimp run. He planned to fish all night and return sometime on Saturday morning, sell his catch, and sleep until it was time to play with the combo on Saturday night. I wish now that we had checked on Rex's boat when we came in from our picnic."

"Hindsight's always twenty-twenty," Janell said. "We thank you for taking time to talk with us. Do you happen to know anyone who went shrimping with Ace that night?"

"I've only met a few of his workers, but Ace introduced me to Santiago Sanchez and said he was one of the crewmen who'd be going out with him that night. I don't know exactly where he lives, but I think it's here in Old Town—if you want to get in touch with him. I'll vouch for Ace's whereabouts on Friday afternoon—stand up in court and swear on the Bible, if that's necessary."

"Won't be necessary," I said. "Ace hasn't been accused of anything."

"Yet," Janell whispered as Gloria walked away.

13

"Nice girl," I said as Janell and I left Pier House. "Ace has good taste in women."

"Agreed," Janell said. "Think it would do any good to talk with Santiago Sanchez?"

"Don't know why it would. The ME said Abra Barrie died on Friday—mid- to late afternoon. Ace was with Gloria at that time. Sanchez could only tell us about Ace's nighttime activities."

"You think Gloria lied to us?"

"No." I sighed. "But let's not take a chance. Let's talk to Sanchez."

"Okay, Kitt. If a guy had murdered someone in the afternoon, he might still be a bit shook up over it that evening unless he has nerves of steel. He might be on edge for a long time. He might even want to talk about it. The cops may have overlooked talking with Sanchez. Our talking to him might point us in a new and different direction."

"You're right. Let's do it—if we can find the guy."

When we returned to the parking lot, the velvet rope was gone and the attendant was nowhere in sight.

"Don't see a tip jar around here anywhere." I grinned at Janell, but before we claimed the car, we walked to a nearby pay phone. Locating Santiago Sanchez was as easy as finding his name in the phone book. I jotted it on a slip of paper and we walked back to Pier House for my car.

Sanchez answered the door at an upstairs, much-in-need-of-paint apartment on Fleming Street a block or so from the library. His head barely reached my shoulder, and I wondered if he used a garlic-scented shampoo. Janell and I both backed off a step or two. What he lacked in height, he made up for in muscle. I could understand why Ace had hired him. He looked as if he could haul in a sixty-foot shrimp net without the aid of a winch. His shaggy hair touched the neckline of his red tank top, and he peered at us from under shaggy eyebrows. He didn't invite us inside. Finding him might have been easy, but getting him to talk to us was harder.

"Mr. Sanchez?" Janell asked.

"Whatcha want?"

"We'd like to talk to you about your boss," Janell said.

"Which one? I work part time for several guys."

"The captain of the *Ace*," I said. "That boss. You go shrimping with him last Friday night?"

"Why ya wanta know? He in trouble?"

"No trouble," Janell said. "You heard about Abra Barrie, the murder victim who died last Friday?"

"I heard." Santiago waited.

Janell and I outwaited him.

"If you think Ace murdered her, you wrong. Friday night, he be out shrimping as usual. Got nothing on his mind but shrimp."

"You a mind-reader?" I asked.

He gave me a scathing look. "You be here trying to get Ace in trouble. I can read it on your faces."

"Now you're a face-reader as well as a mind-reader?" So what if he asked us to leave? We weren't getting anywhere with him.

"You two broads looky here. I ain't gonna let you try to pin no murder on Ace. My living depends on him and his shrimp boat. Mostly."

I wondered what else he did for a living, wondered who else would hire him. I didn't ask.

"Ace, he ain't murdered nobody. Take my word for it."

"Did he seem upset on Friday night?" Janell asked.

"He be calm as low tide on Friday night. And Sattidy morning. Sattidy morning, Ace sell his catch, pay me my wages and head for some sleep."

"He went home?" I asked.

"Didn't say nothin' about home. Ace pay me and we head back to his slip at the dock where he let me out. Boat be his home. He always sleep there, eat there, live there. He think making da boat his home bring him good luck on the water. And that what he did on Sattidy morning. Sleep aboard de boat."

"Thank you, Mr. Sanchez," Janell said. "You've been a big help."

"Didn't intend to be no help at all. I tell Ace two broads came pounding on my door asking nosey-poke questions." With that threat, he disappeared inside his apartment and slammed the door.

I followed Janell down the steps and we headed toward The Poinsettia. "We didn't learn much from that guy, Janell."

"We learned what I wanted to know—that Ace was calm, that he worked the job as planned, that he didn't vary from his usual actions."

"You believe Ace's off the hook?"

"Yes. Don't you? You're the cop. Maybe you think we've learned something that might incriminate him?"

"No. I think you're right. You and Mr. Sanchez. So what do we do next? The morning's melting away."

Janell checked her watch and nodded, but she waited to reply until we reached the carport and left the car. "Guess Phud's alibi's the easiest one to check out next. Let's grab a bite to eat on the drive up to Marathon. His tale should be easy to check out. Said he spoke at a noon luncheon of the garden club. Maybe not so easy to check on what he did or might have done later in the afternoon."

"You think he could have joined the club ladies for lunch and given an erudite lecture, and then driven back to Key West where he murdered Abra Barrie and dumped her body into the sea? He'd have had to have worked mighty fast."

"He said it was a noon luncheon, and most of the ladies in his audience had to return to work by one o'clock. He could have finished speaking by one or shortly after and driven the fifty miles back to Key West by two—if traffic was light. And if he used Rex's boat, he would have had to ease it from its slip without anyone noticing him or questioning him."

I followed Janell to the kitchen. "Maybe we should talk to the people at the marina, asking if they saw anyone borrow and return Rex's boat. Might have been tricky to return a blood-stained boat without attracting some attention."

"You're right. There're a lot of ifs and buts, yet it's not too unusual for a fisherman to return with blood stains on his boat. Fish bleed, you know."

"I don't know a fisherman's routine around here, but wouldn't most boat owners clean up a blood-spattered boat immediately after returning to dock?"

"You're right. But whoever took Rex's boat left it blood-stained. That should have attracted some attention. We can check on that at the marina, but for this afternoon I think we should drive to Marathon and check out Phud's alibi. It might save us from having to hunt down marina people—people who might or might not have seen something unusual that they'd want to talk to us about."

"Okay. I may be the cop, but you're the one who knows Key West and the ways of the natives."

Janell headed toward the countertop telephone. "I need to make a call to Mama G, then I'll be ready to go."

Janell picked up the phone and clicked in a number and I grabbed the chance to walk to the B&B and tap on Hella's door. Nobody answered and I thought she was out, then as I turned to leave, Hella opened her door.

"Kitt? Sorry I was so long in answering, but I was sitting behind my portable sewing machine mending the hem of Rex's work pants. Repairing hurricane damage is hard on clothes. Something I can help you with?"

As if she couldn't guess! "Hella, the glove. The glove! Could your clairvoyance tell you anything about it—about the person who wore it?" I looked around, but I didn't see the glove in sight.

"I spent some time last night with that glove, Kitt. Lots of time. Bad vibes."

"What did the bad vibes tell you? Something about the glove's owner? Maybe something specific?"

Hella went into her bedroom and returned with a plastic bag. She opened the neck of the bag and let me peer inside. I stepped back then looked into her face.

"What are you telling me? That the glove is so contaminated you don't want to touch it?"

She closed the top of the bag and thrust it toward me. "Take it. You must return the glove either to its owner or to the place where you found it. It is bad to keep it in your possession."

"What did you see when you touched it?"

"Evil. Evil that I want out of my house. Return the glove to the spot where you found it and have no further association with its owner. Never."

I took the bag. "I can't hand the glove to Ace and tell him I lifted it from his boat. And I have no reason to return to his boat in order to leave it there. Hella! What am I going to do with this?"

"Perhaps destroying it would be the best thing for everyone."

"Destroy another person's property?"

Hella shrugged. "I think an evil person wore this glove. I can see auras around people, but not around inanimate objects. Yet I feel that the person who wore this glove had an evil intent."

For a brief moment I forgot about the glove. "Hella, do you see a bad aura around anyone who works here at The Poinsettia?"

"Auras tell me many things. Sometimes an aura of a certain color tells me a person is ill—or about to become ill. Other auras tell me the person is upbeat and happy."

"And sometimes a dark aura can tell you a person is evil, right?"

"Sometimes that is true."

"Who have you seen around here with a dark aura, Hella? Tell me. Tell me."

"No."

"No?"

"That's right. No. I will not tell you, because sometimes I read an aura incorrectly. It is like my clairvoyant visions. It is a come-and-go thing. In this instance I prefer to keep my thoughts to myself. Don't want to cast suspicion onto an innocent person. Please take the glove out of my apartment."

I turned toward the door wondering why I had embroiled myself in this situation. Hella had psychic information she wouldn't reveal to me and I was literally left holding the bag.

"Thank you for trying to help, Hella. I appreciate your effort. And if you see into the unknown more clearly, you will let me know, wont you?"

"I'll reveal anything that I feel is important to reveal."

Hella closed the door behind me and I heard the lock snap

into place. Was she afraid I might try to come back inside without her permission? Or maybe she worried that I might open her door and thrust the bag back inside her apartment. The clicking of her door lock unnerved me. I wanted the glove out of my possession, and I acted on the first thought that came to my mind.

Hurrying to the pool, I pulled the glove from the plastic bag, wadded the bag and stuffed it into my pocket. I hesitated only a few seconds before I dropped the glove on the patio near the place where Ace had stood when he came to ask Rex's help with the motor repair. Someone would find it. Maybe Ace— although I didn't know how frequently he visited the poolside patio. I had seen him there only once.

Janell stepped from the kitchen at the same time I started toward the house. My mind was reeling with confused thoughts about Ace. Gloria Bishop and Santiago Sanchez had led us to believe that Ace had nothing to do with Abra Barrie's murder. Yet Hella and her assessment of Ace's glove had sent my thinking back to square one. How much weight could I give to a psychic's words?

I hoped Janell wouldn't ask me where I'd been and what I'd been doing at the pool. And she didn't. Any talk with Mama G seemed to lead to a controversy, and today's discussion concerned the sandwich fillings to be used this evening.

"As usual, Mama G wins," Janell said with a laugh. "Tonight the sandwich fillings will be made from her secret recipe that calls for boiled shark fin broth to moisten tuna flakes, cilantro, and boiled eggs."

"Sounds yucky, but . . ."

"My plan B is a crock full of tuna salad. But tourists usually enjoy tasting something more exotic and Key-sy. They may be totally disinterested in anything as common as tuna salad."

I drove the Prius and we headed toward Stock Island and

then up Highway One. We'd gone only a short distance before we noticed a car following us, slowing when we slowed, speeding up when we did.

"Make a left when we reach Coco's Cantina," Janell said. "It's a low blue building a short ways ahead. Either we'll lose our tail in the parking lot or we'll find out who's following us— who and why."

14

"It's Phud," I said when the tan Ford pulled into a parking slot near us at Coco's. Phud left his car, adjusted his tam and smoothed his silver-gray fringe of hair before he approached us. "Wonder what he wants. He could have called us on his cell phone instead of following us."

"What's up, Phud?" Janell grinned at him. "I didn't recognize your car. You made us nervous."

I looked away when Phud winked at me as if we shared some secret we were keeping from Janell.

"My car's in the shop for a tune-up. I'm driving a loaner."

"So why were you following us?" Janell asked.

"Just wanted to see how a Prius performs on the road. Were you on gasoline or electric, Kitt?"

"Electric. One works as well as the other." Phud irritated me. And I'll admit he frightened me, too. I don't like his winks. I don't like being followed. Maybe he has a dark aura visible only to Hella.

"Kitt'll take us all for a ride one day soon, Phud. That's a promise. We haven't the time for it today. Have to be back in time to get our work organized for this evening's customers."

"Got time to let me treat you to a Coke?"

"Not today, Phud," Janell's voice held a no-arguments-please tone. "Thanks for the offer. We'll take you up on it some other time."

"Where you headed?" Phud asked.

125

"Up toward Miami," Janell said.

"Oh. Well, have a good trip, ladies. You'll have to hurry if you make it to Miami and back before evening." Phud got into his car and pointed it toward Key West.

"Now what do you suppose that was all about?" I asked when we pulled back onto the highway. "I think he wanted something more than a demonstration of my car. And why did you tell him we were going to Miami?"

"I said *toward* Miami. I think he was being nosey, but I think he's really interested in the Prius, Kitt. Why don't you take him for a short ride tomorrow? You know how men are about cars."

"We'll see. I don't like being followed."

We drove on, pausing only for the stop light on Big Pine. Any other time I'd have stopped to take a look at the fishing camp near Spanish Harbor Bridge, but not today. Traffic flowed smoothly across Seven Mile Bridge, and I felt diminished by the vastness of the sea that surrounded us. A few whitecaps on the surface hadn't deterred fishermen. Small crafts with outboard motors bobbed on the blue-green water close to the bridge, and farther away sailboats skimmed along in the wind. We passed the old abandoned bridge where hikers and bicycle riders headed toward Pigeon Key. At the end of Seven Mile, we entered Marathon.

"Garden club headquarters are at mile marker fifty, bayside," Janell said. "Take a left. You'll see the sign directing visitors to the building. It's a beautiful place—a rain forest atmosphere. You can almost hear water dripping from the branches. It's a fairly new spot, but I don't find it as interesting as West Martello."

I drove on a ways in heavy traffic, then had to wait a long time before I could make a left turn, but we soon arrived at the garden club. We left the Prius in a visitor's slot near the palm-shaded entry to the grounds and walked through a gateway.

Inside the clubhouse, the scent of moist earth and rotting vegetation clung to the silence. We approached a slim, svelte woman with slightly graying hair. She sat behind a wicker table wearing a volunteer badge, and when she stood to greet us, her caftan flowed in the slight breeze wafting into the garden. A variety of brochures lay fanned out on the table next to a vase of bloodred hibiscus blossoms.

"The garden club welcomes you." The receptionist smiled and offered us an informational brochure. "Feel free to wander wherever you please, ladies. We have a hundred twenty-six indigenous plants and trees on our grounds and if you have questions, I'll be glad to try to answer them."

"Is there a charge?" I asked.

"No charge, but we do accept contributions." She smiled and nodded toward a box sitting beside the hibiscus.

I opened my purse and dropped a bill into the slotted box while Janell cut right to the point of our visit.

"We're interested in the lecture presented here last Friday, a luncheon meeting where Dr. Whitney Ashby spoke to your members."

"Oh, yes. Dr. Ashby. A charming gentleman. So relaxed and at ease. No public speaking jitters for that man! He could have convinced me he'd been born wearing a white shirt and a silk business suit. And that jaunty little tam! He enchanted the ladies with his manner as well as with his speech."

She rolled her eyes and smiled, and I could imagine the garden club ladies hanging onto Phud's every word. She searched among some papers in a notebook and held a program toward us. "This was our luncheon program. Dr. Ashby spoke on the care and feeding of nephenthes, flesh-eating plants, and how one could use them to the best advantage both indoors and out. Here. I still have a picture of one." She pulled out a glossy print of a plant with two saber-toothed fangs that guarded a small pitcher-like cavity filled with fluid. "Acid in that tiny bowl kills any insect the plant lures into it. Dr. Ashby demonstrated using a cockroach. It struggled and was barely clinging to life by the time the luncheon ended."

I tried not to imagine the luncheon ladies watch the struggling roach as they ate their salad and dessert.

"But even carnivorous plants fall prey to insects," the receptionist said. "I'm trying the doctor's tobacco and soapy water pesticide solution, but it's too soon to tell whether it will be effective." She gave a slight shudder. "Of course, I don't feature carnivorous plants in my garden."

"What time did your luncheon begin?" Janell asked.

"Oh, we always begin promptly at noon," she said. "Some of our members have to be back at their office desks by one o'clock."

"Did Dr. Ashby stay until one o'clock?" I asked.

"Oh, yes. He finished speaking a little ahead of schedule, but he remained until almost two o'clock to talk to a few housewives who didn't have to hurry away. Everyone was gone by two o'clock. Would you ladies care to look around outside?"

"Thank you, but another day," Janell said. "We'll try to stop by again when we have more time."

The woman handed us more brochures and walked with us to the exit. We thanked her for her hospitality as we left, and then once in the Prius, I sighed.

"So he could have left Marathon around two. He could have reached Key West only a bit before three—if traffic was light. But it would have been three-thirty before he changed into his butcher's costume and drove to the marina. Surely he didn't report for that grim duty wearing his business suit."

"I don't believe he could have nabbed the unsuspecting Abra Barrie, forced her into Rex's boat, and taken her to his killing grounds by mid-afternoon," Janell said. "The timing's wrong.

Surely he's innocent."

I started the car. "Let's stop at Publix. If we can find someone who saw him there in the afternoon, we'll know his alibi is sound."

"Be real, Kitt. Who's going to notice one shopper among the hundreds of people who were in the store picking up their weekend groceries?"

"Let's stop. Good cops never give up following every lead— following it and checking it out. You never know what someone might notice. The volunteer at the garden club said Phud was wearing a business suit—a silk business suit and his tam. In the Keys where shorts and tank tops are the dress du jour, a business suit's enough to make a guy noticed. And a tam! That'd make him stand out like a lighthouse on a foggy night."

"No way do I think querying anyone here will get results," Janell said, "but I'll humor you. Let's go inside and ask."

We parked in the Publix customer lot, went inside and looked around for the manager's office. Publix seemed even colder than Fausto's, and when I inhaled, the scent of fresh watermelon made my mouth water. Resisting a desire to buy a slice of it, I followed Janell directly to the manager's office. Once inside the small cubicle, she stood beside his cluttered desk, and I spoke to a man wearing a badge on his white shirt that designated him only as Manager. I wondered if he had a name.

"May I help you ladies?" He rose, pushing his captain's chair aside.

I made our request, mentioning Phud's business suit, tam, and silvery hair.

Manager shook his head. "Can't say that I noticed such a person last Friday, but, you know . . ." He nodded toward the aisles of the crowded selling floor. "Hundreds of people pass through this store every day. Your man would have had to have done something very special to cause anyone to remember him."

We thanked Manager and left the store. When we reached the parking lot, Janell suggested heading for home, but I saw a sign pointing to Sombrero Beach and turned the Prius in that direction.

Janell looked at her watch. I ignored her unspoken hint.

"Kitt, we need to be getting home. Lots of chores to do before we open for customers this evening."

"Phud said he went to the beach," I said. "Do you really believe that? Would a lecturer dressed in a silk business suit spend time at the beach? Probably not. Or if he took time to change into beach attire, he definitely wouldn't have had time to make it back to Key West in time for a murder."

"So let's head on home," Janell said.

"This won't take long. I'm guessing there's a groundskeeper at the beach. Let's find him. Question him."

Janell didn't answer, and she pinched her lips into a tight line while we drove on past the high school and many residences before we reached the beach. Slowing for the pavement humps that prevented speeding along the much-used road, I parked near the first entry gate leading to the sand and beyond that, to the water.

"There's the caretaker's cottage." Janell nodded toward the yellow home surrounded by white sand. "New sand," she said as if that might be important. "They've refurbished this beach following Hurricane George in 'ninety-eight and again after the big blows in two thousand five."

We knocked on the cottage door, and the woman who introduced herself as the caretaker's wife directed us down the beach to a spot where a man was riding on a huge tractor and dragging a piece of heavy equipment that smoothed the beach. I felt sand grit through my sandals and onto my toes while we walked to greet him. His tractor made so much noise that we had to wave to get his attention. He switched off the machine and grinned down at us as I made our request.

"Last Friday? Silver-haired guy? Maybe in a business suit?" He shook his head. "Can't give you any information, ladies. I might have noticed anyone wearing a business suit, but I was in Key Largo last Friday, picking up this machine. Sorry I can't be of help. My wife can't help you, either. She rode along with me to Largo."

"Thank you, sir," Janell called up to him, and we left the beach.

"So Phud seems to have an airtight alibi," I said when we drove onto Seven Mile for the trip home. "But Teach doesn't. And I'm beginning to think there's something strange about Ace's story."

"Seems like we're getting nowhere with our investigation, Kitt. But at least you're getting to see some of the Keys. Sometimes all visitors take time to see is Key West. Too bad. There're a lot of interesting things to see on the smaller Keys."

I felt guilty at having delayed our trip home by insisting on stopping at Publix and then at the beach, but once we reached The Poinsettia, I tried to make up for it by helping Janell with the sandwiches. We barely had time to enjoy Rex's conch chowder and kiwi salad before the combo set up their fronts and customers began arriving.

15

While Hella played drums on the theme song, Ace sauntered toward me. He gave a mock bow then asked, "May I have this dance?"

Even as he whirled me onto the dance floor, I wondered if he would have been so friendly had he known that I'd stolen his work glove, and that only a few hours ago I'd been checking on him, doubting him, thinking that perhaps he might have been the scum who'd murdered Abra Barrie.

"Have a good day?" he asked.

"Great day. Janell and I drove up Highway One a ways and did a few touristy things—a garden club, Sombrero Beach."

He held me closer as we danced to the melancholy tune, and I didn't push away from his embrace. He had such a clean scent, I couldn't imagine him living in the confined quarters of his shrimp boat. I smelled a fragrance like the oil horsemen in Iowa used to care for their riding tack. Maybe fishermen used it, too. I tried to forget about the glove Hella had been so eager to get out of her apartment. Had Ace missed it yet? Or maybe he'd had reason to walk to the pool. Maybe he'd already found it. I tried to push Hella and her misgivings from my thinking.

"Kitt?" Ace gave my hand a slight shake. "Ace to Kitt. What planet are you on? I asked where you went after Sombrero Beach. The country club grounds near there are show places. See them?"

I yanked my mind back to the present. "No. We missed that.

Had to get back here and prepare for the evening, but we had a great day, Ace. Crossing a bridge seven miles long is a big deal for me. Sorta scary if you stop to think about it too long. And I saw enough of Pigeon Key to make me want to return for an on-the-scene visit. And you? What did you do today?"

"My days are pretty much alike." Ace led us farther from the bandstand. "Worked on my boat. Plan to take her out for a long run in a few days. I don't mind the shrimping routine. It's my thing."

His arm around my waist gave me a feeling of being protected. I relaxed and enjoyed it. Why not? His alibi had stood up to my scrutiny—and Janell's. Only Hella's consternation over the glove gave me cause to wonder about it. I hoped his girlfriend wouldn't tell him about our visit and our questions. I wondered how often he found time to take her out on a date.

"You always fish at night? Sleep by day?"

"Right. Shrimp won't show themselves in the daytime. Took Key West fishermen a long time to discover that important fact. For years they never fished for shrimp. Thought no shrimp thrived in these waters."

"How do you keep from getting lost at night? Rex says most boaters try to come in before dark."

"You really want to know? Or are you asking to be polite?"

I looked into his blue eyes. Honest blue eyes, I told myself. "Yes, Ace, I really want to know. You chart your route by the stars?"

Ace laughed. "No way. I'm not that good at astronomy. I have a cane fishing pole mounted in a Styrofoam float and anchor to it with a heavy length of chain. I secure a battery-operated light to the top of the cane pole. When that rig is ready to use, I take the *Ace* to my secret fishing grounds, snap on the light, launch the float and begin fishing while I circle the light in ever-widening rings."

"How far away can you get from the light and still see it?"

"A fur piece, ma'am." Ace laughed. "Never been lost at sea yet. Of course, I have a ship-to-shore radio, too. The Coast Guard's always within signal distance if I should happen to get into trouble."

"Or if your battery in the light gives out?"

"Never had the battery go dead on me yet. I check it out in a battery tester before every trip."

The music stopped before I could ask Ace anything more. I admired his expertise in fishing, his knowledge of boats and the ways of shrimp. *Admit it, Kitt. You enjoy being with him.* The band had played a few more numbers and I was talking to Hella when Phud appeared at the snack bar. Hella turned her back to him and started to walk toward the B&B.

"You're not going to the sunset celebration tonight?" I called after her, hoping she wasn't going to leave me alone with Phud.

"Not tonight, Kitt. I don't go every night. Seems too much like a steady job. I'm a retired lady, you know—enjoying my golden years."

"Golden years!" Phud had joined us uninvited. "Enjoy yourself while you're young, Kitt. Golden years arrive with joint pains, blood pressure concerns, muscles that tire almost before you start using them."

"Welcome, Mr. Gloom and Doom," Hella said. "Count me out of your badmouthing. The golden years are a lot better than no golden years."

"Okay, Merry Sunshine. Keep smiling."

Hella turned, nodded goodnight to me and walked away.

"Have a good day in Miami?" Phud eased closer to me.

"Oh, we didn't get clear to Miami." I backed away from him a step or two and tried to turn away.

"I didn't think you would." He followed me along the edge of the snack bar. "What did you do and see?"

I felt wary. Was he merely being friendly, or was he prying for information he might use to his own advantage later?

"Oh, we stopped by Sombrero Beach. Spent more time there than we'd intended. We'll have to see the sights in Miami another time."

Before I could say yea or nay, Phud pulled me into an embrace and we began dancing. I liked the lime scent of his aftershave. Scents were evoking strong feelings in me tonight. Clean smells. Good feelings.

"I like beaches, Kitt. Sombrero. Smathers. Bahia Honda. Did you stop at the state park beach?"

"The one on Key West or the one on up the Highway?"

"Either one. They're both lovely. Bahia Honda is written up on tour guides as one of the nation's top ten beaches. And you didn't stop there?"

"Not today."

"I like the state park beach right in Key West," Phud said. "Do you like to swim? Maybe we could go swimming some day." Phud laughed. "What I'm really hinting for is a ride to Fort Taylor and the beach in your Prius. I'm dying to ride in that car, dying to drive it, too. Possibility?"

I felt trapped, trapped in his arms and trapped by his questions. "I'll see what Janell has planned for me in the next few days. She did mention something about all of us going out for a ride one day soon—she and Rex and Hella. There'd be plenty of room for the five of us, and I'm sure Janell wouldn't mind if you did the driving."

If my evasive reply bothered Phud, he didn't let on. "Let's make it as soon as possible. If we wait too long, I'm afraid you'll fade away back into Iowa." Phud held me tighter, and I held my head very straight, preventing the cheek-to-cheek maneuver he had in mind. I enjoyed dancing with him, but I felt as if he were rushing me. Rushing me where? I eased from his embrace when the combo took a break. Excusing myself, I left the patio and went inside to run a comb through my hair and sit down and relax for a moment.

When I returned to the patio, both Hella and Phud approached me offering a sandwich and a fresh drink. I tried to peek at the sandwich filling—and it didn't look like tuna salad.

"Thanks, guys, but I . . ." At that moment Teach headed toward us and spared me from having to make either excuses or choices. Even with his hands jammed into the pockets of his blue jumpsuit, Teach gave the impression of standing ramrod straight. His mirrored sunglasses, which he wore both day and night, made me uneasy. I had to look down to meet his gaze, and I never felt sure whether he was looking at me or at someone else. Tonight, for a few moments, he removed that doubt.

"Kitt, I have a question for you."

"Not sure I have any answers." I wished Phud and Hella would give us some space, but they stood listening.

"I've had two cancellations for tomorrow's flight to Dry Tortugas. Since you said you haven't been there for years, I'm wondering if you'd like to go along. I'd be glad to have you aboard."

His question caught me off guard, and I struggled for a reply. "How nice of you to invite me, Teach. I'd like to see Fort Jefferson again, but I'm not sure what Janell and Rex have planned for tomorrow." I wondered if that excuse was growing thin. Or did it ring with sincerity? "I'm sure you must have a back-up list of people who'd like to fly with you."

"Better grab the chance, Kitt," Rex called from his stance behind the cash register where he'd been listening to our conversation. "Teach's a good pilot and a super guide. People

136

sometimes wait days to be able to get a reservation on the *Osprey*."

"Sounds like good advice, Rex, but I'll need to talk to Janell before I make a decision to be away for a whole day. She may need some kitchen help, and we did have some sightseeing plans for tomorrow afternoon."

"Half-day trip," Teach said. "Only a half day."

"Janell's an easy taskmaster," Rex said. "She'll let you go."

Janell stood at the end of the snack bar filling a child's order for a peanut butter sandwich, and I looked in her direction, willing her to meet my gaze. She continued making more sandwiches until I eased away from the others and walked to the counter where she was working.

"Janell, what about our plans for tomorrow?"

Janell turned her back toward Rex and the others and spoke softly. "We were going to check on Teach's whereabouts last Friday afternoon, remember? But maybe if you take him up on his offer it'd give you an opportunity to ask some pertinent questions. Subtly, of course. And not only about his activities, but also about anything Ace, Phud or even Hella and Mama G might have mentioned to him concerning last Friday and Abra Barrie."

"Then you think I should take him up on his offer?" I asked. "I mean . . . I guess if you think it would be okay . . ."

"Afraid of him?"

"Should I be?"

Janell shook her head. "To me, he seems to be the least likely murder suspect I can think of. His size alone rules him out as far as I'm concerned. You don't know when you'll be called back to Iowa, Kitt. Anything you learn about the murder before you have to leave will be serendipity. Anything we might have done tomorrow we can do the day after. Why don't you make plans to go along to the fort and enjoy your vacation while you have this opportunity?"

"My enforced vacation." I felt my dad's medallion in my pocket. "I suppose you're right, sis. Maybe I could help us more on Garden Key than I could here. On the other hand, I don't like leaving you with all the work."

"Forget that. I handled the café scene before you arrived. No problem there. Look at it this way. If you spend a day with Teach, learn some more details of that Friday afternoon, it could take our investigation in a different direction tomorrow and maybe a better direction."

I returned to Teach and the others who now were sitting at a table, and Rex walked to us and drew up a chair for me. I had no more than seated myself when Mama G ended the combo break with a blast on her conch shell.

"Okay, *amigos*. Back on the bandstand. Now. Our patrons want music not chatter." She gave another blast on the shell and basked in the attention of every patron on the patio. Only Ace and Teach ignored her.

Ace had joined the group while I was talking with Janell, and neither he nor Teach looked in Mama G's direction or made any moves toward the bandstand.

"Decide to go along tomorrow?" Teach asked.

"Yes." I smiled at him. "Janell says she can do without my help. So I'll really look forward to joining you."

"Too bad you had a last-minute cancellation," Phud said. "Hard on the ol' pocketbook. Maybe I could help you out and buy that other extra seat. Haven't been out to the fort for a long time."

My heart sank to my toes. I didn't want to spend a day with both Teach and Phud. But before Teach could reply, before I could try to weasel out of the situation, Hella spoke up.

"Teach, you promised me long ago that I could buy your next cancelled seat. You do remember that, don't you? Must have been a couple of months ago."

"Right, Hella. I remember, and you've got dibs on a seat on tomorrow's flight. I'd like to have both you and Kitt along."

"Who else is making the trip?" Hella asked.

"A young couple from Maine. Honeymooners. We probably won't see much of them. Said they plan to spend the day snorkeling. Weather's supposed to be great."

Phud glared at Hella, who returned his glare with one of her own. Mama G blustered across the dance floor, targeting our table, and Teach humored her by standing and taking a tentative step toward his bass on the bandstand. Ace continued to loll in his chair, rising only when Janell hurried toward me.

"Kitt, you have a phone call. Why don't you take it in the kitchen?"

16

I hurried into the kitchen and grabbed the telephone. My mouth felt so dry I could hardly speak, and my whole body tensed when I heard Hank Burdock's clipped tones on the line.

"Brace yourself, Kitt. The Perp slipped into a coma last night. He's not expected to live."

For several moments I couldn't speak. I cleared my throat and took three deep breaths before my partner continued.

"You'll get the news from official sources soon, but I thought I'd call and tell you first so you could be prepared when the chief calls. Kitt? Kitt? Are you there? Have we been cut off?"

"I'm here, Hank. I thank you for calling. Wh-what's going on with the review committee? I've heard nothing."

"Because there's nothing to hear. It's flu season up here, Kitt. Two members of the committee are hospitalized, even though they had shots. Committee won't function without them."

"So I wait." The kitchen began to spin around me, and I managed to sit down at the breakfast table before I fell.

"We all wait. Every person on the force is rooting on your side, Kitt. Rasty Raymore was a no-good. He'd be no great loss to his family, Iowa, the world. A druggie. Been in and out of prison all his life. But you know that. You may have saved the taxpayers the cost of a trial."

"Hank, have you any idea, any idea at all of how it feels to have killed another human being?"

"No. And you don't know either—not yet. The Perp's still in a coma. He's not dead."

"So can you imagine how it feels to have deliberately fired a bullet into another living human being? I think it's a memory I'll never get over, something I'll never forget or recover from anytime soon, if ever."

"I try not to imagine myself in such a situation, but I'll admit I've thought about it. Thought about it a lot ever since I joined the force. All the guys think about it, wonder about it. They may not admit it. But they do."

"And they still stay on the force, don't they?"

Hank didn't answer my question.

"Don't let this get to you, Kitt. What you did was part of your job. You were doing what cops are hired to do—to protect the public from criminals and scofflaws. Far better to have a dead druggie than a dead cop any day of the week. Never forget that. Never."

"You're saying there are exceptions to the Ten Commandments. The do-not-kill one, for example?"

"There are mitigating circumstances. What about the one that says honor your father and your mother? You were certainly honoring your father. Why, I remember when . . ."

"I've got to hang up now, Hank. I appreciate your call, and I'll bear in mind what you've said." The line hummed between us for a few seconds before I could speak again. "Hank . . . do you have a new partner?"

"Yes. But only temporarily. Cops work in pairs. Your place will be waiting for you when that review committee finishes its job."

"Sure, Hank. Sure." I replaced the receiver and sat staring into space, trying to blank from my mind the reality of Rasty Raymore's coma. I blinked, startled when Janell stepped into the kitchen.

"He died, didn't he?" For a moment she stood staring at me.

"No. He's in a coma but not expected to live. If he dies, it'll be my fault. I'll know I've taken a human life."

Rex had followed Janell into the kitchen. "Look, Kitt. You were only doing your job. You were defending law and order."

"I'll try to remember that at night when I can't sleep." I ran myself a glass of water and gulped it down. "Forgive my sarcasm, Rex. I'm not going to let this get me down. I'm going to . . ." I hesitated, not having the slightest idea of what I was going to do—if I ever came to my senses.

Janell finished my sentence for me. "You're going to talk to Teach in a few minutes after you've had time to compose yourself. The combo's about to play 'Harbor Lights,' and he needs to give you some last-minute instructions concerning your outing tomorrow morning."

"Outing. Tomorrow." I let my brain toy with the words until they made sense.

Tomorrow. Fort Jefferson. Dry Tortugas. I stood and returned to the patio. Hella sat playing the drums. The combo was playing "Harbor Lights," but it seemed like a tune I'd never heard before. I forced politeness as I declined Ace's request for a dance, and I busied myself helping Janell and Rex clear off the snack bar.

Teach sauntered toward me once most of the crowd had left the patio. "Got a few tips to help you and Hella make your trip tomorrow go smoothly." He pushed his sunglasses onto the top of his head and looked directly at me, waiting until Hella joined us before he continued.

"I told you this's a half-day tour. We'll take off tomorrow morning from Key West International at eight-thirty, so you'll need to be at the airport thirty minutes ahead of takeoff. My headquarters are a short distance to the side of the main airport terminal. You'll have no trouble locating me. It's one of the few spots on the island where you'll find plenty of free parking space."

"There's no water at the airport," Hella said. "How's a seaplane going to take off with no water?"

"What kind of a plane do you fly?" I asked, thinking more about safety than about the obvious lack of water.

"I fly a top-notch amphibious plane, ladies—a rebuilt Cessna. It has retractable wheels that I pull up into the floats. I use wheels for takeoffs and landings at the airport. When we reach Garden Key, I'll use the floats for our touchdown. Once we dip into the water, helpers will pull the plane onto the beach, where we'll leave it while we explore the park grounds and the fort."

"So we should wear waterproof shoes?" Hella asked. "Or carry dry shoes along in a bag?"

"There're usually park rangers on hand to do the plane pulling." Teach glanced at Hella's Birkenstocks. "Wear what you've got on. You'll be fine."

"Do you always go so early?" Hella asked.

"If it's too early for you, I'll be more than happy to take your spot." Phud joined our group again, elbowing his way past Rex and Janell, who stood listening to Teach's tips. I thought Phud had left for home earlier, and now I held my breath, waiting to hear what Hella might say.

"I'm an early riser," Hella said. "Eight o'clock's fine with me."

I breathed again.

"You're lucky to be going so early," Teach said. "Our flying time will be about forty minutes. Tourists going to the fort by boat will be on the water two to three hours. So you can see we'll be there long before the sea-going crowd arrives and we'll have the fort, the grounds and the beach pretty much to ourselves during that time. There may be a few others who arrive as we do, by amphibious transportation, but not many."

"What should we bring along?" I asked.

"I'll pack you a lunch," Janell said.

"We'll love that, Janell," Teach said. "In real life, we'd have to pack our own lunch, but there are drinks available for purchase at the park. If you plan to swim or snorkel, bring your swimming suits and equipment and your own towels. No air tanks are allowed. Remember that everything we take onto the island, we must take off the island when we leave."

"What time will we be back?" Hella asked.

"Around noon. I have another half-day tour scheduled for afternoon."

"I'll be ready, Teach," I said. "I'll drive Hella and me to the airport, and I thank you again for this opportunity."

By the time Teach finished giving us our instructions, everyone had left the patio—even Phud. Rex, Janell and I finished cleaning the snack bar, leaving it ready for tomorrow night's business. Rex locked the gate, extinguished the torches and clicked off the other lights.

Once inside, I told Rex and Janell goodnight and trudged upstairs to bed for what I feared might be a sleepless night. I took a long, slow tub bath, enjoying the tepid water and rose-scented bath oil until I was able to relax. When my fingers grew pruney, I left the tub, toweled off and slipped into bed.

In spite of the relaxing bath, I lay awake, thinking about the message from Hank and about my guilt in Rasty Raymore's coma and impending death. Those thoughts did nothing to help lull me to sleep. After I'd blocked guilt thoughts into a far corner of my mind, I forced myself to think about tomorrow's flight to Fort Jefferson. Why? Why? Why? Questions continued to pop into my mind. Why had Phud wanted to go along on the flight? He could go to Dry Tortugas any day of the week if he so desired. Why did he suddenly get interested in making the trip when he learned I was going? I could only wonder about his motivations—and Hella's. Of course, Hella said she had put dibs on a seat earlier in the winter.

At first I had welcomed Hella's insistence on taking tomorrow's flight, thinking that perhaps she was trying to protect me from Phud. Maybe he was the person she saw surrounded by a dark aura. Or was I being too trusting of Hella? In our minds, Janell and I had dropped Hella from our suspect list. She was certainly strong enough to have overcome Abra Barrie—or me. But that was crazy thinking. Nothing sinister could happen to me with Teach and two other passengers aboard the *Osprey*.

When I thought more about Teach, I remembered that Janell and Rex had said he had talked with Abra Barrie on her last Thursday night, argued with her, tried to talk her into a trip to the fort. Teach might not have an airtight alibi for the afternoon of her murder, but maybe Abra could have said something to him that might reveal a clue to the identity of her murderer. That's one of the things I'd think about tomorrow. Maybe tomorrow would give me more than an insight into Key's history.

I fell asleep planning questions I'd present to Teach concerning his short contact with Abra Barrie, and it seemed only moments later that I awakened to the jangle of my alarm clock.

"You have to eat some breakfast." Janell punctuated her words with an extra swish of her caftan when I stepped into the kitchen. "You're going to have an exciting morning. You'll enjoy it more if you eat at least a bite or two. Come on to poolside. I'm serving some special cinnamon buns this morning. I already have a pot of coffee ready to pour and there's orange juice out there, too."

"You work too hard, Janell."

"Fausto's bakery and my electric orange squeezer did most of the work today. Come on. Hella's already at the patio."

Today Hella had abandoned her usual long shift for navy

blue slacks and a cotton cardigan. She patted the chair beside her where she had laid a broad-brimmed straw hat. "Don't forget to bring along a sun hat and plenty of sunscreen, Kitt."

"Right," I agreed. "Red hair and sunscreen go well together." I sat beside Rex and tried not to gulp my orange juice, but this trip had me more excited than I'd expected. Even Hella sat on the edge of her chair, trying to gulp coffee that was steaming hot.

"I'll drive you to the airport," Rex said. "No point in letting the Prius sit out there all morning. And we'd better get started right away."

"Want to drive us in the Prius?" I asked.

"Thanks, but no thanks," Rex said. "This early go-to-work traffic is no place for a new car. We'll take our car this time."

I laughed. "Or maybe we could bicycle to the airport."

Janell reached into her pocket and answered her cell phone. "Great, Teach. They'll appreciate." Then smiling at us, she said, "Teach will pick you up at our gate in ten minutes and drive you to the *Osprey.*"

"How nice of him!" I exclaimed.

Rex ran his hand over his bald head. "Don't kid yourself. He just wants an extra few minutes to regale you with more facts about Fort Jefferson."

"I like a fellow who's excited about his job." Hella stood and headed toward her apartment. "Meet you at the gate, Kitt."

Teach arrived in his old Ford and tapped the horn twice, although he could see we were ready and waiting. "Good morning, ladies."

His mirrored glasses reflected the sun, but I assumed he was looking at us. "Morning, Teach." Hella and I spoke in unison as Hella climbed into the passenger seat and I took the seat behind her.

"Have a great morning." Janell and Rex waved and watched

us out of sight.

"We're going to take the highway along the beach," Teach said. "Should find less traffic there."

As Rex had predicted, Teach spouted Fort Jefferson facts all the way to the airport. I found them interesting, but Hella sighed and spent most of the ride gazing out the window at the beach scene. We had passed East Martello Tower and entered the airport gate when Teach slowed the car.

"Would you look at that!"

17

Teach stopped for a brief security check and a "go-ahead" from the uniformed guard, then he drove on toward the *Osprey*, which we could easily see tethered at the far end of the airport terminal. Next to his plane were two humungous Harleys propped on their kickstands with a person relaxing on the ground beside each.

"That must be the Hogans," Teach said. "Pam and Phil. Newlyweds. Every once in a while I get to fly honeymooners to the fort. Only trouble is, they don't pay much attention to the things I try to tell them about the fort."

Honeymoon. I'd tried to shut off all memories of Shelby Cox, but now I found myself envying the Hogans' carefree life, although I knew nothing of them, their problems, their goals. After Teach made the proper introductions, he readied his plane for takeoff. I circled the *Osprey* while he helped the others aboard. This was the first time I'd been close to an amphibious plane and I noted the floats and the retractable wheels that were now touching the ground. Single engine. What if? I tried to bury my apprehensions about the plane—and about its pilot.

"Come on, Kitt," Teach called to me and then helped me up the steps to the cabin. Each of us had a window seat, and I took thc only one left, the one across the narrow aisle from Hella. We buckled our seat belts, and Teach boarded after we did, closed and secured the door before he settled himself in the pilot's seat. He clamped on headphones and started the motor.

I smelled a pleasant mixture of leather and coconut-scented sunscreen and felt the vibration of the floorboard under my feet while we waited for clearance from the tower. At last Teach taxied along the airstrip for a smooth takeoff toward the open sea and Garden Key. Engine sounds roared in the cabin, precluding any small talk, and in spite of my dark glasses I squinted when I looked down at sunshine glinting on the deep blue water of Key West Harbor.

Cruise ships. Yachts. Sailboats. Shrimp boats. Runabouts. In the far distance two gray cargo ships plied the water near the horizon. Had we been flying higher, the crafts below might have looked like bathtub toys, but we were low enough that some of the passengers on the boats below peered up at us and waved. We had traveled only a few minutes before Teach's voice crackled to us as he began speaking over a hand-held microphone.

"Friends, we're leaving Key West Harbor and flying at an altitude of five hundred feet over the Gulf of Mexico. Most of the mangrove islands we pass are charted but many of them are unnamed and unoccupied. We're now flying over the flats where the water is shallow—five to eight feet deep and extending some twenty miles west. Please take time to look down."

What a needless command. The sea water was clear as empty space, and everyone sat with forehead pressed to glass. I saw the dark shape of a stingray, its "wings" undulating in a no-hurry mode that propelled it like an underwater leviathan over sands that looked like a submerged desert.

"Portside, you'll see a shark," Teach announced. "Starboard, two dolphins jumping and diving."

He didn't bother to tell us that port meant left and starboard meant right. After a few more minutes of engine sound, he spoke again. "The water below us here is about thirty feet deep and the islands are the Marquesas, a coral atoll.

"It's near this spot that treasure salvor Mel Fisher discovered the ancient Spanish galleons the *Atocha* and the *Marguerita* along with over an estimated billion dollars in gold, silver and emeralds scattered over an eight-mile area. The area's still a treasure site where divers with the know-how and the proper legal permits continue to seek their fortunes. Look carefully portside and you may catch sight of some sea turtles swimming at the surface. From the size of their heads, I'd say they were loggerheads."

"Their heads are the size of footballs!" Hogan exclaimed.

"Hence their head-oriented name," his wife said.

Teach pointed out a World War II ship, the *Patricia,* that the Navy had sunk for use in bombing target practice, and also the sunken *Arbutus,* one of Mel Fisher's old treasure-hunting boats. Target practice? Was this pipsqueak of a man trying to make me feel like a target?

"Okay, folks. We're almost there. We're going to make a low pass over Fort Jefferson and then touch down for a water landing. Our flight time has been thirty-five minutes. Once we're on land, you're free to enjoy your day in any way you choose. Hike. Swim. Tour the fort. Whatever."

The minute we landed gently into the sea, Teach eased the plane toward the shore. Park rangers splashed into the shallow water, grabbed the plane's struts and pulled us onto the beach. Teach deplaned first, thanking the rangers and then helping each of us onto dry sand.

"Please report here to the plane at eleven-thirty," Teach said. "I'll have you back in Key West around noon."

Key West. Of course we had to go back. But for over half an hour I'd been so occupied with our ride over this exotic area I hadn't once thought about Abra Barrie. Nor had I thought about Rasty Raymore lying near death in Iowa due to my impulsiveness. How could I live with my guilt?

"Great trip, man," Phil Hogan said, reaching into his pocket and producing a tube of sunscreen.

"Loved every minute of it." His wife smiled and donned a sun hat.

"Right," I agreed. "It was a wonderful flight."

"Every bit as wonderful as you're always telling us." Hella laughed and shook one foot to remove sand from her shoe. We all slathered on sunscreen and secured our beach hats, then watched the Hogans for a few moments while they headed for the swimming beach hand in hand and then arms around waists. They stopped a ways from the water's edge to shed their cover-ups, don masks and fins and wade tentatively into the sea.

"What would you ladies like to do first?" Teach asked.

"What do you suggest, Fearless Leader?" Hella asked.

"You're in charge," I agreed. "I'm already fascinated with this place." I looked at a frigate bird soaring high overhead.

"Then if you agree, we'll tour the fort, and then pause for a snack before we hike the perimeter of the structure."

And that's what we did. We crossed the bridge over the moat, entered the dark brick structure through the front gate and then walked into the open area inside the walls. A bevy of gulls screamed from their perch on the ramparts. Palms and sea-grapes shaded parts of the lawn that was sparsely covered with coarse grass. In Iowa we call it crabgrass, an unflattering term. Not sure what the locals call it. I could imagine troops drilling—or troops in parade formations led by a brass band before some general's reviewing platform.

A little farther on, Teach began his lecture by telling us Fort Jefferson was the largest brick building in the Western Hemisphere. I didn't care about statistics. In my mind I planned questions to ask him about the Thursday night before Abra Barrie's murder. I wished now that I'd written out a list. What had they argued about? I guessed the subject matter of their talk concerned more than whether she had time for a trip aboard the *Osprey*.

"In 1812, the government began building a chain of coastal defenses that, if things went according to plan, were to reach from Maine to Texas. Their purpose was to control all navigation headed for the Gulf of Mexico and thus to protect Atlantic-bound Mississippi River trade."

I found everything Teach said interesting, and I was glad I'd made a special effort to read some of his handbook before we made this trip. But I kept glancing at my watch, eager for snack time when he might store his facts for a few minutes and allow me time to talk to him about Abra Barrie. I could hardly guess at what they might have had to say to each other that resulted in an argument.

"How big is Garden Key?" Hella asked when Teach stopped talking a minute to clear his throat.

"Sixteen acres. And the fort covers eleven of those acres."

"Who lived behind these walls?" I tried to be interested in his answer.

"The fort served as a military prison during the Civil War. Its cells held deserters. And it was home away from home, or maybe I should say home away from jail, for four men supposedly involved in President Lincoln's murder. Dr. Samuel Mudd was the most famous of the four."

We walked on and on through the fort, and I found it interesting that one level of floor was about a foot higher than the other. Hella stumbled as she stepped down onto the lower level and Teach grabbed her arm to offer support while he grinned.

"I'm not laughing at you, Hella. I was about to explain that the upper level we just left housed officer's quarters. Enlisted men lived on the lower level. Even in the austerity of the fort, the officers chose that one foot of elevation to make it clear they were in charge. However, in spite of all the money and the thirty years of work that went into its construction, the fort remained uncompleted."

"Why?" I asked.

"Typical government project." Hella snorted. "Spend. Spend. Spend. Even in those days."

Teach interrupted. "Workers weakened by outbreaks of yellow fever slowed building progress, and so did the invention of the rifled cannon. Cannon balls could penetrate the fort's thick walls. Those guns were the chief reason for Fort Jefferson's incomplete state."

We had carried our snack lunches with us, and when Teach suggested we take a break and enjoy our sandwiches, I was first to volunteer to buy us drinks from a nearby concession stand.

"Grape soda for me," Hella said.

"I'll have a Coke," Teach said.

I chose bottled water and once I returned with our drinks, we settled ourselves at a small picnic table in a shady area. Before Teach could regale us with more info on Garden Key and Fort Jefferson, I changed the subject.

"Teach, Janell and I have been thinking a lot about Abra Barrie's murder, trying to figure out who the culprit might be. You have any ideas?"

Teach shook his head. "Don't tell me you suspect me." He scowled at the idea. "The night the police questioned everyone at The Poinsettia I offered proof that I'd been working all day on that Friday. I even gave the detective the names of the patrons I brought here to the fort—Key West addresses as well as their hometown addresses up north. Michigan. Wisconsin."

I said nothing about his returning to Key West for a business appointment. "Be real, Teach. Janell and I never suspected you or anyone else at The Poinsettia, but Janell said you spent some time talking to Abra Barrie when the combo took a break."

"She visited with all of us, Kitt," Hella said. "But, Teach, she followed you to the bandstand for more conversation after the rest of us were enjoying Mama G's sandwiches. Looked to me like you two were having an argument. I'm guessing you were trying to talk her into a flight to the fort and maybe she was resisting. Am I right?"

"A wrong guess," Teach said. "Totally wrong."

I wished I could see the expression in his eyes as he denied Hella's words, but his sunglasses made that impossible. "Teach, will you tell me what you did talk to Abra Barrie about? Why keep it such a secret, since you have an alibi for the crucial time in which the ME says she died?"

"No reason you shouldn't know, I suppose." Teach shrugged. "You probably won't believe it."

"Try us." Hella clipped the words, and Teach's face flushed.

"Ms. Barrie wanted to book a flight over here," Teach said. "She was quite interested in making the trip, but I . . . turned her down."

"Were you already booked?" Hella asked. "Why refuse a paying customer? She didn't expect a freebie, did she?"

"No. She was willing to pay—even said her company might give me a bonus if I could arrange to fly her here on such short notice. She knew I had a waiting list and that she had no reservation."

"Why did you refuse?" I laid my sandwich aside and gave him my full attention, hoping he was looking at me. "That makes no sense. Surely, under the circumstances, you could have worked her into your schedule."

"I had my reasons." Teach lowered his head and I guessed he was staring at his sandwich as if he intended to say no more. I refused to let him get by with that.

"And what were those reasons? It would have meant money in your pocket, would it not?"

Teach sighed and pushed his sunglasses to the top of his

head. "You're right. I seldom turn down a chance to earn more money, but I didn't want that woman to see Fort Jefferson. I figured that if I wouldn't fly her here, maybe nobody else would either, and maybe she wouldn't have time to take the ferry."

"You're avoiding the issue, Teach. Why didn't you want her to see Fort Jefferson?" He replaced his sunglasses and I knew from his tone that he must be glaring at me. "Come on, Teach. Give."

He ducked his head and kept his voice so low we could hardly hear him. "The woman wanted to scope out locations suitable for her company's wind turbines. That's why her company sent her here. When off-shore turbines are set in place, companies face the great expense of working underwater. That means building structures strong enough, steady enough to hold the above-ground turbines in place."

"Sort of like sinking the underwater pilings for a bridge?" I asked.

"Right. Something like that. Miss Barrie wanted to come here to see if Garden Key might be a potential spot for a wind turbine. If her company could set one up here on land, it would save them thousands of dollars, and at the same time they'd reap the advantage of strong off-shore winds."

"And why were you so against that?" Hella asked.

"Give me a break, Hella. My flights are low-altitude ventures. There's no way I'd want to risk flying the *Osprey* near one of those huge turbines. I don't want to see them anywhere near here. And I'm not the only one. Ace agrees with me, too. Ask him if you don't believe me. A huge contraption like Barrie's company is promoting and selling could make changes in this area—all of them changes for the bad."

"But you aren't sure of that," I said. "I'm all for renewable energy sources. I think we need to give new energy-saving ideas a try—unless we want to be dependent on the Arabs forevermore."

"No way," Teach said as if that were the end of the conversation. "I say no to turbines on Key West, Garden Key, or anywhere else in this area."

"Teach, why do you have such a closed mind when it comes to turbines?"

"The government has a way of telling the people all the advantages of a thing and glossing over or sugar-coating what can turn out to be major disadvantages. Take this war, for instance. There were no weapons of mass destruction, not even any plans for such weapons. We taxpayers were taken in. Gullible. And now we're in a war we can't get out of. I didn't hear Abra Barrie mention any negative aspects of having wind turbines in our waters."

"Maybe because there really aren't any," I said.

"And maybe there are lots of them. I'm afraid my potential customers would think several times before booking a flight that went anywhere near an off-shore turbine or an on-shore turbine if it were located on Garden Key."

"On the other hand, maybe they'd be as curious about a turbine as they are about the sunken *Arbutus,* the stingrays, the underwater desert. Many people are curious about things they don't see every day in their own backyards."

"Ace is afraid the vibrations created by such gigantic machines would scare shrimp as well as other fish into a different area. You can't blame either of us for wanting to protect our businesses."

"It's a moot point now, isn't it?" Hella asked. "Abra Barrie's company is unlikely to sponsor any more feasibility studies in this area any time soon."

Had Teach agreed to fly Abra Barrie to Fort Jefferson, he might have saved her life. But I wasn't about to mention that. I might have saved a life, too, had I refused to fire my gun in that Iowa pet store.

"Let's not let this talk spoil the rest of our morning," I said. "Thank you for answering my questions, Teach. I'll say no more about the subject."

And I didn't. I tried to act interested as Teach told us about the army abandoning Fort Jefferson in 1874 and its becoming a wildlife refuge to protect nesting birds and their eggs in 1908, and its being proclaimed a National Monument in 1992. Luckily, nobody would give me a test on those dates.

The Hogans sat in the sand waiting for us at the plane at eleven-thirty, and Teach helped everyone board the craft. Park rangers shoved the *Osprey* into the sea, and I watched sun glint on water that sprayed briefly around the floats when Teach took off and lifted us into the sky. I wondered what kind of an aura Hella saw around Teach. Probably neither white nor black. Gray? Did she see a black aura around me because I'd shot a man? Maybe that was why she felt reluctant to talk to me about auras.

18

Once we were home, Hella headed for the B&B. When I saw Rex and Phud in work clothes and relaxing at poolside, I joined them. My mind was still spinning from the plane ride, from all I'd heard, seen and done in the past few hours. I welcomed the peacefulness of the garden.

"Glad you're back." Rex wiped sweat from his bald head with a bandana. "Been putting up new awnings on the café. That makes it a hot day here—at least for me. How was it at the fort?"

"Pleasantly warm and breezy. We had a great trip, and Teach's a good guide. He must have spent years studying about that area."

"Kitt means he's been talking her ears off all morning." Phud laughed and I wondered why he was still here. Noon was his usual go-home time. He glanced at the headlines on the *Citizen* Rex had laid aside. "Guess the police still have no leads on the Barrie murder."

Rex picked up the newspaper, folded it and tucked it under his arm, clearly not interested in more discussion about the murder.

"Kitt, how about driving Phud and me to Marathon this afternoon? Feel up to doing that? We'd both like a ride in your new car. Janell's going to be busy helping at West Martello, and before I knew she'd need our car for hauling bags of potting soil and fertilizer to the Garden Club, I called the woman in

Marathon who bought that pelican painting."

"She's willing to part with it?" I sat in the empty chair beside him.

"Money talks," Phud said. "In this mercenary world today, there's a price on everything."

Rex ignored his comment. "Didn't mention the painting. Just told her I wanted to talk to her on a business matter. Thought if I drove to her door and made my plea in person, I might be able to persuade her to sell."

"Janell doesn't know this?"

"Right. I'm still trying to make it a surprise. And Phud and I are still interested in a ride in your Prius."

"Right," Phud said.

I didn't mind taking a ride with Rex, but I wished Phud hadn't been included. Something about him made me uneasy. Maybe the fact that he'd followed Janell and me. Or maybe it was Hella's attitude toward him. I sighed. Why was I letting *their* differences over a neighborhood cat bother me? Too late to worry about that now. I saw no graceful way to refuse Phud a ride without being rude to a long-time friend Rex and Janell liked and respected—and needed.

"A ride up the Keys is fine with me. How soon do you want to start? Give me a minute to freshen up, and we'll be off."

"Great day for a ride," Phud said, "Could I talk you into stopping at the Big Pine Key library on the way? It's only a block or so off the highway."

"Don't know why not," Rex said, "unless Kitt has a need to be back here quickly. How about it, Kitt?"

"No problem." I hoped my lie sounded sincere.

"There's a tropical foliage guide in their reference room that I'd like to look at—Reference Room only. No check-outs. I'd like to snap an indoor pic of the library, too. They have a special window treatment that our local library might find interesting as well as practical." Phud pulled a camera from his pocket, studied it for a second or two then thrust it back into his pocket.

"Sure, Phud," Rex said. "It might pay me to stop at the art gallery and talk to the artist who painted the *Pelican*. She might have some tips for me on how to approach the buyer in Marathon."

I ran upstairs, brushed my hair and slipped into a fresh shirt before I joined Rex and Phud at my car. Phud had eased into the passenger seat before I slipped beneath the wheel. I wondered if he and Rex had discussed who was to ride up front. Rex was opening the front gate for our exit when his cell phone rang. I knew from his scowl and terse words that our plans might change. Relief flooded through me. Maybe we wouldn't be going to Marathon after all.

"Police." Rex spat the word after he broke the phone connection. "They want to see me at headquarters one more time."

"What for this time?" Phud asked.

"That's okay, Rex." I spared him from having to answer Phud's nosey question. "No problem. We can drive to Marathon another day—maybe tomorrow or the day after."

"Hate to change the Marathon plans," Rex said. "The lady and her husband plan to leave on vacation tomorrow. She didn't say when they'd be returning. I really wanted to contact her today before . . . Kitt . . ."

I knew what he had in mind, and I wanted to say no, to refuse to drive to Marathon with Phud. But when Rex asked, I couldn't refuse without sounding unsympathetic and unpleasant. A rotten way for a houseguest to sound. Janell and Rex trusted Phud. Why couldn't I?

"Kitt, would you be my emissary? Would you go to Marathon and talk to her? I'll give you a blank check and a note telling her of my need for the painting. Try to keep the price under two hundred if you can. Negotiate. Haggle a bit. But try to bring that painting back this afternoon."

I swallowed a sigh and a quick refusal. "Okay, Rex. I'll go ahead with our plans. But do you think I have a chance to persuade Mrs. What's-her-name to sell me her painting? I'm not the kind of buyer who likes to negotiate and haggle."

"Mrs. Reitz. That's her name." Rex ignored my self-doubts.

"I'm sure you could make a more persuasive plea, Rex."

"You may be right," Rex sighed. "Maybe I'd better phone her and explain the situation—and hope for the best."

"I'd appreciate that, Rex."

"But I'll call her after you've left Key West, tell her why I had to change my plans, and ask her to be expecting you."

Phud grinned. "Surely it'll be hard for her to refuse if you offer more than she paid for the painting."

"Knowing Kitt's made a special trip to her home to pick up the picture should help my cause, too."

"Maybe I could talk to her, too." Phud winked at me, and I looked out the window to keep from scowling at him. "Friends tell me I have a way with the ladies."

Rex and I both ignored Phud's offer and his comment. "How do I find her house?"

"Got the address right here." Rex pulled a slip of paper from his shirt pocket. "Follow the highway to Marathon and turn Oceanside onto Seabreeze Blvd. She's at 1009. You should have no trouble finding it. Or if you should, someone at the post office will be able to direct you."

"Shall I drop you off at the police station?"

"No. I'll ride my bike."

"Flat tire, remember?"

"I'll inflate it. There's a hand pump in the shed. Want to keep a low profile with the police, and your Prius isn't a low-profile car. If you drove me, I'd have to ask for a ride home. Don't want to ask them for favors."

"I can understand that." Phud smiled and shook his head. "Best to keep plenty of distance between you and the PD."

Phud and I waited until Rex brought the air pump from the shed and inflated the bicycle tire before we eased into traffic and left for Marathon. I felt the air inside the car crackle with unspoken words. Mine? Phud's? Maybe both. I couldn't be sure. At last I broke the silence.

"There's an owner's manual in the glove box, Phud. If you've questions about the car, you can probably find answers there. I'm no authority on the workings of any car, especially this Prius. I just know that it conserves gasoline."

"Okay. I'll take a look." Phud opened the glove box, removed the manual, and began paging through it.

From the side of my eye, I could see he wasn't reading it, only flipping casually through the pages like a child searching for the illustrations in a picture book. We'd only driven a few miles before we reached Big Coppit Key. I hung a left and parked in front of a furniture store—Fred's Beds.

"Problem?" Phud asked.

"No problem. I remembered a lamp I saw in here and I've decided to buy it as a gift for Janell." I planned to purchase the lamp and pay by check so the clerk might remember me in case anyone stopped by asking about me later. Paper trail. Maybe I could stop at other stores and leave more checks. That idea bit the dust when I picked up the lamp and my purse and returned to my car.

Phud now sat behind the wheel as if he owned the car. What nerve! I didn't intend to let him get by with that. Scowling, I strode toward the driver's door and yanked it open.

"Out!" I spat the word and pointed to the ground. Phud didn't budge, nor did he show any surprise at hearing my order.

"Out!" I spoke more firmly this time. "Phud, get out of my car. Now. This minute. Out!"

Phud responded by trying to jerk the door from my hand and slam it shut. I stood clutching the car key. He couldn't start the engine, but it infuriated me that he wouldn't budge from behind the wheel. Did he think I'd play passenger and let him drive to Marathon? No way.

"Phud!" I stood back, again jerking on the car door.

A bearded man driving a vintage red Caddy pulled close beside us and lowered his passenger side window. He studied my new car. I studied his old car. For a moment we bonded as car lovers. "You have a problem, lady? Is this guy in your car bothering you?"

Phud laughed and opened the car door, thrusting a camera toward me. "No problem here, sir. I wanted my friend, Kitt, to snap a pic of me sitting behind the wheel of her car—a joke, you know. Wanted to con a friend back home into thinking I owned it. You ever seen a Prius before?"

Phud's easygoing manner, his laugh and his reference to the car distracted the stranger from his original mission—offering me help if I needed it. Men and cars! What chance did a woman have!

"No, I've never seen any car like this one." The old man left his Caddy with the motor running and the driver's door open and began walking around the Prius, giving it a visual probing. "Great-looking vehicle." He returned to where I still stood beside the driver's door. "Why don't you let me snap both your pictures sitting in the car? That should settle your dispute. Okay?"

"Okay, if I'm sitting behind the wheel," I said.

"Spoil sport." Phud grinned and winked at me as if we were sharing a joke before he eased from the car and re-entered on the passenger's side. I slid behind the wheel. The man snapped a shot and returned Phud's camera to him. And that was that.

I felt like asking Phud to leave my car. He could call a cab for a ride back to Key West. But how would I ever explain that to Janell and Rex without sounding foolish, without sounding overly possessive of the car? I could hardly expect them to believe that Phud had tried to commandeer the Prius. I could barely believe it myself. Had I blown the incident out of proportion? That was possible, given my feelings toward Phud—and my car.

We said little on the drive to Marathon. Phud offered no apology for his behavior and I demanded none. I just wanted this trip to end as soon as possible. We passed Sugarloaf Lodge, Coco's Cantina on Cudjoe, Ramrod Key.

"We're coming into Big Pine," Phud said. "To your right you can see the launch that carries passengers to Little Palm Island."

I felt no interest in casual conversation or in Little Palm Island.

When we reached the stoplight on Big Pine, I waited for a red-to-green change.

"Use your turn signal," Phud said. "We need to take a left here."

"Why?"

"Because you told Rex we could stop at the library."

In my anger over the who's-going-to-drive incident, I'd forgotten about that promise and now I regretted having made it.

"Hang a left and take the left fork in the road—and then a right into the Winn Dixie Plaza. It'll only take me a few minutes at the copy machine to get what I want from their book."

"Okay." I felt like a parrot trapped in a cage. If I refused Phud's request, I'd have to make excuses for my behavior to Rex and Janell later.

"The library's right next door to the Artist's Co-op," Phud said. "You might want to take a look at the paintings while you wait."

I pulled into the U-shaped mall and drove down two streets in the crowded parking lot before I found an empty slot near the library.

"I'll wait in the car." I snapped the words.

I had no intention of letting him slip behind the wheel again. Phud had already slammed the passenger door, bypassed a long ramp, and climbed the steps to the library when I realized how silly I must sound to him. Silly and afraid. No reason I should sit here and wait. If I locked the car, there was no way he could get inside and commandeer the wheel as long as I had the key.

I needed to prove to him, and to myself, that I wasn't afraid of him. I'd enjoy looking at paintings while he copied his information, and then we'd drive on to Marathon as planned. If all went well, I'd buy the painting Janell wanted and we'd drive back to Key West.

Entering the co-op, I stood admiring the pictures lining the north wall. Hibiscus blossoms in a porcelain vase. Frigate birds in flight. An old fishing shack. I inhaled the pleasant fragrance of oil paints and turpentine and walked farther into the shop. The artists had painted the scenes at hand. A flock of gulls huddled on the sand facing into the wind. A green parrot in a frangipani tree. After I'd been observing for a few minutes, a volunteer wearing a paint-smudged smock rose from behind her easel and approached me.

"May I help you? We offer both original art and prints." She nodded toward the wall and then pointed to a display rack of unframed prints. "One of our artists also does matting and framing, if you're interested in that."

"Thank you, but I'm just looking today."

"Make yourself comfortable." She pointed to an easy chair. "Stay as long as you please." She nodded toward a coffee urn and some cups on a small table. "Help yourself to a cup of coffee."

"Thank you, but not today. My brother-in-law tried to buy a painting in here a few days ago, but he was too late. Someone had already bought it. I thought I might find something similar, although I'd have to check with him again on dimensions."

"What was the subject matter of the painting?" the woman asked.

"Of course, I didn't see it," I said, "but he described it as a typical Key West scene—a dock with a pelican perched on three posts that were roped together to form a dock piling."

The woman smiled. "The *Pelican.* I think I have a surprise for you. Follow me, please."

I followed her to the far end of the display wall on the other side of the narrow room.

"Does this look like the painting your brother-in-law described? And is your brother-in-law Rex Cummings?"

For a moment I couldn't speak as I stared at the painting Rex told me had been sold. Driftwood frame. Title on a tiny brass plate. What was going on here? Why had Rex lied to us about the painting? Maybe he was the one I should be suspicious of rather than Phud.

19

"But . . . but . . . I thought the painting had been sold." My mind whirled and I sickened at the thought of Rex's lie, its ramifications. Why had he sent me to Marathon on a useless quest? And with Phud! Were he and Phud in cahoots?

"A customer from Marathon did buy the *Pelican* last week. I was gone from the co-op for a few days, but earlier this morning she returned it. Said it didn't look quite right in the location she'd chosen for it."

Could the volunteer see relief turn my knee joints to Jell-O? "And you accept the return of sold paintings—no questions asked?"

"I did this time."

"Maybe the buyer was the kind who wanted to show it off to friends at a special party before she returned it. Maybe she didn't really want to own it."

The volunteer smiled. "I took it back and refunded her money without even calling the artist to discuss the return. I knew I could sell it again immediately." She walked to the business desk and pulled a scrap of paper from a drawer. "Rex Cummings. Key West. Your brother-in-law, right?"

I nodded. "But . . ."

"He came here asking about the painting a few days ago. I tried to phone him this morning to tell him it was available again and waiting for him. But I received no answer."

"He'll be delighted to know this news. I was on my way to

Marathon to try to talk the buyer into selling it to me."

"Would you like to deliver it to Mr. Cummings personally? I can bill him later. It'd save him a trip."

"Yes, I'll be glad to take it with me." I didn't offer the blank check Rex had given me. No point in haggling now.

The woman removed the picture from the wall, and since it was to be a surprise for Janell, I asked her to wrap it in opaque paper. When she finished with the wrapping, she carried it to my car, and I helped her lay it flat on the back seat.

"Thank you so much," I said. "I'll have Rex call you to let you know the painting arrived safely."

Once the volunteer headed up the ramp to the co-op, I followed her and walked on to the library. The room emitted the typical library smell of paper and ink. Women in sundresses stood in line at the check-out desk. Old men sat around a table reading newspapers. Preschoolers with their grandmas and mamas laughed and giggled as they shoved their way to the children's room for afternoon story hour. Three patrons sat at desks using computers. No Phud. I looked in both rooms and up and down the rows of stacks. No Phud.

"May I help you?" a page asked.

"I planned to meet a friend here. Dr. Whitney Ashby. A tall man. Silvery hair. Navy blue tam."

The page began shaking her head and I continued my description.

"He's a gardener and he was wearing work clothes—a camouflage-type jumpsuit. He intended to ask to use your copy machine and a reference room book on foliage plants—a book that must remain in the building."

The page shook her head. "I've seen nobody of that description in here this afternoon, ma'am."

"Perhaps he talked to another librarian."

"Don't think so, ma'am. Just two of us on duty. Sorry I can't be of help. You're welcome to have an easy chair and wait. Perhaps your friend's been delayed."

"Thank you, but I'll go on and perhaps return later."

"And ma'am?" The page's questioning tone stopped me and I turned to face her. "We have no plant books in the reference room that can't be checked out by any patron with a library card. Tell your friend to bring the book of his choice to the check-out desk. If he has a card, it's good in all five of our county libraries. He can take the book with him. No problem."

My head began to throb and my next thought was for the safety of my car and Rex's painting. Had Phud figured out some way to open the car door, hot-wire the ignition, leave me stranded thirty miles from Key West? I ran down the library ramp, my stomach in knots, my lungs feeling like overinflated balloons. Then I relaxed. The Prius sat unharmed where I'd left it. I peered through the rear window and saw the painting still lying on the back seat.

After unlocking the door I slid behind the wheel, trying to calm myself while I waited for Phud to return. Why had he lied to me about going to the library? It made no sense. I had no reason to object to his going to the library. I waited for over fifteen minutes before he returned, carrying a tan cardboard box criss-crossed with yellow tape that held it shut.

"Sorry to have taken so long," Phud apologized, opening the rear door and sliding his purchase inside on the floor. "But, hey! What have we here? A painting on the back seat?"

"Right. The painting. The *Pelican.*"

"By what means of magic did you locate it?" Phud pulled at the paper wrapper until he could see inside the package.

"Pure luck."

"Tell me about it."

I gave him a short version of what had happened, and I sensed he was hanging on my every word and tossing in a question now and then in an effort to distract me from the fact that he hadn't been at the library. When I finished my tale, I looked him in the eye, forcing him to hold my gaze.

"Where were you, Phud? It took me quite a few minutes to find the picture, get it wrapped and into the car. Since you weren't here, I went to the library to inquire. The librarian said she hadn't seen you in there."

"You probably asked for Dr. Whitney Ashby, right?"

"Of course."

"They wouldn't have recognized my name."

"Why not?" I knew he was lying, and I wanted to see just how far he would go to cover his tracks—explain why he hadn't made the library scene as planned.

"You see, I asked a friend of mine who has a library card from this library, Duane Baxter, to take the book to the director's desk and put it on hold—an extra precaution in case someone else wanted to look at it at the same time I did. That way I could stop and, using Duane's name, get use of the book and copy the material I needed."

I said nothing for a few moments, waiting to see if he'd spin more lies. His story was so full of holes I couldn't believe he thought I'd fall for it. "Why don't you go copy your material now, Phud? I'm sure it must be important to you. And we have plenty of time, since we no longer have to drive to Marathon for the painting."

I thought my question and my offer to wait for him might throw him, but he handled the situation deftly.

"Maybe you have the time, but I prefer to get on back to Key West. I'm lucky to have been able to purchase some supplies I've been needing. That's my major accomplishment for today. I'll return to the library another time."

"All right, Phud." I didn't make an issue of his lies. I'd let him think I believed his every word. "We'll leave right now. I'm ready to go."

"Good. We can hurry on back to Key West and maybe Rex can sneak the painting inside the house before Janell gets home."

"That's a plan." I hoped Phud couldn't see my hands shaking on the steering wheel when a biker honked at me as I backed from the parking slot. I gave him the right-of-way and then paused while a rust-colored rooster crowed and took his time crossing our path.

Phud chuckled. "Even on Big Pine the chickens are trying to take over. Wonder if that one flew up from Key West."

I didn't speculate on the why and where of the rooster. I pointed us back to Highway One and tried to calm down.

It irritated me that Phud had the ability to get me so rattled. He was a liar. I remembered his phony story about Janell's plant fertilizer being his idea. I remembered his story about the topic of his speech for the Marathon garden club. And now this tangled tale about a special book he needed to see at the library. White lies? Unimportant stuff? Perhaps. Maybe Phud was the erudite Ph.D. Janell and Rex said he was, maybe he was everything they thought him to be. But I was striking him off my list.

Now Phud had grown talkative. He pointed to a street sign just before we crossed the bridge leading away from Big Pine. "Ship's Way. All the streets opening to the left off Ship's Way are named after great American battleships. *Constitution. Ranger. Independence. Flying Cloud.* Every one is a dead-end street running right into the Gulf of Mexico."

I made no response.

"Pine Channel Estates. That's the name of the area. Some guy got rich developing that land. It's historical, too. A friend of mine says the abstract to his home dates back to King Philip of Spain."

"Interesting, Phud." I forced myself to respond. "Didn't know

Dorothy Francis

you were hooked on history. Thought that was Teach's thing."

"History must be everyone's thing if we're to survive on this planet."

Again, I didn't comment.

We crossed Niles Channel Bridge. "See all those scruffy boats out there?" He leaned forward for a better view. "Some have people living on them. Some of them belong to Cuban spongers—seamen who hook sponges from the ocean bottom for resale to gift shops."

"Oh." I peered beyond the cruddy-looking boats and enjoyed the lime-green waters flowing from the Gulf to the ocean. An osprey flew from its huge tangled nest atop a light pole, dived into the waves and returned with a fish in its talons, which it carried to the nest. I wondered how many mouths it had to feed.

"The osprey mates and nests for life," Phud said, following my gaze. "Did you know that?"

"No."

"The nest grows larger every year."

I didn't respond. It was well past mid-afternoon and I wanted to get home. These lower keys on each side of the highway looked dark and wooded. Secretive. Eccentric. On each key, narrow side roads wind for only a short distance before they disappear into the distance. Who lived on them? Hermits? Druggies? As far as I was concerned, such roads were better left unexplored.

"Ever seen the bat tower?" Phud asked.

"No."

"I'd like to show it to you. It's a short distance off the highway."

"No time today. We need to get on home."

"I think you can reach it if you turn at the road where a pilot has his sign advertising sight-seeing trips. The tower's significant

172

because it's a place all tour guides talk about and take the tourists to see."

I didn't comment, but Phud continued his chatter. "The Keys used to have mosquitoes so large they called them flying teeth but a visiting doctor, a Dr. Campbell, had an idea. He knew that bats ate mosquitoes, so he built a bat tower to make a home for bats, hoping to rid the lower keys of mosquitoes. Big problem. No bats showed up to live in his tower." Phud glanced at his watch. "I think I could spare the minutes to show it to you today."

"Another time. The tower sounds fascinating, but not today." I wasn't about to let him get me even slightly off this highway, and it surprised him when, a few miles later, I turned right and parked in front of Sugarloaf Lodge. Pulling the keys from the ignition, I left Phud and the car and hurried into the lodge.

"May I use your telephone, please?" I asked the desk clerk.

He pointed to a pay phone near the door. "Be my guest. Of course there are phones in every room, if you're planning to book lodging for the night." When he looked out the window and saw my car, his eyes widened, but he didn't comment. I guessed he would like to have the Prius parked here overnight.

"It's a beautiful lodge in a beautiful setting, but I need to call my family and let them know I'm in the vicinity and getting close to Key West."

The clerk smiled. "Here, use the desk phone. It's handier." He pulled a telephone book from a drawer. "What's the family's name? I'll key in the number for you."

"Rex and Janell Cummings. I have the number right here. You're very kind, and I appreciate your offer." It amazed me how the Prius opened doors that had been firmly closed.

"They operate The Poinsettia, don't they?"

"Right. You've been there?"

"Only once. Running this lodge doesn't leave me much time

173

for enjoying Key West or checking out other lodges."

I talked briefly to Rex, then returned to the car, glad Rex knew my whereabouts, glad the lodge owner would recognize the Cummings name if he heard it again. The Prius: he'd remember my car, too—should that be necessary.

When I returned to the car, Phud was still ready to chatter. I let him know that I'd talked to Rex, that the lodge owner knew my name. That didn't seem to bother him, but he said no more about driving off-highway to see the bat house.

When we arrived at The Poinsettia, Rex was standing at the outdoor grill preparing cobia steaks for our supper. The scent of charcoal and fish made my mouth water. Their car wasn't in the carport, so I knew Janell hadn't returned from West Martello yet.

Phud left the Prius, thanked me for the ride and then picked up his purchase and walked toward the front gate.

"Got the painting," I called to Rex before I remembered about his summons to the police station. "What did the police want this time?"

"Just another verification of my former statements." He grabbed the painting, tore the wrapper, and grinned, admiring it while I gave a brief account of my being able to get it without driving to Marathon.

"Good work, Kitt. I'll hide it in the front closet, and when I get a chance I'll hang it in the living room and see how long it takes Janell to notice it. I've already measured the spot."

Rex was so pleased to have the painting that it almost made me forget my scary ride with Phud. I shoved the memory to the back of my mind, determined not to bad-mouth him to Rex and Janell. They respected him, and the fact that I'd crossed him off my list of associates would remain my secret.

20

Right after Janell returned from West Martello, my cell phone rang. I answered, at the same time stepping into the kitchen and then heading upstairs, hoping for privacy. Few people had my cell number. Few people back home knew I was visiting family in Florida.

"Kitt Morgan here."

"It's Hank, Kitt. More news for you."

My hand grew slippery on the phone as my grip tightened. "Give, Hank. Give. I hope the news is good."

"Rasty Raymore died early this morning. Today his doctors are releasing his body to his family for burial. Consider this good news, Kitt. Another scofflaw with a gun off the streets."

For a few moments I couldn't respond to Hank. Good news? How could he be so callous? Didn't he realize I'd killed a man? I was a murderer. The Perp was dead. Rasty Raymore. Now he had a name I'd never forget.

"I really appreciate your calling me, Hank. That's all I can say for now."

"I wanted you to hear it from me before you heard it from someone else. A little lead time helps a guy plan a careful response."

"And I will certainly need a carefully planned response. Fate plays a big part in our lives, doesn't it? I'll be better prepared to respond when I receive official notice from the chief—and/or the review committee." I heard myself rattling on and on until

Hank broke in.

"Look for the positive side of this situation, Kitt. I'm wagering you'll be reinstated on the force soon. Of course, I wouldn't mind changing places with you for a week or so right now. It's been below zero in Iowa for over a month with no warming trend in sight."

"I'm not interested in a weather report, Hank. Weather comes and goes. Killing another person is something that will live with me, something that will stay in my mind forever."

"Try to believe that life is going to go your way, Kitt. Believe it. You shot in self-defense. Make peace with yourself."

"I'll try." The words hung in the airwaves between us. I knew Hank wanted to hear me say I'd welcome my job back, that I was ready to come home, but I couldn't lie to him. I wasn't sure what I wanted to do with the rest of my life. Maybe Rasty Raymore's death was a warning for me—a warning that I lacked the emotional stability to handle a police job or any job involving a lethal weapon. It might be very easy to stay here in South Florida close to my family, stay here and avoid facing anyone who'd ever known me in another life, first as a failed singer, and now as a failed cop.

Wherever you are, God put you there. Wherever you're going, God is sending you there for a purpose. Those words had been favorites of my minister's at First Methodist on Cherry Street anytime either Dad or I faced big decisions in our lives. And he'd also said, *People don't meet accidentally. They meet when they need each other.* Had there been a need for Rasty and me to meet on a cold night in an Iowa pet shop?

The connection between Hank and me hummed then the line began to crackle with static.

"Kitt? Kitt? You still there? Can you hear me?"

"Still here, Hank. And thanks again for calling." I broke the connection.

After I hung up, I revealed nothing about the nature of Hank's call to Rex or Janell. And they didn't pry. They both were in light-hearted moods. No point in my spoiling that. A night's work ahead of them in the beautiful Florida Keys. I welcomed the routine of supper, the clean-up.

"Hola," Mama G called to Rex and me when we stepped outside to light the patio torches. Their glow flickering in the warm trade wind turned the world into an exotic wonderland, a wonderland where I could forget a police force in Iowa.

"Hola!" Rex and I shouted to Mama G in unison. I held my breath to avoid the odor of the lighter fluid.

"Hella!" Mama G shouted when she saw Hella approaching from the B&B. "Get your bones on the bandstand if you intend to sit in on the first number. Ace! Teach! Get those music fronts in place. Pull the first three charts." She tapped her wristwatch. "Pronto!"

Hella was the only one of the three who hurried to obey. I looked at Rex and rolled my eyes. "How *do* you and Janell stand that woman? I'm surprised the guys put up with her."

"Where else could Teach or Ace find a steady moonlighting job?" Janell asked, joining us. "Where else would I find exotic and delicious sandwich recipes? We at The Poinsettia need Mama G."

While Hella sat in on the first number, Ace brushed strands of wayward hair from his forehead and strolled across the patio to ask me to dance. It surprised me to realize I'd been hoping he would. As usual, he looked at me with a smile and a sparkle in his eyes that bordered on amusement. I smiled back. I felt comfortable and protected in his arms, and I tried to forget how vulnerable I'd felt on the ride with Phud that afternoon and during the phone conversation with Hank. My phone conversation with Hank lay close to the surface of my mind, but I didn't have to face its implications right now.

"You got big plans for tomorrow morning?" Ace asked after we'd danced in a comfortable silence for a few minutes.

"Nothing big. Just the usual activities."

"Then how about doing a bit of sightseeing with me? Janell and Rex are too busy to spare much time for sightseeing, and my boat's in dry dock for repairs tomorrow. I'd like to show you more of the island."

"What do you have in mind?"

"I'd suggest a ride on the Conch Train, but you've probably done that many times."

"Yes, a long time ago, but surely you've viewed the Conch Train scenes many times. Janell says that's what the locals do when visitors come—take them, or, better yet, send them, on a Conch Train tour."

Ace laughed and guided us farther from the combo. "Yeah, I've had a few Conch Train rides. Any place specific that you'd like to see? Maybe one you haven't seen before?"

"Your choice. You know the most interesting sites, maybe places overlooked by a lot of visitors."

Ace thought for a few moments. "How about the Military Lighthouse Museum? It's right on Duval Street. But lots of people bypass it—especially women. I think the word 'military' turns them off. They see the Hemingway house across the street, and by the time they finish the tour of that house and count the six toes on one of the cats, they're ready for a break. They forget about the lighthouse."

"Too tired to climb lighthouse steps, right?"

"Right. Think you'd like to do that? Think you feel up to the climb? You'll get a great overview of Key West from the top. Of course, I suppose it won't compare to the view from Teach's plane."

"Maybe not, but Teach focused his trip on the sea between here and Fort Jefferson. Gave us no chatter about Key West."

"So if you'd like to visit the lighthouse, I'll stop by for you tomorrow morning. No parking problems. I'll bike over from the *Ace,* and we can do the Duval crawl—walking to the lighthouse from here."

"Do you really live aboard the *Ace?*"

"Sure do. I'm a low-maintenance sort of guy. Why pay rent when I own a floating bunk and a galley?"

"No reason. No reason at all." It sounded like a fancy-free life to me, a life to envy.

"About tomorrow, Kitt. A visit to the lighthouse. Sound like a plan?"

"Let's go for it. But right now, Hella's vacated your drum seat. You'd better go for the bandstand before Mama G explodes with wrath."

"That woman!" Ace gave my hand a squeeze before he left me near the snack bar and strolled to join the combo.

The next morning I dressed in tourist's uniform of white pants and flowered shirt and dropped my cell phone into my pocket before I went downstairs to help Janell serve our poolside breakfast. Watermelon balls. Guava juice. Orange marmalade pastries. Who cared about such Iowa fare as bran flakes or oatmeal soaked in soy milk? Hella and Rex, that's who. They both ate hearty breakfasts that sometimes included bacon and eggs. I was content with a glass of juice as I watched a gentle trade wind sprinkle bougainvillea blossoms into the pool where they floated on the surface like pink confetti. Why would anyone in their right mind give this up for the snows of Iowa?

A paper carrier delivered the *Citizen,* and Rex shared it, keeping the sports section, giving Janell the front page and letting Hella and me peruse the want ads and the crime report. I found nothing of interest in either section. I saw no news about Abra Barrie's murder, and I had little interest in who had been picked up last night for petty theft, disturbing the peace, or for drug and alcohol violations.

Ace arrived around nine.

"Okay if I leave the bike on your carport?" he called to Rex.

"A good plan unless you want it stolen." Rex turned toward me as he opened the gate for Ace. "Kids pick up bikes, ride them to their chosen destination, then abandon them for the next kid needing a ride to somewhere else. It's a vicious circle. Last month I lost mine three times and each time I'd left it locked to a light pole."

"How'd you find it again?" I asked.

"Went to the police station. They store the unclaimed bikes there. Identify it, and it's yours. Kitt, if you want to, you can borrow a bike from us and ride with Ace to the lighthouse."

"Thanks, but no thanks. I think we'd be safer walking."

"Agreed," Janell said. "And in a collision between flesh and concrete, concrete always wins. You two have a good time. Rex will be here if you should happen to want a ride home, but I'll be at West Martello, pinch-hitting for one of the subs who has to be out of town today."

Ace and I walked along Whitehead Street, passing Kelly's, the Banyon, Truman Annex. We turned a corner and strolled toward Duval. Bells from St. Paul's tower pealed pigeons into the sky. Ace's chatter kept me from concentrating on window displays at Chico's and Fast Buck Freddie's.

"Has Janell taken you to the gazebo at the top of the hill at West Martello?"

"Yes. Beautiful spot. You've been there, too, I suppose. Or do the locals bother to seek out the tourist attractions?"

"Been to West Martello only once. I'd heard there was a lignum vitae tree growing at the top of the hill there. I wanted to see it up close and personal."

"Right. I saw it among some thatch palms. Gnarled. Bent.

Recognized it from a picture I saw in a tourist brochure. The one at West Martello looked like it was on its last legs. Or should I say its last roots?"

"The tree's old, that's for sure. But those in the know say the wood's still strong. Guess that's why it's called ironwood."

"Strong, I suppose, but it's no tree of great beauty."

"Agreed. But I wanted to see it because there aren't many left on Key West—or on any of the Keys. Tour guides like to point out the one at West Martello. My drumsticks are made of lignum vitae. I told you that, didn't I?"

"I suppose so, but I'd sort of forgotten the connection between your sticks and the tree."

Ace laughed. "Whenever I hear the words lignum vitae, I think of that hilltop tree and of my two-hundred-dollar drumsticks."

We stopped as a Conch Train turned the corner in front of us. Tourists waved to us and we waved back.

"A lighthouse may seem like a strange place for a museum," Ace said after the Conch Train passed, "but there's a lighthouse keeper's cottage on the premises. The place is stuffed with historical goodies and a few priceless antiques."

"Such as?"

"Models of old ships. War uniforms worn by military men of another age and time. I guess the things that interest me the most are artifacts from the battleship *Maine* and the mystery that surrounds that ship."

"The first warship designed and constructed by Americans, right? A big player in the Spanish American War."

Ace looked at me in surprise. "How did you happen to know that? I'm the one supposed to be giving the guided tour."

I grinned up at him, refusing to tell him I'd read about both the lighthouse museum and the lignum vitae tree in a brochure I found on the Cummings's bookcase last night. "Oh, I paid attention in history class now and then, but I can't remember the events leading up to that war."

"There's still disagreement on that. That's the mystery. In those days, the Cubans were rebelling against Spanish domination, and the Spanish were set on maintaining their control. The *Maine* sailed into Havana harbor geared for war. It remained there peacefully for three weeks."

"Then it mysteriously exploded," I said. "Guess nobody ever figured out exactly why, but it sank in fifteen minutes."

"And a few weeks later America was at war with Spain. But enough history. Let's just enjoy looking at the artifacts."

We passed Hemingway House Museum and crossed the street to the lighthouse. Outside on the grounds we saw various kinds of torpedoes, depth charges, and gun mounts.

"Will they just rust away?" I asked.

"Could be," Ace said. "Everything down here rusts."

We looked at a replica of a Japanese submarine that patriots had taken on a tour of the country, collecting money to raise the ships sunk at Pearl Harbor. Guess their fund drive didn't pay off. I remember Dad saying he saw those ships still underwater when he took a vacation to Hawaii.

At the doorway to the lighthouse keeper's cottage I pointed out a series of stakes joined with twine.

"Must be the spot the city has claimed for Phud's landscaping project, his decorative plantings."

"Could be," Ace said. "Phud and I don't have much in common." Ace paid our admission, and we looked through the interior of the musty-smelling cottage at more naval artifacts and pictures of old-time ships and the heroes that sailed aboard them.

"Let's go up," Ace said, breaking into my sober thoughts, which had gone back to Pearl Harbor, where my great-uncle had died on the *Arizona*.

"How many steps?" I asked.

"Eighty-eight. But who's counting?"

"Me. I'll be counting every step and breath."

We began our ascent, gripping the black handrail while our shoes scraped and clanged against the iron of the circular staircase. We stopped every few moments to catch our breath and to enjoy the view both above and below. Overhead a small plane pulled a parasailor buckled into a kelly green parachute. He dangled precariously above the sea and above a small runabout ready to rescue him, if needed. Thank goodness Ace hadn't suggested we go parasailing! I might never feel up to trying that sport.

Below us we heard car horns honking. By peering through the branches of a Spanish laurel we saw impatient drivers lined up behind a slow-moving horse and buggy carrying six passengers. Some tourist attraction! I felt sorry for the horse.

At one rest stop we heard laughs and giggles punctuating the footsteps of a group descending the stairs. We pressed ourselves close to the railing so the group could pass us without mishap.

"What's so funny?" I asked a chubby woman leading the group.

"We're not telling," one of the group said. "Big surprise in store for you in a few minutes."

More giggles. "Oh, you'll see it when you get up higher."

After we climbed twenty more steps, we could look down onto the flat roof of a building near the lighthouse and see the scene that had instigated laughter. Below us nude sunbathers, all male, were lying on mats and chaise lounges catching the rays with no worries about their clothing creating unbecoming tan lines. I wished I knew how to keep from blushing.

"Oh, my." I tried unsuccessfully to keep from staring at the scene below.

Playfully, Ace covered my eyes with his hand and urged me

on up the steps. We were both panting when we reached the top and stepped onto the circular viewing platform that overlooked Key West and the harbor. When we had caught our breath, Ace looked down at me with an amused gaze.

"You still don't remember me, do you?"

In spite of his smile, I felt a frisson of unease. Now I saw a phoniness in that smile instead of bland amusement. "No. I don't remember you. Should I? You mean we've met before?"

"Many years ago, Kitt. I'm glad you don't remember me or the circumstances of our meeting. I owe you a belated apology."

I wanted to back away from him, but I saw no place to retreat except over the safety rail or back down the steep stairs. "I have a hard time believing we've known each other in the past, Ace."

"Let me start my apology by telling you I gave my pet snake to the zoo years ago when I began feeling sorry for all those white mice. I'm sorry now that I enticed you from your yard to watch me feed the snake, sorry I scared you, sent you screaming home to your mother."

"Donald!" I spat the name at him, somehow managing to keep my composure when I felt the heat that flooded my face as I remembered when and where we'd met years ago.

"Right. Donald Brewster."

In Key West I'd heard nobody say Ace's full name. Ace was the only name I'd heard. Now I understood his strange smile, his knowing looks. Ace was the person who lay at the root of my nightmares. The textbook I'd been studying said that a person who enjoyed inflicting suffering on animals could be a person without a conscience. A sociopath. A person who could kill and feel no guilt.

I'd pegged the Donald of my childhood as a sociopath long ago, never thinking I'd meet him again under such terrifying circumstances. Had this man murdered Abra Barrie?

21

Run!

I knew I had to run for my life even if it meant plunging down a steep flight of spiral steps. The only other escape would be to jump over the safety railing—to concrete below. Certain death. No. I began sweating at the thought of the impossible choices. Maybe I'd be faster on the stairs than Ace. Maybe I could phone 911 for help. I pulled my cell phone from my pocket and started taking the stairs two steps at a time. It was my only chance to escape and live. I managed to key in 911, but before the dispatcher answered, I stubbed my toe and the phone flew from my hand and over the handrail. I heard it thunk on the ground below.

I kept running. Maybe I'd reach the bottom first—reach it in time to scream for help. But why wait to scream? The sound from my throat shrilled so loud and piercing, I could hardly believe I had produced it.

I clutched the stair railing, turned and stumbled on down the steps, screaming as I ran. In my mind's eye, I saw Ace's glove in a plastic bag and heard Hella calling the glove an evil thing. I remembered Donald Brewster, the boy who had tortured mice. I heard Ace behind me, Ace Brewster, the man who had tortured Abra Barrie, the man who wanted to torture me?

"Stop!" Ace shouted. "What's the matter with you, Kitt? Stop!"

When he almost grabbed my arm, I visualized my death. His

fingernails had scratched my skin, but I escaped his grip. I heard him lunge at me. The steps spiraled in my mind like a multiplicity of iron traps and I imagined myself falling.

"Stop!" Ace shouted from close behind me. "Kitt, what's the matter with you? Stop!"

I sensed his nearness. When I glanced over my shoulder to see if I had a chance of escaping, I stumbled and almost lost my footing, found it, lost it again, this time turning my right ankle. For a moment I floundered, my handhold on the railing the only thing that saved me for those few seconds—seconds that let Ace lessen the distance between us. My throat ached from screaming, from gasping for breath.

"Kitt!" Ace yelled at me again. "Stop running. I'm not chasing you. I'm not going to hurt you. Stop!"

Did he think he could trick me? I wasn't about to stop and let him overtake me, try to make it appear to anyone watching that all was well between us, that we were playing games with each other. For a moment lack of breath forced me to slow down. I listened. My footsteps were the only ones I heard. But his ruse didn't fool me. I guessed he was pausing, waiting for me to give up and let him overtake me. Adrenalin shot through my body like rocket fuel and I fled, unable to scream any longer.

"What's going on here, lady? Better slow down before you kill yourself—or somebody else."

Startled into even greater fear, I stared down into the brick-red face of an angry tourist. Fat man. Hawaiian shirt. Short shorts. Backpack. Camera slung over backpack. Where had this jerk come from? I hadn't thought about other people trying to use these same stairs.

"Let me past!" I shouted. "You son of a witch! Give me room! Let me by! Stop Ace. Stop the guy behind me. Please. Please. He's trying to kill me." I continued hurtling downward.

Openmouthed, the man jammed his pudgy body against the

handrail, stopped climbing long enough to let me by. I felt the heat from his stomach press against my hip. He didn't try to stop me or to slow me down. Lucky for me! His presence did slow Ace's pursuit.

"Stop that woman!" Ace shouted at him. "Catch her! Stop her before she kills herself!"

"Are you two out of your minds?" the man yelled. Then he must have realized we weren't teenagers playing games. He shouted. "Security! Security! We need some help up here! Stop these two crazies! Security!"

But no security person responded. Why would an old lighthouse have need of a security guard?

"Out of my way!" Ace ordered. "Mister, let me past."

"I'm going to report you," the man said. "You haven't heard the last of this. I've got a cell phone. I'm going to . . ."

His voice trailed into the distance and I continued catapulting downward, but I knew the man had let Ace pass him. My toe caught in the grillwork of the next step, and again I almost fell, but I regained my balance, clung tighter to the handrail and continued my descent.

When I rounded the next spiral, I felt Ace clutching at my shirt. The sleeve ripped and dangled against my lower arm, threatening to loosen my grip by falling between my fingers and the handrail. I yanked my arm free from Ace's clutch and kept running, my shirt sleeve dangling, flapping in the breeze like a flag of defeat. At last, the bottom of the steps came into sight. For an instant I considered jumping the rest of the way down. But no. The shock of landing on my fanny would make it impossible to rise quickly and run again.

"Stop, Kitt," Ace called. "Please stop and let me talk to you. Listen to me!"

"No way!"

"You've nothing to be afraid of from me, Kitt. You're being

187

your own worst enemy. Stop. Please."

I stopped running for a moment. Right. He was no longer chasing me. Good. I'd use this break to reach the ground, moving at a safer pace. But once I started down the steps again, Ace was a bloodhound narrowing the gap between us.

When he grabbed my arm, I knew my life was over. I couldn't jerk loose from his grip. He pushed. He clawed. I couldn't tell if he was trying to hold me back or push me on to the ground. My mind spiraled with my steps and I felt myself losing my balance. Using my last bit of strength, I clutched the handrail again and broke from his grip. When my feet touched ground, both ankles were wobbling, but I steadied myself and turned to face him, thrusting out my hand to strong-arm him and keep distance between us.

"Stay where you are, Ace. Stay there or I'll call the police."

"You dropped your phone, remember?"

I heard a taunt in his tone.

"But forget the phone. You don't need the police."

Right, I had no phone, but I'd call the police the minute I reached the safety of the caretaker's cottage. There had to be a phone there, right? Maybe the hostess, the ticket seller, would make the call for me. I felt too winded to talk.

"Kitt, chill out." Ace took a step toward me and I backed off, ready to run again the minute I caught my breath.

"What do you plan to tell the police, Kitt? Consider that. Think. I don't know what you're imagining, but you have no reason to be running from me, or to be afraid of me. I tried to stop you before you fell and killed yourself. You'll make a fool of yourself and of Janell and Rex if you call for police help."

The horrible truth of Ace's words bruised my eardrums. He was right. What could I tell the police? He hadn't harmed me—yet. Of course, he'd accosted me and I had a torn shirt to prove that. Yes, I'd call the police. Maybe the call would help get Rex off the hook the police seem to have him hanging from. In spite of Janell's and my investigation that seemed to prove otherwise, maybe Ace was the person, the sociopath, who had murdered Abra Barrie. Or maybe my mind had snapped. My mind. What was wrong with my mind?

I didn't run again. I couldn't. But I walked at a brisk pace around a corner and toward the caretaker's cottage—and right into Phud. This couldn't be happening. I wasn't up to it. I wanted to kick his shins—or something higher.

"Kitt!" Phud took one look at me and pulled me into his arms. "What's happened to you?"

"Phud! What are you doing here?" I tried to jerk free, but Phud held me tight for a moment. Even when he relaxed his grip, he still trapped me in the circle of his embrace, keeping his arm around my waist, letting me know that although I had escaped from Ace, I now stood in his power. For a moment I stiffened, glaring at him both in fear and amazement. What *was* he doing here? Had he been suspicious of Ace all along? Had he come to save me from Ace? Or were he and Ace working together? Were they both after me? At that moment Ace rounded the corner of the caretaker's cottage, stopped for a moment and stared.

"I heard someone screaming." Phud looked down into my eyes, holding my gaze. Seconds passed before I could look away. "Can you speak? What's the problem, Kitt? Has Ace been bothering you?"

Now Phud's eyes held a knowing look, a threatening look. For me? For Ace? Ace stepped forward, then stopped a few feet from us.

"Okay, Phud," Ace said. "Buzz off. Kitt and I were having a private argument when . . ."

"Private! You're joking."

I looked around us. Strangers stood gawking. Some began to

push closer to us. I felt vulnerable, but I tried to will calmness into my being. I needed the safety in numbers. The safety of witnesses.

"Explanation, please." Ace took a step closer to Phud. "How do *you* happen to be here?"

Phud dropped his arm from my waist and grabbed my hand as he pulled himself to his full height and glared at Ace. "I happen to be working here for a few days. You got a problem with that? Care to explain what you and Kitt were doing that resulted in this?" Phud lifted my torn sleeve then let it drop again.

"Whatever you're thinking, you're wrong." Ace's voice turned into a growl, low and deadly, and when he tried to pull my hand from Phud's, I jerked free from both of them and turned toward the door of the caretaker's cottage.

"Hold it, Kitt!" Ace's command renewed my determination to escape. I dashed to the cottage door at the same moment the door opened and Mama G stood, arms akimbo, glaring at me.

"*Hola!*" She blocked the doorway. "*Hola!*"

"Let me in! Let me in! These men . . ."

Mama G's eyes widened when she saw the three of us. She yanked me inside the cottage and stepped in front of me, shielding my body with hers.

"Lucky for you this be my lighthouse day for to clean." Then eyeing the crowd that was gathering, she shouted. "*Vamanos.* Be gone. All of you! Stop your gawking!"

Her words failed to deter the onlookers.

She plunked me onto a chair, then returned to block the doorway. In those few minutes while she ranted at Ace and Phud, I thought about my situation. Were both Phud and Ace after me? Out to do me harm? Could there be two murderers at large in the Keys, two men intent to kill and dismember women? Ace had apologized to me, told me he'd given his snake to a zoo. Said he'd felt sorry for the doomed mice. Sociopaths never felt sorry—unless it involved feeling sorry for themselves. And Phud? I remembered his lies, but Janell and Rex trusted Phud, counted him as a friend. Maybe I'd been looking for trouble where none existed.

The crowd outside began to disperse. Mama G glared at people. "Away with you! Move on! Stop your gawking. Move on!"

When the sidewalk began to clear, she turned and faced Ace and Phud again. "Explain. Explain yourselves. Both of you. Explain *muy pronto.* Why you cause Kitt to run from you?"

The crowd had obeyed Mama G's orders, but Ace and Phud, having been exposed to her invectives on a daily basis, ignored her. Phud stepped around her, grabbed my wrist, and pulled me back outside where he headed for his Chevy parked a few feet distant in a metered slot. Ace tried to dash after him, but Mama G blocked his way with her stout body, tripped him with a thick ankle and sent him floundering for balance once he regained his footing.

"Follow me into the car," Phud shouted at me and grabbed my wrist.

"No!" I dug my heels in and pulled back, but he flung the car door open and jumped inside onto the passenger seat, yanking me after him. I banged my head on the door frame and slumped for a moment, stunned, while Phud slid over to the driver's seat, pulled me after him, reached across me to slam the car door. He started the motor.

I felt my forehead. No blood. Where would he take me? I had to get out of that car, but when I grabbed the door handle, dizziness sent my world spinning, forcing me to hang onto the car seat for support.

"Stay with me and you won't get hurt," Phud said. "I don't know what Ace has or had in mind, but I'm driving you to The Poinsettia."

Oh sure, I thought. Some fat chance of that. If only I hadn't dropped my cell phone! My head throbbed so hard I could hardly bear to keep my eyes open. Traffic flowed slowly, but in a heavy stream. In the moment Phud started to nose the car ahead of two guys holding hands in a pink convertible, I looked back and saw Ace shove Mama G aside. She blustered and chased him, but he dashed toward us, and even with the Chevy moving forward, he managed to yank the rear door open and slide onto the back seat.

Car horns blared. When we neared Southernmost Point, a police car sat waiting at an intersection stop sign. I tried to signal the officer, but he didn't see me and left his patrol car to talk to two girls whose moped had stalled. Phud drove on and turned a corner onto Simonton Street. For a moment I relaxed.

Maybe he did intend to take me to The Poinsettia. At least we were headed in that direction when a police car nosed into the traffic directly behind us, lights flashing and siren wailing.

22

Key West's narrow streets and heavy traffic make it hard for drivers to pull over to the side for any reason—police car, fire truck, ambulance. At the next corner, Phud hung a quick left onto a side street with the patrol car riding our rear bumper, its siren still wailing.

"Stop, Phud. Stop before you get us killed!" I held my breath. Did he plan to pull over and stop, or was he going to make a break for freedom? I grabbed the leather handhold above the door and braced both feet against the floorboard in preparation for a chase. A chase to where?

"You dumb head!" Ace shouted, leaning from the back seat to shake Phud's shoulder. "Highway One's the only route out of the Keys! You're going to get us all jailed!"

"Please stop, Phud," I begged. "We can't escape for long." The police car still followed us, lights still flashing but with the siren silenced.

At last Phud hit the brakes and slowed the car, stopping in the closest place available and lowering the window. Nobody spoke. Nobody moved. Drivers behind us honked, shouted, and gave us the bird, but drove on past. Looking into the rearview mirror, I watched the policeman fling his car door open and approach us. Only seconds later, the squad car's rear door opened. Mama G stepped into the street and blustered toward us.

"May I see your driver's license, please?" the officer asked Phud.

Officer Lyon matched the name on his badge. He filled out his size large uniform with no fabric to spare, and his tawny mane of hair matched his hazel eyes. He reminded me of the picture of a lion fish I saw once in an encyclopedia. Impaling Phud with his direct gaze, he waited for an answer, saying no more to any of us.

Phud dug into the pocket of his jumpsuit and pulled out his billfold, flashed the license to the officer who took it and examined it carefully.

"Dr. Whitney Ashby?" Officer Lyon asked. "Are you Dr. Ashby?"

"I am."

"May I see your car registration, please?"

Phud reached across me, opened the glove box, and after fumbling through its contents for a few moments, produced a plastic envelope that contained the pink registration slip. The officer studied it as if memorizing it for a test.

All this time Mama G stood at the officer's elbow, breathing like a winded whale while she clenched and unclenched her fists. Then, unable to keep quiet any longer, she pointed at Phud and began spouting her complaint.

"He be the one, Officer. Him behind the wheel. He force the woman into his car. Kitt Morgan. That be her name. Kitt, she pull back. She no want to go with him. I can tell that. But he stronger. He jerk her inside the car. He slam car door to keep her from falling into street, then *varoom-varoom* he zoom forward." She nodded toward Ace. "Big guy jump in back seat, Ace Brewster, he grab back car door and leap inside with them one *momento* before they *varoom.*"

The officer waited until Mama G finished her high-volume spiel before he spoke to Phud. His low-key voice contrasted with Mama G's tirade in a way that drew our undivided attention.

"Dr. Ashby, this witness has reported seeing you force your companion into your car against her wishes. Is this true?"

"Yes, it's true!" I said. "I never wanted to get into this car, and I want out of it right now!"

"Did the man injure you?" the officer asked me.

I hesitated. "No, but . . . I didn't want to get into this car."

"I notice your torn shirt. How did that happen?"

I hesitated again and Phud spoke up. "Ask the sport in the back seat. I'm guessing he can tell you about the torn sleeve."

"Sir?" Lyon bent lower to look at Ace.

"No comment," Ace growled.

Phud spoke again. "By chance, I was a bystander on the scene at the lighthouse. I'd gone there to fulfill my contract with the city to add some landscaping to the museum grounds. Ms. Morgan dashed toward me, running from her assailant. I shoved her into my car for her own protection—to escape from him."

"Is this true, Ms. Morgan?"

"I . . . I'm not sure, sir."

"I planned to take her home," Phud said. "That's where we were going when you stopped us."

The officer peered into the back seat at Ace. "May I see your identification, please."

Ace presented his driver's license, which the officer read as carefully as he'd read Phud's before returning it to him and peering at me.

"Where do you live, miss?"

"Iowa, sir. For the past few days, I've been a house guest of my family, the Cummings, at The Poinsettia bed and breakfast inn."

The officer raised an eyebrow. "The Poinsettia. I believe a murder victim, Abra Barrie, had been staying there before . . ."

"Right!" Mama G exclaimed. "The dead one, she stay at The Poinsettia. These two men in car. They work at same inn. That's

195

why I call police when I see the bad stuff coming down between them this morning."

"Miss . . . Miss Morgan, right?"

I nodded.

"Miss Morgan, are you afraid of these men? Either of them? I'm not sure what's going on here, but if you feel frightened, I'll drive you to your relatives and hold these men for further questioning."

"Is good plan. *Mucho bueno.*" Mama G punctuated her words with a slap on the car fender before I could respond. "I walk back to my museum job. Kitt go to The Poinsettia. Men go to station for more questions."

"Miss Morgan, please answer my question. Are you afraid of these men?"

For a few moments I lowered my head and covered my face with my hands, saying nothing. The officer stood at the car window waiting for my response. I wasn't sure of my feelings. I'd felt terrified on those lighthouse steps, but now my head throbbed and my mouth grew so dry I could hardly swallow. Nor could I pinpoint exactly what had happened at the museum or what had caused all the hubbub. Maybe I'd misinterpreted Ace's apology. Maybe the memory of my horrifying nightmares caused me to aggrandize his apology out of proportion to its importance. Maybe this. Maybe that. My mind felt muddled.

And what about Phud? I wasn't sure of my feelings toward him, either. Maybe today's ruckus was fallout from my frightening trip with him to Big Pine yesterday. Why did I always have to keep reminding myself that Phud was Janell and Rex's friend, that Ace was their trusted friend and employee? When I lifted my head, Mama G still stood beside the officer, both of them awaiting my answer. Surely if I'd witnessed the same scene Mama G had witnessed, I'd have reported it to the police, too. She'd only acted on the spur of the moment and done what she'd considered to be her duty. I couldn't fault her for that. My mind flashed to Rasty Raymore. I knew a lot about quick actions and doing one's duty. More than I wanted to know.

"Officer," I said. "I believe this trouble's the result of several past misunderstandings. Mama Gomez has tried to be helpful to me and I'm grateful for her concern, but I'm really not afraid of either of these men. They both work for my Key West family as trusted friends and employees, and I'd like you to overlook today's disturbance."

The officer smiled. "Then, I'll ask you to get into my car, and with your permission, I'll drive Mama Gomez back to the lighthouse before I drive you to The Poinsettia. I'll trust Dr. Ashby and Ace Brewster to get wherever they're going on their own. If any of you have anything more to say about this incident, you may call me at the police station. Ask for Detective Lyon."

"Detective?" I asked.

Lyon blushed. "I've been promoted. Got the word a short time ago this morning. From now on it's Detective Lyon."

"Congratulations, sir. And thank you for your help." I left Phud's car and got into the police car with Detective Lyon and Mama G. We rode to the lighthouse museum in silence where Mama G left us, head held high.

"I'm sorry to have caused this disturbance, Detective," I said as we drove to the B&B.

"No apology needed. Please remember my name if you have any additional problems."

"Yes, sir. And thank you again."

Janell rushed outside when she saw the patrol car stopping in front of The Poinsettia. "Kitt, what's happened to you?" She eyed my torn sleeve when Lyon opened the car door for me. "Where's Ace?"

"I'll explain everything, Janell." I turned to thank Officer Lyon once more for his help, for the ride, and then I turned to

Janell. She motioned for Rex to join us, and he left his carpentry project on the patio and strode toward the house. The morning had grown warm, and Rex's bald head gleamed with perspiration. When we stepped into the kitchen, he wiped his head with his work glove and then removed both gloves and tossed them into the laundry alcove on top of the washing machine.

The gloves! I recognized them from the yellow stain and the worn fabric on the thumb of the left glove. That was the same glove I'd snitched from Ace's boat, given to Hella for study, and then planted at the poolside, hoping Ace would think he'd dropped it there. How did Rex happen to be wearing it now? I wanted to ask a few questions, carefully worded questions, but Janell and Rex were brimming over with questions of their own.

"Where's Ace?" Janell asked. "Has something happened to him?"

"Were the two of you in an accident?" Rex asked. "What happened?"

Janell filled a glass with ice cubes. Rex pulled a pitcher of tea from the refrigerator and filled the glass, then poured one for Janell and another for himself. I'd almost forgotten my torn sleeve, but now I ripped it from my shirt and stuffed it into my skirt pocket.

"Give," Janell said, joining us at the kitchen table.

I tried to make my explanation to her brief, but Janell insisted on hearing every detail. When I finished, neither of them spoke for several moments.

"I had no idea that Ace knew you from childhood years, Kitt. You never mentioned anything about him when you were growing up—at least nothing that I can remember."

"I told you I was too scared to tell anyone about him because I'd disobeyed Mom by leaving our yard to meet him."

"And you've held that secret and those horrible memories for years. It's no wonder you've had nightmares. Maybe today's fright happened for the good. Maybe you'll have no more bad dreams now that you have a better understanding of what happened all those years ago."

"I hope so. Ace apologized to me. Now that he's an adult, I'm vowing to forget those rotten things he did as a child. Forget that I disobeyed Mom. Live and let live. We all have lots of growing up to do."

We finished our tea, and I intended to go upstairs to shower and change clothes, but I hadn't forgotten about the glove—the glove that had seemed to frighten Hella so much that she wanted it out of her apartment. I stepped toward the countertop where Rex was picking the gloves up now in preparation for returning to his project on the patio.

"Those look like Ace's gloves," I said, forcing a laugh that I hoped sounded realistic. I touched the worn thumb and the mustard-colored stain. "Didn't I see them that day we went aboard his boat?"

"Probably did," Rex agreed. "Guess I laid them down in the wheel house. Ace returned one of them to me and I found the other one by the pool." Rex slipped the gloves on and had started out the back door when the phone rang.

"The Poinsettia," he spoke into the phone. "Rex Cummings speaking."

I had headed on upstairs when he called me back.

"It's for you, Kitt."

Both Rex and Janell left me alone with the phone. I hadn't told them about Hank's call, about Rasty Raymore's death, nor had I mentioned the possibility that I might be getting news concerning my job soon. My hand shook as I reached for the phone.

"Hello."

"Greetings, Sergeant Morgan. Chief Gilmore speaking."

He didn't need to say that. I recognized his voice. I held my breath.

23

"Sergeant Morgan? Are you there?"

"I'm here, sir."

"I have two pieces of news for you. Rasty Raymore died this morning."

"I'm sorry." The words hung between us for a few moments before he spoke again. I could hear his breathing on the other end of the line.

"I've saved some better news for last," Chief Gilmore said. "The review committee has reached a verdict after considering your case." Tension grew in the silence following that announcement. Did he expect me to respond? When I didn't speak, Gilmore continued. "They ruled that you shot Raymore in self-defense. They recommended that no charges be filed against you and that you be reinstated in your position on the police force—if you so desire."

Again, silence. Raymore's death was a real downer. The decision of the review board was an upper. But both events left my mind spinning. I kept my own counsel. As a child, I used to wonder what that phrase meant. Now I knew. I monitored my words carefully.

"How soon do you expect my decision, sir?" Again, the line between us hummed. Had he expected me to leap at the chance to return home, return to the small-town gossip that would follow this case? Did he expect me to be eager to return to the scrutiny of my community and my co-workers?

"You were suspended with pay, Sergeant. If you need more time, you may have another week—without pay. At that time I'll expect your decision."

"Thank you, Chief Gilmore. And thank you for giving me this news. These past days have not been easy ones for me, for you, or for our community. You will hear from me soon."

"I'll be expecting your call, Sergeant. The force is ready to welcome you back."

I replaced the receiver and sat deep in thought, relieved that the review committee had exonerated me. Now I'd have to exonerate myself. That would be harder. I wasn't sure I could do it.

Thirty-four years and I never fired my gun.

My dad's words played like a threnody in my mind. Maybe I wasn't level-headed enough to handle a job involving the possibility of taking a human life. The decision to return to Iowa would take a lot of soul searching. But not now. Janell and Rex knew this call had been an important one, important to all of us. They deserved to know the decision of the review committee immediately. I had started to leave the kitchen to give them the latest news when the telephone rang again.

"I'll get it," I called as I picked up the receiver.

"The Poinsettia. Kitt Morgan speaking."

"Kitt! It's Shelby. Howya doin? Been meaning to give you a call."

Shelby Cox. A voice from my past. A voice missing since the night I shot Rasty Raymore. A voice missing during all the days the review committee had been in session. A voice I had no interest in hearing now.

"Kitt? Can you hear me? I'm on my cell. Can you hear me now?"

I replaced the receiver.

"You okay, Kitt?" Janell stuck her head into the kitchen.

"That last call? You okay?"

"Yes, I'm okay." Rex followed Janell into the kitchen. "Everything's okay. The first call was from Chief Gilmore. Rasty Raymore died, but I've been exonerated. Chief Gilmore wants me back on the force."

Janell rushed to me, giving me a long hug before she backed off. "And you'll return, won't you, Kitt? You'll reclaim your position?"

"Don't rush her," Rex said. "Give her some thinking time."

I smiled at Rex, but all at once everything fell into place in my thinking. Maybe my decision had been there all along and Chief Gilmore's call, Shelby's call, had given me the incentive to put my misgivings aside and declare that decision. I must return Gilmore's call. Today. My singing career might have flopped through no fault of my own, but my police career was still up and going. I might change my mind about it later, but for now I was still Sgt. Kitt Morgan.

"Yes. I'm going to return to my job. That night in the pet store, I could have doubted my need to defend myself. I could have wimped out and let that guy take a shot at me. But I didn't. I made a split-second decision to pull the trigger. I shot a man. Sometimes I can still hardly believe I did that."

"You did the right thing," Rex said. "Believe it. You did the right thing—the only thing."

"And after I shot the man, I could have chosen to resign from the force right then. I didn't have to let keeping my job hang on the decision of a review committee. I could have resigned on the spot. But I didn't. I chose to fight for myself and my career." I lowered my voice. "The memory of killing a man will live with me forever. I'll have to learn to deal with it. Some way. Somehow. But for right now, I'm ready to keep on fighting."

"It's what Dad would have done, Kitt."

"I'm glad you said that, Janell. It confirms the rightness of my decision. It helps me move forward. You, Rex, Chief Gilmore, the review committee—and God. You've all given me grace. I thank you."

Rex took my hand and gave it a squeeze. "Grace is fine, Kitt, but you're going to need strength, too. Strength to move forward and face your future."

"Yes. Much in life depends on our personal choices, doesn't it? In addition to returning to the community, the guys on the force and my friends, I'll be returning to . . . to myself. That's the person nobody can run from—one's self."

"We're proud of you, Kitt." Janell gave me another hug. "Why don't you go upstairs and rest a while. You've been through a lot today."

"Right. I need some minutes to myself, but first I have to make a call. Don't run off. Stay right here. I want you to hear it, too."

I called Chief Gilmore and claimed my job, my place on the police force. Next I called my partner and told Hank my decision. Then I left the phone and headed upstairs, knowing that for now I had no place to go but forward.

Once in the shower, I let the water sluice over me, carrying away the grime from my body as well as the grime in my mind. I felt humbled by my decisions, yet stronger for having made them. After I toweled off and eased into a robe, I slipped Dad's medallion around my neck. I felt as if I'd been on a long journey and I welcomed the cool bed as I lay down to rest for a while.

Janell and Rex were busy readying the patio for the night's business when I returned downstairs, and I went to Hella's apartment. I had made decisions that would make my return to Iowa less painful, but the question and the horror of Abra Barrie's death still hung over everyone at The Poinsettia.

When I knocked on Hella's door, she answered immediately. I told her of my imminent return home. "I'll be leaving as soon as I can pack and get my car checked over to be sure it's ready for the long drive."

"My best wishes to you, Kitt. It's been nice having you here, and we'll miss you when you leave."

"I wish we could help solve the Abra Barrie murder before I go, Hella."

"A huge wish." Hella shrugged. "We have tried. We have failed. But it's not our responsibility. Leave it to the police. That's the best thing to do."

"We do that, and her murder becomes a cold case. The paperwork will be dropped into a folder, filed away and forgotten."

"Maybe that's where it belongs."

"I think we can do more. Everyone deserves answers. And Hella, I think you can help us find them if you really want to."

"I've done all I can."

"You told me that in Des Moines you lived in a castle, a haunted castle. Did you ever see any of the ghosts?"

Hella shrugged. "Other people claimed to have seen him, not I."

"Him?"

"Yes. In the 1920s, Senator Leslie Francis and his family lived at Balmoral Castle. His young son, Merwyn, died of bone marrow disease. The senator insisted for years that Merwyn's ghost still lived in the home."

"But you, a psychic, never saw him?"

"I've never been into ghost hunting, Kitt. Sometimes the best thing a psychic can do is to keep her silence."

How could she be so disinterested in helping us! Anger heated my face, but I kept my voice calm. "Will you try one more time to see Abra Barrie's killer?" I thought she was going to go inside and close the door on me so I blurted my plan. "If I bring you a possession from each person living and working at The Poinsettia, will you hold those things in your hand and try one more time to see and feel what those items might have to tell you?"

"My readings aren't an exact science. I've tried to explain that to you, but you refuse to listen."

"I understand your feelings, Hella, and now I hope you'll humor me one more time before I leave here. Somewhere there's an answer to our question. Will . . . you . . . try . . . one . . . more . . . time . . . to . . . find . . . it?"

Hella sighed. "Under certain conditions, I will try again."

"Fair enough. What are your conditions?"

"The first and main condition is that you never bring that work glove to me again."

I wanted to blurt one word—*why*. But I squelched the question. Hella had said the gloves held a dark aura. She had used the word evil. So an evil person had owned the glove—a person evil enough to murder? We had thought the gloves belonged to Ace because I'd lifted one of them from his boat, but now I knew they belonged to Rex. That changed everything. Could Rex be the guilty one? Is that why the police had called him back for questioning so many times? I didn't mention Rex owning the glove. Maybe Hella already knew that. Rex was almost like a son to her. She catered to him. Maybe, like me, she couldn't bear the thought of Rex having anything to do with Abra Barrie's murder.

"It's a deal, Hella. We'll forget the glove for now. I'll find some much-used possession from everyone connected with The Poinsettia and bring those things to you."

"All right."

Hella's agreement came wrapped in reluctance, and I reassured her before she could change her mind.

"I'll leave right now and try to have possessions ready for you tonight, if possible."

"No gloves. Remember I say no gloves. Remember I promise you nothing from this endeavor."

"Agreed. One more thing. Hella?"

She gave another deep sigh. "And what is that?"

"I'd like to be present when you hold the items I bring to you. I want to hear what you have to say about each item. Is that possible?"

"Yes. That's possible. Your presence will not interfere with what my mind's eye tells me."

"I'll try not to interfere. Perhaps we can meet tonight while the combo is playing, while the others are busy keeping the customers happy."

"That is a good plan. You may come here to my apartment once you have gathered the individual possessions you feel are necessary."

I left Hella feeling that my plan represented my last opportunity to help in finding Abra Barrie's killer.

Some of the items I needed were easy to find. I went to the kitchen first and pulled a plastic grocery bag from the supply Janell kept on hand.

"What's up, Kitt? Thought you were still resting."

"I feel rested enough—at least for now. Janell?"

"Yes?"

"I'm really disappointed that our investigation concerning Abra Barrie has turned up so little information and evidence. I've been talking to Hella just now, and I asked her to do some psychic detecting."

"You really believe in that sort of thing?"

"Yes. There may be a lot of fake psychics in the world, maybe especially in Key West, but I think Hella has a special ability to see what others cannot see." I explained my plan to Janell.

"Okay, Kitt. I'll help you gather the things you want to take to Hella. How about my green caftan? How about Rex's chef's apron?" Janell stepped into the laundry room and lifted the garments from the laundry basket near the washing machine. "And you can take one of Mama G's dish towels—one she frequently uses to cover her bowls of sandwich fillings."

"Great. And I have the book on Fort Jefferson that Teach used to carry in his pocket. So we still need something personal belonging to Ace and Phud. I'll look around the bandstand and inside the tool shed out back."

"Ace keeps extra drumsticks on the bandstand."

"True, but those are the ones Hella uses. I need something that belongs only to Ace and he seldom lets his black drumsticks out of his sight."

We walked to the bandstand to take a look. Music folders. Drums. Teach's bass fiddle.

"How about the cushion from Ace's chair?" Janell asked.

"No. Won't do. Hella sits on it, too. Guess I'll have to get something of Ace's later. Don't know how long it takes Hella to 'see' into the depth of each article. Maybe I have enough things for her to work with tonight."

After I left Janell, I walked to the tool shed at the back of the garden and looked at the array of items it held. Which ones belonged to Rex? Which ones did Phud have personal claim to? Or maybe they shared them. I couldn't be sure. Maybe I'd have to wait until tomorrow morning and pay special attention to the tools the men used.

For now, I carried the collection I'd gathered in the grocery bag to my room. I'd take them to Hella later tonight. I stared at the bag after I tossed it onto my bed. Had a murderer held something in that bag? The question creeped me out.

24

Later that night after I'd helped Rex light the patio torches, I stood for a few moments, entranced. Such moments as these would soon be only memories—scenes from my past.

The lighter fluid emitted a pungent odor and heat from the flames warmed my cheek. I watched the torches point slim fingers of flame to the sky before the trade wind caught them, broadened them, and sent them undulating like golden dancers shimmying this way and that into the night. I stood there caught up in this picture postcard scene and dreaming, knowing I'd remember The Poinsettia long after I returned to the snow and ice of the Iowa winter.

I forced myself to put all thoughts of Rex and the stained glove from my mind. Nor did I dwell on the fact that I would be leaving Janell alone with him in Key West. There had been no indications that Rex might harm her or that he might have thought of harming her. Nor did I believe Rex had harmed Abra Barrie. No. No such thoughts at all.

I refused to let such ideas take root in my mind. Rex was my brother-in-law, a loved and highly respected member of our small family. Maybe Hella had been wrong about the glove reeking of evil vibes. She was first to admit that she was sometimes mistaken about the things her mind's eye saw. Or maybe she hadn't been mistaken. Maybe other men had also worn that glove in the past. Maybe someone had grabbed it and slipped it on in a time of need.

I helped Janell arrange sandwiches at the snack bar until I heard Mama Gomez count 1a, 2a, 3a, 4 and give the signal to start the music. When I heard the opening strains of "Harbor Lights," I knew Hella was sitting at Ace's trap set. From the corner of my eye, I saw Ace striding across the dance floor in my direction. I took a deep breath and steeled myself for whatever might come next. No way was I going to make this encounter simple for him. No way would I make his first words to me any easier for him. Then, feeling ashamed of myself and my negative attitude, I turned, looked directly at him and met his gaze.

"K-Kitt, will you please let me apologize again?"

"No more apologies necessary, Ace. I shouldn't have jumped to such crazy and uncalled-for conclusions."

"I'm really sorry our lighthouse trip turned into such a fiasco and caused us both so much anxiety and pain."

"But it's all behind us now. Let's leave it there, okay?"

"Deal."

"You could have been killed jumping into Phud's car the way you did."

"And I hate to imagine what might have happened to you if you'd fallen down those steps, thinking I meant to hurt you."

I swallowed before I spoke. "Let's call it one total misunderstanding. Perhaps a decade of misunderstandings." I smiled.

Ace smiled back. "When I was a child, I spoke as a child. Now I'm a man, I've put childish things behind me." Ace's smile quirked into a grin. "That's not an exact translation, but I remember hearing words something like those from a Bible-belt minister back in Iowa. Anyway, I mean the words sincerely."

"Thank you, Ace. And I accept them as you intended."

"How about a dance before the tune ends? We're still friends, aren't we?"

"Of course." I took a step toward him. I was about to tell

him that I'd be leaving Key West soon, but he surprised me by mentioning it first. Did everyone at The Poinsettia know? I hoped everyone didn't know the why of my visit. I wasn't ready to share those intimate details just yet.

"You're leaving soon, right?" Ace asked when I hesitated in replying.

"Right." I wondered if he even guessed at the problems I'd face back in Iowa. This was no time to think about that. I let him ease me onto the dance floor. "Yes. I'll be packing my suitcase soon with layers of mixed emotions. I love Key West and The Poinsettia. I hate to leave, but vacation's over. I can't stay any longer." I offered no further explanations. Ace didn't pry. But why should he? People took vacations. Vacations usually came to an end sooner or later. Nothing about my time here really required any explanation.

We glided across the floor to a far corner of the patio. Eyes closed, Ace had buried his face in my hair and I could feel his warm breath against my neck. From the side of my eye, I saw Janell give me thumbs-up and a huge grin.

"Kitt," Ace murmured. "Someday I'd like to visit you in Iowa. Think that might be a possibility?"

"Maybe we could arrange that. I'll have to think about it." I hoped he couldn't feel my heart thudding. "It's a long ways to Iowa. And there's your boat. Who'd take care of it and your shrimp business?"

Ace ignored by question. "You got a boyfriend back home, Kitt? I mean, I can't imagine that you don't have several guys there awaiting your return. Wouldn't surprise me if one of them isn't hurrying you home right now. Guess it wouldn't surprise me to learn that you're engaged."

"No boyfriends. No engagement." I didn't elaborate, didn't want to spoil the evening by thinking about Shelby Cox. When Ace nestled me more closely into his arms, I welcomed his nearness and enjoyed dancing in silence until the music stopped and Mama Gomez shouted.

"Back on the bandstand, Ace. You're on. Move it. *Pronto.*"

At the sound of her voice, Ace jerked his head up in surprise so quickly he banged his forehead against my nose. My nose spurted blood. I tilted my head back, but blood dripped on my lip, my chin and then onto my shirt. Ace yanked a bandana from his pocket and offered it to me. I took it from him, but I didn't try to stop the flow of blood. He grabbed his bandana back and tried to wipe my face clean.

"Kitt! I'm sorry. Stand right there. Let me go to the faucet and dampen this thing with a little warm water."

I grabbed the bandana again. "Thanks, Ace, but I've had nosebleeds before. I'll take care of it in the house. No point in letting the patrons see blood."

"Okay. Go. But I am sorry."

"Enough of apologizing. Mama G will have your head on a platter if you don't get back to the bandstand."

"That woman doesn't scare me, Kitt. She's more bark than bite."

"But go. I'm okay. I'm okay." I held his bandana to my nose. "Get back on the bandstand before your fearless leader has a stroke." I pushed him toward his trap set. "Go. Go. I'll be fine in a few minutes."

Ace rejoined the combo without a glance at Mama G's scowling face, and they began their next number. I hurried across the patio toward the house, still tilting my chin to try to stop the flow of blood. Janell grabbed a paper towel and held it under my nose until it stopped bleeding.

"Your shirt's a mess, Kitt." She threw the paper towel into a trash basket. "Better go douse those stains in cold water. They should come right out. Why didn't you finish blotting the mess on Ace's bandana?"

"I'm not worried about blood stains at this point." I lowered my voice to a whisper. "Now I have a personal item from Ace to show to Hella."

"What if he asks for it back? Don't think I've ever seen him without a bandana hanging from his hip pocket."

"If he asks, I'll tell him I'll toss the bandana into the laundry and return it to him later. Surely he has more than one."

"Good. And fast thinking on your part."

I hurried on inside the house, stopping at the refrig for an ice cube to press on my upper lip. I held it in place until the bleeding had totally subsided before I hurried to my room and added Ace's bandana to the grocery bag of items I'd managed to collect for Hella.

Going to the closet, I pulled out a fresh shirt and donned it before hurrying into the bathroom and running a basin of cold water. I submerged my blood-stained tee, squishing it around and squeezing it until it was thoroughly soaked. Although fresh, the blood stains didn't give way to the water quickly. I had to add stain remover, rub each spot with hand soap and scrub, scrub, scrub.

I'd been making so much noise with the shirt and the running water that even the combo music sounded sporadic. After I eased the shirt onto a plastic hanger and hung it over the tub to drip dry, I opened the bathroom door. I had been so preoccupied that I hadn't heard anyone come upstairs and I jumped, startled when I saw Rex waiting for me in the hallway. He had a strange gleam in his eyes and he held a hammer in his right hand.

"Rex?" I backed off, bumping into the wash basin as he stepped forward, blocking the doorway. For a few seconds he stood looking at me with that weird glint in his eyes. I wanted to run, but he stood between me and the door, and I couldn't squeeze past him to reach the hallway, and the stairs.

"Kitt, I want to tell you something." His voice came out a raspy whisper, and his demeanor made me back farther into the bathroom instead of approaching him and the door. Three steps back and now there was no more space. I was trapped against the shower stall. Shades of the Bates Hotel! All I could think of was *Psycho,* that memorable Hitchcock movie, the stained glove Rex claimed as his own and the hammer in his hand. And mixed with all that, I recalled TV programs in which the killer murdered his victim in a bathroom and drained her blood down the shower drain until there was nothing left for the police to find.

Rex's next words were real shockers.

"I want this to be a surprise for Janell."

My death? Some great surprise! "What are you talking about, Rex? Have you lost your mind?"

I forced myself to stand taller and straighter until I was only a bit shorter than Rex, but my hands were slick with cold sweat. Fear held me mute.

25

Rex's next words brought me to a confused sort of attention.

"Kitt, I can't thank you enough for finding the painting, bringing it to me."

The painting? I began to relax, to throw off my crazy fears. Maybe Rex didn't intend to murder me after all. I forced a smile and tried to forget his gloves and the hammer in his hand.

"Since you'll be leaving soon, I want to have a small party tonight after we close the patio, just the band and our workers. Janell's busy with customers right now, and I've let Hella take over the cash register while I've been hanging the *Pelican* in place on the dining room wall."

"So that's the surprise!" Could he see the relief on my face?

"Yes. I want everyone to get to enjoy Janell's reaction when she sees the picture in place for the first time."

"Wonderful, Rex!" I managed to make the two words sound sincere, and I hid my previous and unfounded fright.

"Right now, I hope you'll come on downstairs and take a look at the painting and its placement. I need a woman's eye and viewpoint. If you think there's a better place to hang it, I'm willing to make the change. I can fill nail holes later."

I followed Rex downstairs and stood across the dining room to view the *Pelican* from a distance.

"I think it looks great right where you've placed it, Rex. Of course, if Janell has different ideas, you can make changes later."

"Then for now, I'm going to leave it where it is. Thanks for your input. You ready to join us on the patio again?"

"Ready and eager." I followed him outside, sat at the snack bar and sipped a soda, still feeling a need to calm down.

"You okay?" Janell asked. "You and your shirt?"

"Everything's fine."

The word had spread about my upcoming departure, and it was the first thing Phud mentioned after he pulled me onto the dance floor. I didn't resist. I'd be leaving soon. No reason I couldn't be nice to him for another day or so.

"Sorry to hear you'll be leaving so quickly, Kitt. We were just getting to know each other."

"All good things must come to an end." I repeated an old cliché, unable to think of a fresh retort. "Phud, I want to thank you for trying to rescue me from Ace earlier today."

"*Trying!* Seems to me I *did* rescue you. I'm still not sure what Ace Brewster had in mind. I can't believe he had your best interests at heart. You both looked so wild-eyed! I'm not convinced he wasn't trying to harm you and that you weren't running for your life. Care to give me the true story?"

"No. I don't. It was all a big misunderstanding on both our parts. There's no true story that's more interesting than the scene you saw playing out at the lighthouse museum." I couldn't bear repeating the Donald-and-the-mice tale again, especially not to Phud. A murderer still walked at large in or near Key West, and in my thinking that person could live or be employed right here at The Poinsettia. In my mind, the evidence was beginning to point directly at Rex. I didn't want that to be true. Nor did I want to discuss it with Phud.

What I really wanted from Phud tonight was his tam. I'd never seen him without it, no matter how warm the weather. What kind of man wore a tam in the South Florida heat? I wondered if he wore it throughout the summer, too. Surely it

216

was a bit of clothing Hella could use in her effort to pinpoint a killer.

"Tell me about your tam, Phud. Since you wear it all the time, it must be very special to you."

"It is. I bought it many years ago in Paris—when I was a young man still searching for my niche in the world. At that time I was fresh out of college and my grandparents had given me a trip abroad as a graduation gift. I didn't get much farther than Paris."

"I've never been abroad. You must have had a wonderful trip."

"Yes. Wonderful." Phud chuckled, as if remembering pleasant pastimes. "I met artists, and one of them introduced me to his teacher, a beautiful lady who showed me the city and offered to give me some painting lessons."

"You could paint?"

"Who was I to say I could or couldn't? I'd never tried it before. She helped me buy the necessary supplies, and I insisted on buying this tam. Who could convince himself he was an artist without wearing a tam?"

"I don't know. Who?"

"Certainly not I." Again, Phud laughed. "The lady helped me find and purchase the tam and she invited me to her studio for lessons."

"And did you produce some sketches, a painting?"

"Of course. She was a good teacher. But my painting turned out to be a dismal failure in the eyes of other artists. I was the only one who cared for it. I discarded it even before I left France, but I've kept the tam all these years to remind me of Paris and my beautiful teacher."

"Do you still keep in touch with her?"

"No. She lives only in my memory."

"Maybe Key West with all its art and artists will inspire you to try painting again. Maybe you were too hard on yourself with your criticisms of your initial effort."

"No. I'm no artist. I'm a botanist. My passion lies in working with living plants."

I wanted to reach up and snatch the tam from his head and run to Hella with it. I quashed that ridiculous idea, wondering if it might be possible to find a way to get him to willingly part with it for a short time.

I put my thoughts about Phud's tam on a back burner, danced the final theme song with Ace, then helped Janell and Rex douse the torches and close the patio for the evening. The combo members were packing their music folders and stands when Rex clapped his hands for attention.

"Okay, gang. You've all heard by now that Kitt will be leaving soon. Before that happens I want you all to join Janell and me inside for a short farewell party. It's hard to find a party time when we have day jobs and work here every night. Do come on inside. I have a surprise for you."

26

Once everyone stepped inside, crowding the kitchen, Rex led the way into the dining room and invited the seven of us to sit at the table. He stood before us, holding everyone's attention when he lifted a bottle of champagne from the ice bucket. Playing his role to the hilt, he took his time wrapping the dripping bottle in a towel.

"What's going on here, Rex?" Janell asked, but without waiting for his answer, she hurried to the corner cupboard, brought out crystal champagne flutes and set one before each guest. Then she disappeared into the kitchen, returning in moments with paper napkins.

"Wow!" Ace exclaimed. "Champagne! Some great farewell party! I like it. I like it."

"I hope it doesn't mean you're glad to see me go," I said.

"Kitt," Rex said, "in all honesty, the champagne isn't meant to celebrate your departure. That's just happenstance."

"I'm relieved." I laughed.

"Who's good at opening champagne bottles?" Rex asked.

Phud reached for the champagne. "I'll do it, but I better take it to the kitchen." He carried the bottle and his glass to the kitchen sink, grabbed another towel, and worked with the cork while everyone craned their necks to watch. At the sound of a resounding "pop," the sparkling liquid frothed into the glass, which he had at the ready, half filling it with the golden treat.

Returning to the table with the bottle still wrapped in the

towel, Phud handed it to Rex. "The honor is all yours."

"Thanks, Phud." Rex walked behind his guests, reaching over their shoulders to fill each glass. "First a toast to Kitt, who has given us the joy and pleasure of her company for the past few days."

We clinked glasses and everyone took a sip of the champagne before Rex spoke again. "Now hear ye, hear ye! A toast to another important occasion."

Rex's guests looked at each other in surprise.

"A toast to the *Pelican*." Rex raised his glass and nodded to the wall. "My gift to Janell for her upcoming birthday."

Everyone turned to peer at the wall, and when Janell saw the painting, she rushed to Rex and gave him a lingering kiss.

"How long has that painting been hanging there, Rex? If you tell me I've walked past it a dozen times without noticing it, I'll feel terrible."

"Then don't bother to feel terrible. It's only been in place a few hours. I slipped inside and hung it while you were making more sandwiches and while Hella took over the cash register for me."

"Beautiful painting," Ace said. "It's a scene I see almost every morning of my life. That bird looks like Old Bigmouth. The same pelican hangs around the *Ace* every A.M. waiting for a handout."

"It's hanging crooked." Teach rose, walked to the painting and tilted it slightly toward the ceiling. "There. Isn't that better?"

"Looks perfect to me," Janell said. "I thank you all for coming inside to make the hanging so special. There's a long story behind this painting, but you can hear it another time. Right now, I know you've all had a busy day. Again, let me thank you for your good wishes. You've all made my birthday celebration a very happy one, although a bit bittersweet because Kitt will be leaving us soon."

"Thanks for inviting us in, Rex," Hella said. "The new painting enhances your home."

When everyone began shoving their chairs away from the table, Mama G thumped on her champagne flute, catching their attention.

"Wait. Wait," she said. "I have a suggestion."

When Ace and Teach kept moving toward the door, I blocked their way.

"Listen, guys. Mama Gomez has something to say."

"Mama G to you from now on, Kitt. Only strangers call me Mama Gomez. For those who come to me for help, my name is Mama G, and I never saw anyone in more need of help than you were this morning, Kitt."

"You're right, Mama G. I needed you, and I thank you again for being there for me. Now what suggestion were you going to offer?"

"Our Kitt, she walk into The Poinsettia in aftermath of murder. It's likely that she go away to Iowa without that murderer being found. But hear me. There's one thing we can do."

"Oh, come on!" Ace growled. "There's nothing we can do to solve a murder. It's a police thing—has been a police thing right from the beginning."

Mama G glared at him. "You're probably right. But we can do one thing—with Hella's help. We can prove to ourselves, if not to the police, that nobody connected with The Poinsettia is guilty."

"Forget it." Teach drew himself up to his full height and took a step toward the door. "There's no way we can do that."

"There is a way, and you will listen to me. Now! Hella has a great gift. She can see things the rest of us cannot see."

"Okay, Hella," Ace said. "Tell us who done it."

221

If Hella hadn't looked as surprised as I felt, I'd have suspected that Janell and Mama G had been talking over the plan Janell, Hella and I had already been trying to put in place.

Teach took another step toward the door. "Since when have you become such a Hella-the-Psychic fan, Mama G? Since when?"

"That be a personal matter between me and Hella. It be none of your business. You will listen to me now if you want to continue playing your big fat fiddle in my combo."

"*Your* combo!"

Ace and Teach spoke in unison.

"Okay, guys." Rex urged both of them back from the doorway as he spoke. "Let's give Mama G a hearing." A nod along with a sweeping arm gesture signaled Mama G to speak again.

"I want each of us to give Hella something we use every day of our lives. I want Hella to hold each item. I want her to agree to use her second sight to determine the innocence of each of us."

For a moment everyone greeted this idea with total silence. Then Teach spoke up and would have left the room had Rex not blocked his way.

"You're not getting anything from me."

"Your reluctance might lead us to suspect you're hiding something from everyone, Teach," Phud said. "Like you, I remain unconvinced that Hella has such a special talent, but I find no harm in playing this little game with her if it makes everyone happy."

Ace gave a deep sigh and shook his head. "Count me in to cooperate. Mama G's idea can't hurt anyone. And it might help." He sighed again.

"Don't see what it could hurt," Rex said. Janell nodded her agreement.

"What do you say, Hella?" Janell asked the question as if we hadn't already talked it over with Hella.

"With reservations, I'm willing to try your idea, but I promise nothing."

"We know, Hella," I said. "Seeing into the future is a sometime thing, a thing you can't depend on." I presented her negative comment before she had a chance to say it herself.

"Okay, so it's decided." Rex stepped into the kitchen and returned with a small box. "I'll start the contributions with . . ."

Rex hesitated, thinking, and I held my breath, fearing he would suggest contributing his gloves and thus make Hella refuse to cooperate.

"I'll let Hella work with my shirt." He unbuttoned his shirt, slipped it off and dropped it into the box. "I've worn this shirt all evening, and it's one you've all seen me wear many times."

Good, I thought. The shirt's even better than the apron Janell had suggested.

Janell took the box, stepped into the laundry room and returned with her yellow caftan. "My contribution," she said, dropping it into the box.

Ace scowled at Mama G, but he slipped from his t-shirt and tossed it on top of Janell's caftan. When the box reached Phud, he removed his tam and dropped it in. At first Teach backed away from the box, then he relented and added a pair of his sunglasses.

"I have others at home. But I want this pair back when you're finished with this crazy experiment. And what about you, Mama G? What do you plan to add to this mix?"

"This towel." She dropped the towel she'd used to cover her sandwich mix on top of Teach's glasses. "And that does it." She gave the box to Hella. "See what you can do with these things. Tell us what you can learn about their owners."

"How soon can you do this, Hella?" Janell asked. "Kitt and I plan to go to Searstown tomorrow to have a mechanic check over her car before she leaves on that long drive to Iowa."

"Please don't give me a deadline. I don't work at all well when there's a time limit involved."

"Of course," Janell said. "We don't want to rush you. We'd much rather you take your time and give this project your best effort. If you could tell us about just one item tomorrow at breakfast, it would be a strong start."

"I make no promises about when, where—or who." Hella lifted the box, and we watched her pick her way across the stepping stones to her apartment.

27

The next morning after I'd dressed for the day, I went downstairs when I heard Janell and Rex moving about in the kitchen. Rex had carried in a basket of oranges from their tree, and I pulled the electric juicer from the cupboard and began juicing them. Janell made coffee and warmed sweet rolls in the microwave. Except for the whir of the juicer, we worked in silence.

"Do you suppose Hella's up yet?" I peered in the direction of the B&B and asked the question uppermost in our minds.

"Not yet," Rex said. "We're going to have to be patient and bide our time. No point in risking upsetting her by rushing her."

"How can you be so sure she's not up?" Janell asked. "On an ordinary day she's usually out and about before we are."

"But this is no ordinary day." I added a few ice cubes to the orange juice. "She knows we're eager to hear any opinion she may have about the items we gave her last night.

"I know she's not up yet because Voodoo's still hanging around her doorway waiting for a handout." Rex broke off a piece of sweet roll and popped it into his mouth. "She may tell Phud she doesn't feed that cat, but I've seen her do it. Not that I care. Its presence around here helps discourage the tree rats."

"Tree rats?" I stopped juicing oranges.

"Guess we didn't tell you about that little glitch in paradise. They're pests to us, and we'd like to get rid of them, but some species are endangered, protected by law. It's illegal to try to eliminate them, no matter how much we'd like to. But cats can't read so I'm guessing Voodoo manages to catch one now and then."

"Hella likes to torment Phud. Don't know why, but it's like a game they play." I readied a tray for the orange juice and glasses.

"And he likes to torment her about her psychic abilities," Janell said. "Sometimes I think they're jealous of each other."

After Janell finished slicing fresh avocado and papaya into a bowl, we carried our breakfast to poolside. Two geckos were playing tag in the morning dew that coated the picnic table until Rex scared them away and found a towel to wipe the table and chairs dry. In the distance gulls screamed their greeting to the morning, and closer at hand a mourning dove cooed, letting us know we had disturbed its day.

We spoke in ordinary tones as we ate, hoping our presence, our voices, might draw Hella outside. But her window shades remained drawn, and Voodoo had the nerve to come to poolside to beg for tidbits, winding himself around our ankles and mewing for attention.

"Maybe she stayed up late last night working on the items we gave her," Janell said. "Maybe she overslept."

"Or maybe she didn't see anything special about them." Rex helped himself to another sweet roll. "That's probably what happened. Maybe Phud's right about her. Maybe her psychic ability is a figment of her imagination."

"Shhh." I raised an eyebrow. "She'll hear you."

Janell looked at her watch. "Rex, do you want me to call the Sears store and ask if they have a mechanic available today? It's one of the few automotive places open on Saturdays, you know."

"No, don't call. Kitt, why don't we drive there and talk to whoever's on duty? Sometimes eye-to-eye contact is more effective in getting attention than a telephone call."

"Right." I agreed with Rex. "It's harder to say no to an in-your-face person than to drop a telephone receiver back into its cradle. And maybe, since it's early morning, they'll have time to look the car over while we wait. It's been running fine. I don't think there's any problem that needs attention, but I'd like someone to take a look-see before I start out on a long drive."

"Alone," Janell added. "Maybe I should drive to Iowa with you and fly back. I'd like to see the old home place again."

"No way, Janell. I'd love to be able to enjoy your company on the trip, but winter's no time to be visiting Iowa. Think about June or July. Besides, you're needed here. I'll be fine."

"So let's drive on over to Searstown, Kitt." Rex stood, popped another sweet roll into his mouth and walked toward my car.

I didn't feel as comfortable with Rex as I had before I discovered the glove that had upset Hella belonged to him. But neither could I believe he was guilty of murder. And what could happen to me between here and Searstown? I stood, ready to follow Rex to my car.

"Shall we leave the juice and goodies on the table for a while in case Hella shows up?" I asked Janell. "She always enjoys breakfast, and I'm guessing she'll join you before long."

"I'll cover the rolls and leave the juice, but I'm not waiting around any longer." Janell stood. "I've things to do inside this morning. When I see Hella come out, I'll join her for a second cup of coffee."

"Good." Rex turned to me. "Ready to go?"

"Let's do it. I'll have to go inside for my car keys."

After I returned to the garden, I tossed Rex the keys. "Want to drive? I'll open the gate."

Few people were out and about this early on a Saturday morning, and Rex grinned at me as we turned toward Highway One. "Let's take the scenic route past the beach, okay?"

227

"Sure. I won't be seeing any beaches in Iowa until summertime."

Rex drove slowly. The guy selling parasailing rides waved to us. Even at this early hour, teenagers were using two of the volleyball courts, and closer to the water a boy tossed a yellow Frisbee to a brown lab who caught it and returned it to him. Near the curbside, a vendor prepared breakfast for early risers. The fragrance of frying bacon made my mouth water even though I'd just eaten.

Farther on toward the airport, an old man stood knee deep in the sea, flying a kite shaped like a pirate's flag—white with black skull and crossbones. Nearby a teenager opened a shed, set out a FOR RENT sign, and began lining up beach chairs and umbrellas for his future customers.

"Great day for the beach. I hate leaving all this behind, Rex." In the back of my mind, I thought about Ace and admitted that I'd miss him, too. But I didn't mention that to Rex.

"Didn't see you spending much beach time this past week. One afternoon with Janell. Think we kept you too busy."

"I've enjoyed every minute of my stay. Every minute."

"Remember it, Kitt. I know facing your job, your friends, is going to be a tough scene when you get back to Iowa. Never forget that you did the right thing. The only thing. And whenever you need a break from the police force, you can come back here. We'll be glad to have you."

Rex's words were a comfort, but I welcomed the three-day drive I faced. I'd have plenty of time to plan just how I'd greet my old friends and neighbors as well as the guys on the force.

In a few minutes Rex turned toward the main highway and drove on toward the Searstown mall. Shopkeepers were unlocking and raising their storefront grillwork, and people were carrying their weekend groceries from Albertson's. Rex stopped in front of the Sears automotive area and cut the motor.

"You wait here, okay? I'll go inside and see if I can talk to the mechanic on duty. Even on a Saturday people can count on Sears."

I sat in the car for a few minutes, then I got out and walked around the parking lot, gazing at the gulls perched on coral rocks in the shallow bay across the highway. When Rex returned. I knew the news wasn't good.

"They can't take the car until early Monday morning. Thought the guy might be eager to look under the hood of a Prius, but no. Well, yes, he was eager to see your car's engine. But no. He had no time to work on it until Monday."

"That's okay, Rex. I'll still have plenty of time to make it back to Centerville before my week's leave is up."

When Rex tried to get back onto the highway we heard sirens and stopped to look and listen. Police car. Ambulance. Fire truck. More police cars.

"Someone's getting lots of help," I said. "Suppose they're headed for Mallory Dock? I can't see if they're turning toward Old Town."

"Could be a problem anywhere in the harbor," Rex guessed. "Few emergencies worse than a boat on fire. Especially a fiberglass boat. Fiberglass goes up like tinder."

"Think Janell read in the paper that a cruise ship was due to dock early today. The Costa line. Oh, Rex! What if it's caught on fire? Or what if some passenger's had a heart attack?"

"No use speculating. How about turning on the radio? You're more familiar with the knobs than I am. We'll know what's happened soon enough."

I snapped on the radio, but I couldn't find any news broadcast. No special bulletins. Cars and RVs seemed to come out of nowhere to try to bull their way in line behind the emergency vehicles.

"I'm waiting until the traffic thins," Rex said.

"Good idea. We're in no big hurry."

Rex had to wait several minutes before the traffic let up enough to allow him to make a left turn and join the throng. As we grew closer to Garrison Bight, cops on foot motioned drivers to turn left, to stop following the crowd. We turned.

"I hate to get into traffic like this," Rex said. "It's a good place to get a new car scratched or a fender dented."

I saw a twinkle in his eye and knew he was trying to get a rise out of me.

"You're joking, right? Or maybe not. I'm glad someone's getting the emergency help they need from the ambulance crew and the cops, and I intend to take my Prius home scratch and dent free."

"Worry not," Rex said. "I'm teasing."

We followed the diverted traffic to Duval and then on to Whitehead. At last we managed to turn toward Caroline Street. Then we both reached the same realization at the same time when we saw motorcycle cops in the distance clearing the way for the police cars.

"Rex! They're going to pass right by The Poinsettia."

"Wrong. They're not passing by. They're stopping." Rex hit the brakes. Cops were directing the sightseeing drivers to move on, to leave the area.

"Keep it moving, buddy," an officer shouted. "Move it! Give the emergency crew room to work!"

"I live here, Officer. Rex Cummings. I own this place."

"Tough luck, buddy. You've got a problem, but get your car off the street. That's an order."

"I'll get the gate." I jumped from the car and opened the gate while Rex drove into the garden. I closed the gate and started to follow him to the carport, but I stopped when I saw two officers unrolling yellow crime scene tape and attaching it to the front fence, then pulling it in place around the house, the patio, the back fence and the shed.

Janell saw us and ran toward us with tears streaming down her face.

28

Rex leaped from the car and Janell rushed toward us screaming. "Hella's dead. Dead! She's been murdered!"

I stiffened my spine, lifted my chin and started running toward Janell. Rex reached her first and she flung herself into his arms. It chilled me to realize I'd known what Janell was going to say even before she spoke. I'd had that sinking feeling in my stomach that, for me, prefaces bad news. My heart began thudding as if it might leave my chest. I took deep breaths to try to control it.

The clues had been in place. Hella, an early riser, hadn't shown up for breakfast. Voodoo had been hanging around waiting for the tidbits she usually offered. The blinds across her windows had remained closed in spite of the noise of our voices, the scraping of chairs against concrete. We should have knocked on her door. But no. We would have been too late, but at least that action would have spared Janell from being left alone to find Hella's body.

"Janell!" Rex kissed her forehead and clasped her to him. "Are you all right? Were you in danger? Do you know what happened?"

I suddenly felt icy cold in spite of the warmth of the sunny day. Gooseflesh rippled along my arms and thighs, and I had to clamp my teeth together to keep them from chattering.

"Hella's dead. Hella's dead." Janell repeated the words again and again, sounding like an old-time phonograph with a needle unable to go on to the next groove.

"Who found her?" Rex whispered as if he didn't believe what Janell was telling him. "Were you the first to . . . ?"

Before she could answer, a man joined us, barking orders and urging us toward the house. Detective Lyon. No uniform today. Plain clothes. I hardly recognized him. But he was the same tawny-haired guy who'd brought me home from the lighthouse museum in his squad car yesterday. Today the trade wind blew his neatly styled hair askew as he yanked the back door open, stepped in behind us, and ordered us to enter the kitchen and then the living room as if he owned the place.

"Sit down, please,"

"Look here, fellow," Rex said. "You're trespassing. This's my property. You're trespassing in my home. I don't need you to order me to sit down in my own living room. You're . . . what's the meaning of this?"

"Sit down, please." Detective Lyon repeated his order. And he waited.

Rex took Janell's hand and led her to the living room couch where he waited until she sat before he took a place beside her. They seemed to have forgotten I was there, but Lyon motioned for me to take the chair at the side of the couch.

"Your name, sir?" Detective Lyon looked directly at Rex while he pulled a dog-eared notebook from his pocket and waited, ballpoint poised, ready to jot down an answer.

"Rex Cummings . . . sir. You do realize that this is my house? That I'm the owner?"

"I realize that," the detective said. "And your name, please?" He looked at Janell, wrote down her name when she replied, then turned toward me. "We've met before, I believe. Kitt Morgan, an Iowa visitor at the Cummings's home, right?"

"Right."

He faced Rex once more. "Your wife called 911 a few minutes

ago to report a death on your property. Where were you at the time she made this call?"

"Do I need a lawyer?"

"You're not under arrest, and you may call a lawyer if you so desire. My questions at this time will be informal ones. I believe the victim, Miss Hella Fuller, is a renter here at your inn."

Hella! Dead! I could hardly believe it. Why Hella? Why a spinster retiree playing out her golden years in the Florida sunshine? I looked at Janell as if the answer might be written on her face. By now she had managed to stop crying, but her face was still so red and blotched I could hardly tell where skin ended and hair began. Redheads are seldom beautiful when they cry. But why were such crazy thoughts racing through my mind at a time like this?

"Who found Hella's body?" Rex asked.

"I'll ask the questions if you don't mind." Lyon stood as if memorizing our faces for a few moments before he spoke again. "Janell Cummings found the body. Janell made the 911 call. Under ordinary circumstances, the person who finds a corpse is of special interest to the police, but in this case . . ." Lyon's voice trailed off into the silence of the room.

"Why in this case?" I blurted, in spite of knowing it was not my place to try to take over the questioning.

"Because the body was badly mutilated. Mutilated in a manner I don't believe Mrs. Cummings is physically cable of doing."

Looking out the window, I saw a photographer with camera at the ready striding past the pool and the B&B as he headed on toward the tool shed and the back fence. I guessed the man following him to be the medical examiner. Nothing much would happen until those two finished their work.

Detective Lyon stepped between me and the window, blocking my vision of anything else that might be taking place in the yard. I guessed he had done this on purpose.

"Who was present at this address last night?" Lyon asked, directing his question at Rex.

"Many people, sir. Our café and dance patio are open to the public until ten o'clock. We had a large crowd yesterday evening, and we don't ask for names, addresses or other types of identification."

Lyon did not change his expression. "I understand that, Mr. Cummings. I'm more interested in your employees than in your customers. What employees were present?"

"Hella Fuller, for one," Rex said.

"She works here?"

"Part time every night. Full time if our regular drummer has asked for the evening off."

"Please give me the names of all your employees—either full-time or part-time workers."

Rex responded with the names, giving no further information.

"I understand your establishment was involved in another recent murder. Is that correct?"

"It is not." Rex ran his hand over his head.

"Abra Barrie." Lyon spat the word. "She was murdered while renting one of the rooms at your inn? Is that not correct?"

"She was not murdered on these premises," Janell said. "Strangers found her body washed up on the beach. She was not murdered here."

"I stand corrected." Lyon tucked his notebook and ballpoint back into his pocket without any words of apology and without taking his gaze from Rex and Janell. "I want all three of you to remain in this room until I or another officer grants you permission to leave. Is that understood?"

"Is that really necessary?" Rex asked. "We operate a business here. We have work to do."

235

"Probably not as much work as you think," Lyon said. "Crime scene tape will be in place until a police investigation of the scene is complete. Your business may be closed for tonight—perhaps closed for the next few days. State police will be called in. Maybe even the FBI if they think this murder may be in any way connected with what may be a rash of serial killings in Florida and Georgia. I'm ordering you to remain right here in your living room until you have official permission to leave."

Nobody spoke for a few moments after Detective Lyon left us alone. I was afraid if Janell began weeping again I might join her. Who? Why? I kept asking myself questions that had no answers.

"I'm sorry you were the one to find Hella's body." Rex eased toward Janell, taking her hand in his. "A terrible thing. How . . . can you bear to tell us what happened?"

"I knew things weren't right," Janell said. "The orange juice was getting hot sitting there in the sunshine. In spite of the plastic wrap, the sweet rolls had to be drying out. I thought Hella might have decided not to try working with the items we gave her last night—thought she might be reluctant to tell us, to disappoint us. So I decided to talk to her. I walked around the B&B toward her door, and . . ."

"Don't relive the horror," Rex said. "Sorry I asked. Try to block the scene from your mind."

"Can I get you something to drink?" I stood and headed toward the kitchen. "Coffee? Juice? Piece of toast?"

"Thanks, Kitt. But no. I may never be hungry or thirsty again. Not ever."

"Who do you think could have done this?" Rex looked at both Janell and me as if we might be privy to answers withheld from him.

"We know it wasn't one of us," I said. "So that leaves . . ."

"That leaves everyone in Key West," Rex said. "Nobody can

say the murderer is someone who was present last night, someone who works here. Our gate's never locked. We built the fence to beautify our property, not to repel criminals."

"I hate being a prisoner in my own home." Janell rose and began to pace. "I hate realizing that two people closely associated with The Poinsettia, two people we liked and whose company we enjoyed, are now dead. Rex, one of us could have been a victim. Nobody is safe around here anymore. We're all in danger. We have no idea what enemy might be targeting one of us next."

Janell's voice shrilled and Rex went to her, pulled her back to the couch.

"Don't panic, Janell. We have to keep level heads." For a few moments he rubbed Janell's wrists with a brisk touch, and then he brought her a cup of coffee, which she set on the coffee table without tasting.

Rex had leaned over her, urging her to sip the drink when Detective Lyon knocked on the door and then entered the house uninvited.

"The ME has tentatively set the time of the victim's death at shortly after midnight last night."

Nobody spoke. I shuddered when I saw four men carrying a stretcher holding a body covered with a blanket toward the ambulance, sliding their burden through the open rear doors, slamming the doors.

"You're free to go wherever you choose at this time," Lyon said. "But don't leave the city without police permission. I'm the detective assigned to this case. My partner Detective Brooks and I can be reached at police headquarters should you need help or want to make an additional statement. Do not plan to open for business tonight."

"We have nothing more to say," Rex said. Janell and I nodded, backing up his words.

"I've called a meeting for two o'clock this afternoon here in this room," Lyon said. "I'm getting in touch with your employees. You and they will be asked to answer general questions concerning last night's murder. You will be read the *Miranda* warning. You may refuse to answer our questions or you may have a lawyer at your side—or both."

Again, nobody spoke. Lyon let himself out of the house unassisted.

29

Rex glanced at his watch. "We have an hour to prepare ourselves for this question-and-answer event. I'm surprised that Lyon would leave us alone—free to discuss this tragedy, free to agree on our story—if we felt a need to concoct a story other than the truth."

"How dare that man to plan a question session here in our own home without asking our permission," Janell said. "Is that legal, Kitt? Is that how such a thing would happen in Iowa? Why not question everyone at the police station? Isn't that where suspects are usually questioned? Rex, they kept calling you back to police headquarters for questioning about Abra Barrie. What do you think, Kitt?"

It wasn't like Janell to spout so many rapid-fire questions. I tried to calm her down. "Don't know what Key West police procedural rules are, but my suggestion is to go along with any reasonable request the detectives make. Do you think it would be any easier to answer questions at the station?"

"Probably not," Rex said. "Let's cooperate without making a fuss, okay?"

"What about a lawyer?" Janell looked at Rex. "Anything we say can be used against us in a court of law. Isn't that what the *Miranda* warning says? Maybe that detective's trying to trick us into saying something that we'll live to regret later."

"The police can ask tricky questions," I agreed before Rex could speak. "Do you have a lawyer?"

"Of course. We didn't survive all the legalese of getting our business established without the help of a lawyer." Rex picked up a telephone and punched in a number. "Hubble and Hubble. I'll give Kran Hubble a ring."

A ring was all he gave him. No answer. No answering machine requesting that he leave a message. "Let's wing it," Rex said. "A lawyer at our side might give the detectives the impression there's something important we're trying to hide."

"Just tell the truth," Janell said. "The truth, whatever it may be, will come out sooner or later."

We were still in the living room when the others began to arrive. Mama G blustered in first.

"*Hola!*" She flounced across the room and stood glaring down at Janell on the couch. "Hella! Hella dead! What do you know about this? Who could have done such a thing?"

"That's what we all want to know." Rex took Mama G's arm and eased her toward a chair.

"*Es malo. Muy malo.*"

Mama G accepted a glass of water from Rex and then lapsed into silence until Phud arrived. Rex pulled a chair from the dining room table into the living room and without speaking motioned Phud to be seated.

Teach and Ace arrived together and Rex pulled in two more chairs. "May I bring anyone a glass of water?" Nobody answered.

Before sitting, Ace passed my chair and dropped my cell phone into my lap. "One of my tech friends fixed it. No problem." He grinned. "I programmed my name first on your speed dial."

"Thanks, Ace." I tucked the phone into my pocket, glad to have it back even though I didn't plan to be making any calls.

"No lawyers?" Teach asked. "Does that mean we're all sure we won't incriminate ourselves?"

"I'm not worried about incriminating myself." Phud looked

around the room, letting his gaze touch each of us. "Are any of you concerned about that?"

"We need to take care," I warned them. "Listen thoughtfully to each question, and don't hesitate to ask questions of your own if you think they're necessary. Think carefully before you speak."

Detectives Lyon and Brooks arrived in an unmarked car, parked in the tow-away zone, then strode to the door. Rex admitted them before they had time to knock. Lyon smoothed his hair, checked his watch and then with slow, deliberate motions he pulled his notepad and ballpoint from the pocket of his tan suit. Detective Brooks, a giant of a man, darkened the room like a rain cloud. He wore a charcoal gray suit, gray shirt, gray tie and black Nikes, and he stood blocking the doorway. Did he think one of us might make a sudden break for freedom?

"Thank you all for gathering here promptly," Lyon said. "The sooner we get your statements, the sooner you'll be free to leave. Detective Brooks will read you your rights."

Detective Brooks cleared his throat before he recited the *Miranda* warning as if he had done it a million times and could repeat it in his sleep. After getting each of our verbal agreements that we understood the warning, Lyon proceeded with the questioning, letting his gaze fall on each of us before addressing Rex.

"In your own words, tell us what happened here last night after your café closed for business."

I squelched a smile, wondering whose words Lyon thought Rex might use other than his own.

"You closed a little after ten o'clock, right?" Lyon prompted. "Can you give me the exact time?"

"I can." Rex rose to his feet, walked around the couch and stood behind Janell. "Paying patrons left the patio at ten o'clock. None lingered. Everyone who had worked here last night came inside at my invitation, and we had a brief celebration. I'd planned a mini-party and a couple of toasts in honor of Janell's upcoming birthday and in honor of Kitt Morgan, who will be leaving us soon to return to her job in Iowa. I served champagne, but that was all. No hard drinks. No other refreshments." Rex took his time telling the whole story of our evening.

I watched the others as he spoke. Janell buried her face in her hands, and I couldn't tell whether she was weeping or trying very hard to keep her composure. Phud looked out the window. Mama G squirmed in her seat and gulped the rest of the water in her glass. Ace and Teach slouched on their chairs, trying hard to look bored and failing to bring it off.

Detective Lyon looked directly at Rex all the time he spoke, taking time at the end of his story to jot notes. "It is my understanding that each of you here in this room works in some capacity at The Poinsettia. Is that correct?"

"It is," Rex said, speaking for all of us. "Ace Brewster, Teach Quinn and Mama Gomez form the dance combo. Hella Flusher sometimes joined them, playing drums. Dr. Ashby is our gardener. Kitt Morgan our houseguest."

"So the combo plays in the evenings?"

"Right," Rex replied.

"You, Janell and Miss Morgan work at your café in the evenings, right?"

"That's correct," Rex said.

"And Dr. Ashby, your gardener. When does he work?"

"He works in the mornings—when it's cool."

"So why, sir, were you present last night?" Lyon looked at Phud.

"I came to enjoy the music, the evening, the refreshments and to dance with Kitt Morgan."

Lyon started more direct questioning with me.

"Where did you go and what did you do last night after the

celebration ended, Miss Morgan?"

"I went upstairs to my room and retired for the night."

"Any witnesses?"

"Janell and Rex were also upstairs, but I didn't see them again. I had closed my bedroom door, and I went directly to bed."

"You stayed in your room? You didn't leave the house later?"

"I remained in my room. I had no reason to leave my room or the house."

"When was the last time you saw Hella Flusher alive?"

"She was one of the guests at the party. I saw her walk out our back door, head across the garden stepping on the flagstones on her way to her apartment at the bed and breakfast inn."

"You didn't see her enter the inn?"

"No. Her entry is on the back side of the building."

"No front entry?" he asked.

"Yes. There's a front entry, but Hella usually used the back entry, perhaps for more privacy."

"That was the last time you saw her?"

"Yes."

"And what time was it?"

"Around eleven-thirty."

"You looked at your watch?"

"No, sir. After I snapped off the light and retired, I looked at my bedside clock that glows in the dark."

After Lyon asked everyone in the room the last time they had seen Hella alive, it became clear that Rex saw her last. He said he had gone to the pool about 11:45 to make an adjustment on the filter system and had seen Hella's shadow on the window shade as she moved about in her apartment.

"Did you speak to Miss Flusher at that time?" Lyon asked.

"No, sir. I did not. I had no reason to speak to her."

"Mrs. Cummings, you found the body this morning. Is that correct?"

"Yes."

"Will you describe the scene?"

"I object to that question." Rex drew himself to his full height and then laid both hands on Janell's shoulders. "My wife gave you her statement about finding Hella's body earlier this morning. I consider it harassment on your part to require her to relive that experience."

"All right, Mr. Cummings. I'll skip that question for now, but your wife may be required to answer that question many times and under many circumstances before this case is solved."

"Thank you," Rex said.

Detective Lyon looked around the room, allowing his gaze to rest on each of us for a moment before he spoke again.

"Dr. Ashby, Mr. Cummings mentioned that you worked mornings. When you came to work this morning, did you see Hella Flusher's body?"

"No, sir. I never work here on weekends."

Lyon jotted words in his notebook before he let his gaze rove around the room, touching briefly on each of us. "Who were Hella Flusher's enemies?"

"Who say Hella have enemies?" Mama G demanded, her nostrils flaring. "I say she have no enemies."

"She must have had one," Ace said. "She pretended to be a psychic. Maybe she gave a patron a reading that patron didn't like."

"Pretended to be?" Lyon asked. "You question her ability?"

Ace shrugged. "I think we all had our doubts about Hella's psychic abilities."

Teach and Phud nodded in agreement, Rex and Janell looked straight ahead, but Mama G jumped to her feet. "Hella have true ability to see the future. She tell me things about my life that helped me. Help me *mucho.*"

"I think she was bilking the tourists with her fortune-telling act at the Mallory sunsets," Phud said. "I'm surprised some of her victims didn't complain and have her arrested."

"Was there any fortune telling going on at last night's party?" Lyon asked.

"None," Janell said.

"But . . ." I hesitated.

"But what?"

Lyon's gaze bored into my eyes, making me regret having spoken.

"Miss Morgan?"

"At the party, we began discussing Abra Barrie's murder and the fact that it remains unsolved. Janell and I had done a little investigating on our own this past week—to no avail."

"You wanted to give the police some assistance in finding the culprit?" Lyon asked. Nothing in his voice or his demeanor suggested that he might be making fun of our efforts.

"We would have been pleased to have pinpointed the identity of the culprit," I said. "But since that didn't happen, all of us here this afternoon talked about trying to prove that nobody connected with The Poinsettia was guilty." I told Lyon about our plan, about Hella agreeing to help us with her psychic ability.

"So where are the items you gave Hella to 'read'?" Lyon asked.

"She took them with her," Rex said. "I'm assuming you'll find them in her apartment."

Lyon didn't reply, but I sensed that he had not found the box or the items in Hella's room.

Teach spoke up, pushing his sunglasses to the top of his head. "So maybe Hella was on to something. Maybe someone didn't want her delving any more deeply into his or her life."

"I doubt that." Phud laughed. "Who'd believe such silliness?"

"I would." I felt all eyes on me. "Our police department in Iowa once benefited from the work of a psychic. And Hella once revealed to me happenings from my past that she had no way of knowing except through extrasensory perception. I believe she had a very special ability. Would it be possible for the Key West PD to work with a psychic?"

"Perhaps we can discuss that at a future time," Lyon said. "For now, this will end the informal questioning. You will be called to headquarters later and asked to make more complete statements. At this time you are free to go on about your chosen activities. Do not leave Key West without telling me of your plans."

30

Once the detectives walked to their car and drove away, The Poinsettia workers stood and prepared to leave.

"Well!" Teach exclaimed. "What did you think of that? Are we all suspects? Just because we happen to work here, worked with Hella?"

"That's how it appears," Phud said.

Ace shrugged and headed for the door. Even Mama G had little to say when she left the house.

"I still can hardly believe Hella died in this cruel way," Janell said. "Can't believe we're all caught up in the aftermath of her murder."

"I can believe it," Phud said. "Never did like that woman, and I'll tell the police that if they should ask." He headed for the door. "I'm outta here."

Once the three of us were alone again, Janell excused herself and went upstairs to rest, and Rex followed her. I heard water running in the shower, then all was quiet.

Yes, we all were suspects in Hella's murder. I went to my room and began packing my suitcase, stowing things I knew I wouldn't need until I reached home. Home. What if the police wouldn't let me leave? How long could they hold me here? While I worked, the idea of the police talking with a psychic ran through my thinking. I doubted that Detective Lyon believed in Hella's talents, at least believed strongly enough to plead with the PD to engage a psychic for help in solving the two recent murders. But there was no reason I couldn't talk to one on my own. Couldn't hurt. Might help.

I glanced at my watch. A little after four. By now, the buskers and artists would be starting to gather at Mallory to present their acts, their paintings and crafts. No reason I couldn't approach a psychic with my questions. Several of them usually set up tables and chairs near the dock—tarot card readers, crystal ball gazers, tea leaf readers. Hella had pointed them out to me the evening I went there with her. They welcomed anyone with a few bucks to spare. I tucked some twenty-dollar bills into my billfold, stuffed it into my fanny pack and tiptoed downstairs.

Had it been dark, I'd have been apprehensive about leaving The Poinsettia alone, but in broad daylight I felt I'd be in no danger. I agreed with Teach. Someone who had learned of our plans had wanted to prevent Hella's future readings. And who could that have been except someone at last night's celebration party? I buckled on my fanny pack, left a note for Janell and Rex on the kitchen table telling my plans and headed for Mallory Dock.

The late afternoon sun warmed my head and shoulders but a slight chill in the onshore trade wind hinted of a cool evening to come. Had I not smelled the fragrance of popcorn a block away from the dock, I might have returned to the house for my sweater. Instead, I pulled a couple of dollars from my billfold and approached the nearest popcorn wagon. Two wouldn't do it. I pulled out a third, thinking of twenty-five-cent popcorn I enjoyed at the band concerts in Iowa.

Munching this favorite treat, I savored the taste of butter and salt and popped corn and forgot about needing a sweater later on. I strolled along the dock with an eye out for crystal ball and tarot readers. The sun glinting against the water all but blinded me, so I walked with my back to it.

Passing the man with the trained cats, the contortionist and a silver-painted mime standing motionless on a silver pedestal, I approached Fondetta the Famous. Fondetta was offering palm readings and tea-leaf readings for ten dollars. For an additional ten, her sign mentioned the sharing of visions she might see in her crystal gazing ball. The heavy aroma of gardenia-scented incense wafted around her, and a black cat that could have doubled for Voodoo purred in her lap.

When I paused, looking down at her table and her paraphernalia, she smiled up at me. That mannerism drew attention to two cheek dimples as well as her cleft chin. Dressed in a red satin gown that touched her ankles and a shawl that covered her dark hair but not her golden earrings, she whispered her come-on. All the while she ran her carefully manicured fingernails through her cat's silky fur.

"Missy. Missy. Come. Do not hang back. Come to me. I tell you where your true love awaits you, Missy. I give you his name. This information presently known only to me will add great happiness to your life. Only twenty dollars, Missy. Only twenty dollars for the name of your one true love." She stopped petting the cat and held out her hand, palm up.

"Do you guarantee your visions, Fondetta?"

"Yes. Yes. Indeed yes, Missy. I guarantee the truthfulness of my crystal ball."

Before she could say more, the bagpiper near the end of the dock began to blow a penetrating melody superimposed on a heavy drone bass.

Fondetta's earrings jangled to the rhythm of her enthusiastic proclamations, but the bagpiper's talent for loudness forced her to abandon her whispery voice. "I guarantee all visions, Miss," she shouted. "I guarantee. Within one short week your true love will appear. Your soul mate. Do not pass up this opportunity for enlightenment. Fondetta will introduce you to a new life and give you her blessing."

"Fondetta, did you know Hella Flusher?"

A look of fear crossed her face and she cuddled her cat on her shoulder, burying her face in its fur. "No. I d-do not know Hella Flusher."

Her face flushed, and I knew from that and her stammer she was lying. Or maybe she was afraid—afraid someone might have a special penchant for murdering psychics. I turned to walk on.

"Missy. Missy. Do not leave. Do not . . ."

"Maybe another evening, Fondetta. Another time." From the corner of my eye I saw her shoulders slump when I turned and walked on down the dock, putting distance between us. I paused to look back. She had lowered the cat to her lap and sat pulling her shawl tighter around her head. She might be Fondetta the Famous, but more likely she might also be Fondetta the Fake. I couldn't imagine Hella ever having used such blatant bits of self-promotion. Nor did she ever guarantee her work. Hella almost encouraged people to disbelieve her.

Walking on, I almost missed seeing Levanah, who had set up shop for the evening in front of a small cream-colored tent partially hidden by a seagrape tree. Zodiac signs covered the tent canvas and Levanah sat in the tent's opening wearing a leopard print caftan, a matching turban, and at least a dozen necklaces and chains that jangled when she moved. She pointed to a canvas chair that matched her own, both chairs also in leopard print canvas. Peeking inside the tent, I saw a man in the dimness, lounging on the ground in a brown beanbag chair. He sat almost out of sight of passersby. Bodyguard? Watchman? His gaze never left us.

"Your fortune, miss?" she called. "Your true path through life is written in the stars. I will point it out to you."

Levanah's leopard print, zodiac symbol approach seemed even phonier than Fondetta's satin robe and whispery-to-screaming voice. I started to walk on, still munching on popcorn.

"Only twenty dollars, miss. Your future revealed in full for the small sum of twenty dollars."

"No thank you, Levanah. Maybe another time." I walked on.

"Special price for you today, Missy," Levanah called after me. "Sunset celebration special—fifteen dollars. Just fifteen dollars for a reading to help you find your true path through life—and your true love."

I hesitated and then walked back toward her. Beanbag Chair Man never took his eyes off of us. "Levanah, were you acquainted with Hella Flusher?"

In one fluid bit of motion, Beanbag Chair Man rose and stepped from the tent, joining us and placing his hands on Levanah's shoulders. "Why are you questioning my wife about Hella Flusher? We know nothing about her death. Nothing."

"But you know she's dead," I said. "How did you learn that?"

"Radio. And we take care. We watch our backs."

"Then you knew Hella." I made it a statement I hoped he wouldn't deny.

"People in our business know each other," Levanah said.

Beanbag Man nodded. "We knew Hella Flusher. We respected her."

"So can you tell me if she had any enemies that you know of?"

"That we do not know," he said. "We did not know her well. She told us little of her life or her acquaintances."

"We only saw her at sunset now and then," Levanah said. "She didn't come here every night. Maybe she had a day job to help her pay expenses. Who knows?"

"Is she a friend of yours?" the man asked.

"Past tense. She was a friend. Thank you for talking with me."

"Missy, I tell your fortune. Listen to me. Maybe I see something about Hella Flusher in your future." The man shook

251

his head, eased back into the tent and slumped once more onto the beanbag chair.

"Thank you, Levanah, but not tonight." I turned and walked on.

"Fool!" She spat the word at my back. "Tightwad!"

The sun still hung above the horizon, and its fiery globe made an eye-catching backdrop for the sailboats that paraded in front of it. With practiced skill, they tacked to catch the wind, turned to keep their photogenic position. Tourists, with cameras at the ready, pushed and shoved as they vied for an unobstructed view. I wondered if the city paid the sailors to create this send-a-picture-back-home scene. I had to admit that it made me wish I'd brought my camera along.

Today's sun was not long for today's world, and I wanted to return to The Poinsettia well before dark, so I almost didn't stop at Faith Brimwell's space crammed between two eight-foot tables where vendors stood selling tie-dyed t-shirts. I thought those had gone out of fashion with the hippies, but both women were doing business, stuffing shirts in sacks, pocketing bills.

Faith Brimwell's booth consisted of one tiny table and two three-legged stools. A lace cloth covered her table, bare except for a crystal ball and a small stack of business cards. She wore white jeans, golf shirt, and a visor that shielded her eyes from the sun.

"May I help you this evening, ma'am?" She spoke to me only after I'd picked up one of her cards. "Faith Brimwell," I read. "Professional Psychic."

"Yes." Faith smiled. "May I help you?"

I smiled back at her, really interested in what she might have to say.

"If you think I may be of help to you this afternoon, please sit down and make yourself comfortable and we'll talk."

I wondered just how comfortable she thought I could get on

a three-legged stool. But at least she wasn't trying to give me a hard sell on her abilities.

"What is your charge?"

"My charge will not exceed twenty-five dollars. It depends on your questions, of course, but the charge may be less. Never more. However, I do impose a ten-minute limit on my reading."

"Of course," I agreed, as if I was quite familiar with all psychics' penchant to set prices and time limits.

"What is it that you wish to discuss with me this afternoon?" Faith asked.

"I'm concerned about the recent murders here on this island."

Faith's gaze met mine and held it. I don't think I could have looked away had I wanted to. And I didn't want to.

"Ma'am, are you in some way connected with these deaths, these horrible murders?"

"Only marginally." I explained my relationship to Janell and Rex and The Poinsettia. "Have you thought about these murders?"

"Not professionally. But I think everyone in Key West has thought about them to some extent. What is it that you want to ask me?"

"I want to ask if you can visualize, see in your mind's eye, the person who might be guilty?"

"Ha!" She spat the word. "If I could see that so easily, I would have rushed to the police with the information."

"Hella Flusher, the woman who was murdered last night at The Poinsettia, was also a psychic. I knew her. I've been a guest at that B&B for a few days. I think Hella might have been able to see, to give information, about the person who murdered Abra Barrie, the murder victim of a week or so ago."

"And why do you think that?"

I knew I'd said enough. Maybe more than enough. "Miss Brimwell, I'm a police officer from Iowa, from a town where the

PD drew on help from a psychic to assist in solving a case. I've suggested to Detective Lyon at the Key West PD that he might want to consult a psychic for help with the solving of Hella Flusher's murder."

"The police haven't contacted me," Faith said. "I'm not eager to become involved in a murder investigation."

"If the police contacted you, would you try to help them?"

"I might. I don't know. I'd have to think about it."

"May I give Detective Lyon your business card?"

"Of course," Faith pushed the stack of cards toward me and I took another one to add to the one I already held. "If the police get in touch with me, I'll have plenty of time then to make the decision concerning whether I might be able to help them."

"Thank you," I said. "That's all I'm asking of you—to hear them out if they come knocking on your door."

"I'm here every night," Faith said, "but I live on Big Pine Key—about thirty miles up the highway. It's a quiet spot, a quiet island. I prefer it to the noise and clamor of Key West. Serenity gives me time and space to think."

I had started to walk away when she called to me.

"Miss?"

"Yes?" I faced her again

"Were you a personal friend of Hella Flusher?"

I thought for a moment about my relationship to Hella. "I'd known her for about a week. Yes, I was her friend. We had differences of opinion and sometimes we rubbed each other the wrong way. But I'll always count her as a friend. And I miss her."

I smiled at Faith Brimwell, tucked her business cards into my fanny pack and walked again along the pathway, jostling my way through the tourists crowding around the vendors' booths. I found a quiet spot next to a safety railing between the sunset watchers and the Gulf and held the flat of my hand toward the sun.

Years ago a Girl Scout leader had shown my troop the trick of judging time using the horizon and the sun as guides. Each finger you could hold between the bottom of the sun and the horizon equaled fifteen minutes of time before sunset. This afternoon, I could fit two fingers into that distance. Thirty minutes. I turned and headed toward The Poinsettia. No point in my being out after dark, or even in the twilight preceding dark.

A half hour allowed me ample time to get back home, and I strolled along without hurrying. I had turned my back to the dock, walked down the alleyway used by motorists ready to pay their parking fee and drive on to other events. When I stepped onto Front Street a man joined me, strode along beside me. The angel Gabriel? The guy's skin gleamed with silver paint. He wore a wide belt with a skin-tight leotard that looked as if it had been painted on, too. At first I thought he was the mime I'd seen posing on a pedestal at the dock. But no. A silver yachting cap sat on this man's head and a silver mask hid his features.

I stopped in front of a t-shirt shop and turned to face him. "Who are you? What do you want?"

31

"Just keep walking," he ordered. "Show no surprise." The mask muffled his voice, but the tiny silver pistol he pulled from beneath his belt and jabbed into my side fit into his disguise and carried his message loud and clear. Anyone noticing us would think he was a busker who had finished work for the evening and was leaving the dock early. But there were few people around right now to notice us or to speculate about the man or his intentions. The climax of the celebration was at hand. Now that the sun was about to sink into the harbor, everyone was on the dock intent on watching its demise.

"I'm on my way home," I said. "People are waiting for me, expecting me. Leave me alone. Go before I call a cop."

The man chuckled. "What cop do you think could hear you above the clamor of the dock? Walk along beside me. Pretend we're best friends."

He linked his left arm through my right arm, and as he did that I felt the sharp prick of a needle. I jerked away from him, but too late. He grabbed me back. A pink syringe the size of a thumbnail dropped from my arm and he kicked it into a gutter where it disappeared into a scattering of fast-food cartons, candy wrappers and cigarette stubs that lay caught against a storm drain.

I tried not to imagine what this stranger had injected into my arm, but I knew I had to act fast, act before the substance could take full effect. Already, I could feel my heart pounding. That could be from fright, but my eyes were beginning to burn and my mouth felt so dry I could hardly swallow. I knew I should scream, but his gun would speak faster than my scream that might never be heard.

"What are you trying to do?" I felt as if I were pulling each word from a quagmire of wet sand.

"What does it look like I'm trying to do? I'm using gentle tactics to persuade you to come along with me quietly. You try to call anyone for help, and my tactics may turn less gentle. A lot less gentle." He jabbed me with his gun. "Keep moving forward. You won't be able to walk much longer. Just keep putting one foot ahead of the other."

I wished I could hear his voice unmuffled by the mask. He wore nothing but the leotard and a pair of silver sandals. And now he tightened his grip, slipping his arm more tightly through mine, making it look as if we were lovers strolling away from the crowd, seeking a quiet place to be alone.

I tried to hold back, dragging my feet as he tried to continue his forward motion, but with one firm jerk he propelled me along beside him, and again I felt the nudge of metal against my ribs.

"Where are you taking me?"

When he spoke, his voice seemed to be coming from a great distance. I blinked and tried to force myself to listen. "To a wonderful and beautiful spot where we can be together and enjoy the scent of the sea, the pumpkin-like hue of the rising moon before it glows silver. Imagine. Just the two of us melding our bodies cooled by the trade wind and brushed by starlight. I'll take you to places you've never seen before—to a secret niche suitable for our never-to-be-forgotten interlude."

"Who are you?" I whispered, trying to save my strength and my voice. "Why are you disguised as Gabriel?"

"Gabriel? I like it. I like it. Gabriel! But in reality, I'm no

257

trumpeting angel, only a mere man you've met quite casually. A mere man, but a man who'll claim your heart—in a way you'll never dream possible, a man you'll never forget."

My knees threatened to buckle when my captor paused beside a silver Ford, opened the passenger door and motioned me inside with a subtle flourish of his gun. I craned my neck, trying to get a glimpse of the license plate. Local? Out of state? I couldn't focus on the letters or the numbers. They wavered. I felt as if I peered at them through a vat of water.

"Don't bother squinting at the plate, Kitt. Won't tell you a thing. The wheels are stolen—from a rental at the airport. I thought a silver vehicle was in keeping with my costume."

I knew the shot he'd plunged into my arm was curdling my brain. But somewhere in the working gray cells that remained I knew I'd rather be dead on this Key West street than dead at some place of this crazy man's choosing.

Don't get in that car. Don't get in that car. Don't get in that car!

The words formed a mantra that gave me courage. Mustering what strength I had left, I braced myself against the car door and gave Gabriel a shove that sent him reeling in surprise—and anger. Adrenalin must have kicked in because I took off running and screaming, my Nikes pounding the pavement. Or was that my heart pounding? I expected to feel a bullet in my back at any moment. On any other street in the world, this scene would have attracted someone's attention, maybe the attention of a crowd. But not in Key West. Not at Sunset Celebration time. Sounds and sights wavered in my waning consciousness.

"Hey, looky there." A woman appearing from nowhere pointed at me and shouted to her escort. "I'll bet those two are actors from Waterfront Playhouse or maybe the Red Barn. You know that theater back on Duval."

"Some publicity stunt," her friend replied. "Want to stop at

Hospitality House? See if we can still get tickets?"

Was I dreaming this horror? I felt my steps slowing, faltering.

"Help me!" I screamed. The couple looked at me and smiled, and the guy tossed a bill and a few coins in my direction as they disappeared inside Hospitality House.

My head ached and my whole body throbbed from my sudden exertion. I knew I shouldn't waste time looking over my shoulder, but the temptation was too great. When I took a quick glance, I saw that my shove had injured my abductor enough to draw blood. A red stream washed away silver paint as it trickled down his arm and side. It must have slowed him down. Maybe he hit an artery. Did arms have arteries? My mind wouldn't focus. I knew I was moving slowly, barely creeping along.

I could hardly drag one foot ahead of the other.

"Police!" I shouted. "Police!" Blood or no blood, the guy was gaining on me, and no policeman or woman came to my rescue. I tried another idea.

"Fire! Fire!" Most people were interested in fires. Someone might respond to that shout. Wishful thinking. I tripped on the rough brick of the street, tried to gain my footing again. But it was too late. I went down.

Now my captor grabbed me, yanked me then half carried me along with him back to the Ford. A man stopped in front of us.

"Got a problem here, buddy?" he asked. "Need some help?"

"No problem," Gabriel replied. "The broad's the one with the problem. Can't hold her liquor worth a damn."

"Where you headed?" the Good Samaritan asked.

All the time, my mind was shouting, *Help me. I'm not drunk. Please help me.* But I was the only one who could hear my voice, my addled brain trying to make contact with the outer world. Now Good Samaritan took my arm and Gabriel allowed him to help drag me along between them. This was my chance. Maybe my last chance before I died. Deep inside me, I knew I lived on the threshold of death—on the edge of a deep and endless chasm. I had to make this guy listen to me.

"Not drunk. I'm not drunk. Listen to me. Believe me." But he didn't hear me.

"Think she's trying to say something," he said to Gabriel.

"Probably asking for another beer."

"Hey, buddy. You're bleeding. You know that? You're hurt. Better let me get you some help." He dropped my arm and I sagged to the pavement with only Gabriel holding my other arm.

"I'll be fine," Gabriel said. "It's just a scratch."

"You're dripping blood," the Good Samaritan said. "I'm going for help. City has rules. Law says they have to keep a few first-aid kits around here somewhere. I'll find a cop. He'll know where they keep them. Think you probably need a couple of bandages and some disinfectant."

By now we had reached the car and I heard Good Samaritan take off at a run. Gabriel opened the car door and tried to thrust me inside. I couldn't shout. I couldn't even whisper. My strength was gone. But in one last effort I tried to kick him.

Didn't even hit him. Instead hit my leg on the car. Yet I felt no pain. My brain had turned off. Good news? Bad news? I fell into the car and Gabriel hoisted me onto the seat and once he had me in a sitting position, he rammed my head onto a pillow. A pillow? I had to be dreaming, didn't I?

I lolled against the pillow and the door while Gabriel must have walked around the car. Couldn't focus on him any longer. Heard the car door slam. Heard the engine start. Was I dying? They say hearing's the last sense to go. Heard him lay rubber when we wheeled from the curbing. Heard him stop at the gate to the parking lot, pay the attendant.

"Looks like you've got a sick one there, fellow," the attendant said.

"Just a little upset stomach. She'll be fine once she gets home and to bed."

How was he hiding his bloody arm? Maybe the parking guy would call for help. Maybe. I drifted away with only traffic sounds in my mind. For a short distance I tried to keep track of our turns. Crazy thinking. I couldn't keep track of anything. My brain was a blank. I couldn't see or think. Or hear.

32

No. I'd been wrong. I could still hear what was going on around me. Something must be wrong with the car. I heard water dripping. No. Water flowed somewhere near me and I lay on something very hard and cold. The scent of night-blooming jasmine almost sickened me with its cloying sweetness. Where was I? My head throbbed. My tongue felt glued to the top of my mouth. Every part of my body ached. Someone groaned. In the next moment I felt a foot nudge my ribs and I realized I was the groaner.

An atavistic instinct warned me to play dead, to keep my eyes closed.

"Okay, Kitt Morgan. Time to rise and shine."

I opened my right eye a slit. Nighttime. But a night silvery with moonlight.

Where was I? Who was with me? I closed my eye and listened. Somewhere nearby water flowed into a pool. My hand touched something smooth. A plate? Again, I opened an eye and this time my surroundings came into sharper focus. Moonglow lighted a pool where water flowed over rocks and splashed against water lilies. I was lying on tile. A giant ficus tree guarded a bricked archway. Now I knew. West Martello. I lay inside the garden center. Janell? No. Janell wouldn't be working here after dark. The gates closed at sunset.

Crazy thoughts ran through my head. I could hear Janell telling me about garden club ladies sharing plants from their personal gardens to get this center started, getting tile from Cuba. Tile from Cuba. Was that possible? My mind wouldn't let go of the thought. Garden Center. Cuban tile. In the distance I could hear traffic sounds. And in the next moment I knew why I was here.

"On your feet, Kitt!" He prodded me with a pistol.

Whose voice? Still muffled. Memories drifted back to me. Gabriel. The silver man. The silver car. The shot in my arm. This guy held me captive. In my mind I ran from him. In reality I lay frozen in place.

"On your feet, broad. I have a big night in store for us."

I didn't struggle, and my limpness made it hard for him to haul me to my feet while clutching the pistol in one hand. I refused to stand, letting my body remain limp. He dropped me. My head hit the tile before he kicked me in the ribs and picked me up again. Broken ribs? I couldn't tell. Pain radiated through my chest. Now he dropped me onto a bench and I slumped there, trying to get my bearings. Moonlight gleamed against the silver of his skin and leotard. Now his yachting hat was gone and moonlight glazed his bald head.

My mind churned. Bald head? Rex!

Rex planned to kill me.

Nausea washed over me. I gagged.

A man I respected, trusted and considered my friend had betrayed me. Hella? Abra Barrie? Had Rex murdered both of them? Clearly, I would be his next victim. I had to escape. Had to warn Janell. My mind began to clear, but not enough.

My brain still balked.

I was still befuddled and in no position to defend myself, let alone warn anyone else of their danger.

"Make it easy on yourself," Rex muttered through his mask. "Make it easy on both of us. Just obey orders. Do what I say. We're going to have a wonderful time—at least I am."

"Rex! What are you doing to me? Think about this."

"I have thought about it. Been planning it for days, since the first day I met you."

Now he wasn't making sense. Rex had met me when I was a teenager. Maybe his mind had snapped. Maybe if I went along with his craziness, I could talk myself out of whatever plans he had for me. I remembered my cell phone in my fanny pack. Maybe I could pull it out and call help. Or maybe he'd grab it away from me and fling it into the pool. Keep him talking. Maybe I could keep him talking, reason with him.

"Rex, why don't you drive us both to The Poinsettia? Let's go back there and talk over our problems. You need to explain all this to me—and to Janell." And the police, I thought. "At home you can tell us all what you've been thinking and what's been bothering you."

"Ha! I can tell you what I've been thinking right here and right now, but I'm tired of talking through this mask."

I watched astounded and frozen with fright when Rex reached up and pulled off his mask. With it came his bald head.

Rex?

Silver gray hair shone in the moonlight, and I stood facing Phud. He tossed the silver pistol aside, reached under his belt, and pulled out a machete. Relief that the man wasn't Rex thudded with my realization that I again faced Phud.

"Come along with me, Kitt."

Now he prodded me with the knife tip. Then he grabbed my hand and yanked me with him along cold damp corridors, through archways where snake-like vines clutched at me. I heard myself groaning until we left the fort and faced the hill outside.

"Go ahead of me now," he ordered. "Move it!"

I stepped ahead of him, walking as slowly as I dared and feeling the prick of his machete whenever he wanted me to move faster. While I was walking I fumbled with the zipper on my fanny pack and pulled out my cell phone. He heard the zipper sound.

"What do you think you're doing?"

"Nothing." Before he could see what I was doing I managed to click the phone on and push the speed dial. Ace's number. He had programmed it when he'd had the phone repaired. But once we reached the top of the hill, Phud stepped around me on the path and faced me head on. When he saw my phone, he grabbed it, tantalized me by holding it just out of my reach.

"Forget about calling help. I own the phone now. It's mine. All mine."

"Phud, listen to me. Forget your plans whatever they are. Take me down from here and I'll make no trouble for you."

"You women all use the same line. That's what Abra said. That's the same line Hella used. I thought maybe you could think of something more original."

"You killed Abra Barrie and Hella?" I asked.

"Oh, yes. Those two and others. And nobody will ever guess. They'll just be shocked that Kitt Morgan also has fallen to the hands of a murderer. Look around you, Kitt. Isn't this a lovely spot to spend your last hour, your last minutes?"

I was looking around, trying to stall when I saw it—the tan box with yellow tape, the box he'd brought from the Winn Dixie the day I drove him to the Big Pine library. He hadn't carried it up the hill with him just now. He must have planted it here earlier. I saw no way that I could get my phone away from him. I had to keep him talking.

"What's in the box, Phud?"

"A surprise. Just for you, Kitt. Want to see?" He walked to the box and gave it a hard kick. It remained closed. He bent and slashed it open with the machete. "Take a look."

I looked, but I didn't give him the satisfaction of screaming. The box held a length of clothesline rope and two rolls of gray duct tape. I knew he'd planned this scene earlier, but my call to Rex from the Sugarloaf Inn had thwarted him—saved my life, for the moment.

I had to keep him talking. Ace might have his phone turned on. He told me that he kept it on most of the time so he wouldn't miss calls from customers wanting shrimp, or workers who might want to hire on for a run with him. Ace might hear this conversation between Phud and me.

But he'd have no idea of where we were. Once I tried to make an obvious statement, Phud would guess my intent and destroy the phone. As it was, he might remain satisfied to tantalize me with it, to hold it just out of my reach.

"Yes, Phud, you're right. This is a wonderful spot. The moonlight. The sea." I wanted to say "the gazebo," but that might be a giveaway word that would alert him to danger. I was even afraid to say the word "hill," because there were so few hills in Key West, that "hill," too, might be a giveaway.

"How many women have you murdered, Phud?"

"Why do you ask?"

"Just curious. How many?"

"You'll make number ten."

"All in Florida?"

He laughed. "No, I get around quite a bit. Two in Georgia. One in Alabama."

"And nobody has ever suspected you?"

"Of course not. The image I've built for myself is too respectable."

"Why do you do it? Why? Did you hate those women? Did I do something to make you hate me?"

"I kill women because it gives me indescribable pleasure to kill. I have special rituals I perform before a victim's death, and an extra-special one I perform after each death. That final one gives me more pleasure than you can imagine. I remember that pleasure a long time. But when it wanes, I begin looking for my next victim. But don't think about that, Kitt. Enjoy your last minutes. Look at the beauty all around you."

I had an idea that might work! Although Phud had his knife at the ready in his right hand, I walked in front of him, stopping at the tree beside the gazebo. I didn't care if he saw my knees shaking. It would be normal for a woman to be afraid under such conditions, wouldn't it? And what did it matter if he caught onto my plan? He'd marked me for death sooner or later. I might be hoping in vain that it would be later.

"You're a plant expert, Phud. Tell me about this tree. It's so crooked and gnarled, it looks as if it's been here a thousand years. Ironwood, right?" I waited, hoping his plant expert ego would prompt him to say the true tree name.

And he stepped into my feeble trap.

"Lignum vitae is the proper name. That's what professionals call it. Lignum vitae. Only amateurs call it ironwood."

"Lignum vitae." I repeated the words as if I had trouble saying them or remembering them. "Lignum vitae." Did I dare say it another time? No I wouldn't take that chance.

Phud approached me now with his right arm pulled high over his right shoulder, ready to plunge the blade into my heart.

"Phud, did you know I'd killed a man?"

"You? You've got to be kidding!"

"It's the truth and I'm not bragging about it."

Phud lowered his arm. "The guy's death gave you no pleasure?"

"That's right. None at all. I'll never get over the fact that I took someone else's life. It's made me rethink my career choice. It's something I'll carry with me the rest of my life."

"The rest of your life is going to be very short, Kitt. And I'm a killer in control. I'm the person who'll decide your fate. I've already decided where. Now I'll decide when. But I want to hear more of your story. How did you happen to kill a man?"

"I want a promise from you."

"You're in no position to be asking for promises."

"You're in no position to ask me to tell you about the most horrible time in my life. I don't want my family to know how hard it is for me to think about the experience."

Phud shrugged. "I want to hear your story. Every minute you talk on the subject will delay your death. That's what you want, isn't it? So talk. Did killing the guy give you a buzz? The big O?"

I talked. I hated the subject matter, but maybe Rasty Raymore could save my life. "In Iowa I was a cop, a cop on a small-town police force. And one night I shot a man." I recounted the whole story of the snowy night, the pet shop, the drug bust. I elaborated on every small detail, making the tale last as long as possible. I talked until I was so hoarse I didn't think I could say another word. I felt all strength and will leaving me.

"So what's the big deal?" Phud tapped his knife against his thigh. "You shot in self-defense."

"Right. Society says, 'You're a cop. Handle it, but don't change.' Cops can't be wimps. It's an impossible job—not changing. I'm barely handling it, and I know I've changed."

I saw the police climbing the hill to the gazebo, saw Ace behind them, before Phud saw or heard them. They were making some noise, but it was almost as if my story had mezmerized Phud. I looked toward the sea, trying to get his gaze to follow mine.

And for a few moments it did. And in those minutes the police took over the scene.

33

Ace rushed to me, kissing me and burying his face in my hair. I clung to him until Janell and Rex joined us, standing to one side of Ace. I reached for Janell's hand, gripping it so tight that my ring cut into my fingers. By that time the police had disarmed Phud, arrested him and handcuffed him, arms behind his back. Nobody spoke until Phud tried to jerk away from the police. An officer retaliated by holding him in place while another officer locked shackles around his ankles.

"You can't arrest me!" Phud shouted. "Nobody read me my rights. You're not blaming anything on me. Nothing. This woman asked me to bring her here to enjoy the view of the sea. She's the one. She's been flirting with me all week. She's the one who's caused all this trouble. Don't know who called you guys onto the scene. It's not my fault. None of it."

"We have your confession, Dr. Ashby." Detective Lyon tapped my cell phone that he had taken from Phud. "Ace Brewster called us the minute he answered his cell and heard Miss Morgan's voice. You saved us a lot of trouble by confessing to Hella Flusher's and Abra Barrie's murders."

"Thank God you arrived in time to save Kitt," Janell said to Detective Lyon. "And who knows how many other women you may have saved in the future!"

"I confessed to nothing," Phud said. "Nothing. You're trying to trap me, and you won't get by with it. Nobody read me my rights. That's a law!"

Dorothy Francis

"Come with us," Detective Lyon ordered.

"No!" Phud shouted as if he could stop them. "Where are you taking me?"

"We have a holding cell for you, Dr. Ashby. It may be holding you for a long time."

Although he stood handcuffed and shackled, Phud cast a murderous gaze on each of us.

I winked at him.

With a great crashing in the hillside thicket, the officers took Phud away. Who was that man? University professor emeritus? Respected lecturer? Much-read newspaper columnist? Serial murderer? The sociopath next door? I shuddered.

"Miss Morgan," Lyon said. "Please wait and we'll send a car for you. We'll want to see you at headquarters."

"If it's all right, I'll drive her to headquarters," Ace said, "along with Janell and Rex. We all drove here together."

"Fine," Lyon said. "We'll need to ask you all some questions."

We groaned at the thought of more questions. But we got in Ace's car and rode to headquarters. I guess it was because the police had Phud's confession that their questions didn't take as long as they had taken this afternoon. By the time they had finished questioning us, I had calmed down from the horrors of the evening. For the first time since arriving in Key West, I felt safe. Detective Lyon drove Rex and Janell home, but Ace invited me to ride with him and I accepted.

"Wish you didn't have to go back to Iowa so soon." Ace drove beside the sea to the White Street Pier, easing his car into a slot at the park across the street.

"I wish I could stay longer, too. But I have to get back."

"Feel like taking a short walk on the pier?" He looked at the sky. "I can promise you an endless sea and a full moon."

"It can't get much better than that."

270

He took my arm and I welcomed his touch, his support. Waves crashed on the rocks beside us, and we walked to the end of the pier where Ace led us to a bench overlooking the water.

"Why are you so determined to get back to Iowa, Kitt? You need a few more days to unwind and enjoy our island. You sure you have to hurry back?"

For a few moments I didn't reply, then as he drew me closer to him, I started to tell him about my job—all the details. He stopped me.

"I heard the life-saving litany you told to Phud. You are indeed a brave woman, Kitt Morgan." He held me tenderly. When his lips found mine, we shared a long and passionate kiss.

"Stay here, Kitt. Turn in your resignation to the Iowa PD. You can find a job in Key West, an apartment, a . . ."

"No. I must go back. I'm no quitter. I'll return and face whatever I have to face."

"For a while, maybe." Ace kissed me again. "But perhaps not forever."

"You might want to come to Iowa for a visit, Ace. After all, it's your home state, too."

"You might be able to talk me into that." Ace stood and pulled me to my feet. "There's a special place there I'd like to see again. Maybe you'd like to go there with me."

"Where is that?"

"It's called a Field of Dreams. Perhaps it could be our Field of Dreams."

"Let's call it a plan, Ace. A plan to look forward to."

ABOUT THE AUTHOR

Award-winning author **Dorothy Francis** writes novels and short stories for children and adults from her home studios in Iowa and the Florida Keys. She is a member of Mystery Writers of America, Sisters in Crime, Short Mystery Fiction Society, Key West Writer's Guild, and the Society for Children's Book Writers and Illustrators. Her first four novels for adults, *Conch Shell Murder, Pier Pressure, Cold Case Killer,* and *Eden Palms Murder* have received critical acclaim from *Booklist, Publishers Weekly,* and *Crime Scene Magazine.* Her husband, an educator, avid fisherman and jazz saxophonist, was recently inducted into the Jazz Hall of Fame at the University of Northern Iowa.

For more information, visit her Web site: www.dorothyfrancis .com or send her an e-mail: dorothy@dorothyfrancis.com.